She had just run out of the bathroom, her bare legs flashing, one hand holding the towel closed at her breasts, when she saw him in the hall. Jim came toward her, a wicked smile forming.

"I like your outfit," he said lazily, his eyes lingering on her legs, then moving up to the knot she clutched for dear life. "Very fetching."

Marijane saw the storm building in his eyes, but couldn't look away. When the towel began to slip, she tried to reach for it, but Jim held her arm back.

"What are we going to do about this?" he asked softly as the towel fell to her feet.

She looked at him warily. "What do you mean?"

"Isn't it obvious? Something's developing here. Something we're going to have to make a decision about...."

ABOUT THE AUTHOR

Muriel Jensen is a full-time book-store
manager as well as a part-time author, now
living in Oregon. She is also a cat collector—
both live and porcelain. She began writing
stories in the sixth grade and never stopped.
This is her first romance novel.

Winter's Bounty

MURIEL JENSEN

Harlequin Books

TORONTO • NEW YORK • LONDON
AMSTERDAM • PARIS • SYDNEY • HAMBURG
STOCKHOLM • ATHENS • TOKYO • MILAN

Published October 1984

ISBN 0-373-16073-9

Chapter One

Marijane Westridge glanced away from the snowy road to the hand-drawn map pinched between her gloved thumb and the steering wheel. A snaking line off the straight one indicating the highway was marked "Scotch Broom Road," and at the end of the line an elaborate X in her mother's spidery hand was marked "Home."

"Home," Marijane said aloud, dropping the map onto the seat to negotiate the turn onto the road indicated on the map. Then she uttered a skeptical grunt. As far as she was concerned, home was the low, rambling redwood house nestled in the Hollywood Hills where she had been born and raised, not whatever could appear on this forbidding landscape in this frozen Northwest wasteland.

She had suspected six months ago when her mother married Terrence Sullivan and moved to the wilds of Oregon that the woman had lost her mind. Now, as she looked about her at the interminable snow and fir trees, she was convinced.

It was hard to imagine Katherine Westridge, former star of television comedy, the toast of Laguna Beach summer stock, the sun worshipper who spent every vacation glued to a chaise longue in Santa Barbara, content in the Oregon woods with a man who owned several lumber mills.

But her letters sang with both a peaceful serenity and a pulsing excitement. *She has every right to be happy*, Mari had told herself again and again since the wedding. The shock and annoyance she felt that her mother could have fallen in love with a man so different from the man who had been Mari's father, and only a brief year after his death, was something she kept to herself.

Her two sisters, Althea, younger than Mari by two years, and Jasmine, the eldest of the three, supported their mother's position.

"Imagine being *without* a man!" Thea had lamented at the wedding, her heavy makeup and her curvaceous body gaining her many second glances as she led the way to the punch bowl. "Poor Mom must be dying of frustration, even at her age." Then she emitted a seductive growl as the newlyweds emerged from the house under a barrage of welcoming shouts. "But Terry looks like he could end that for her in no time at all."

Mari and Jasmine exchanged a speaking glance. Althea was notoriously glandular in her reactions to men, young or old. But Jasmine's eyes drifted to the couple, and she said with a wistful sigh, leaning close to Mari, "Thea's panting aside, he is very handsome and we should give him a chance."

Mari had glanced from her mother, ablush in a lacy lavender dress and broad-brimmed matching hat, to the bearlike man who held her possessively in the curve of his shoulder. He was dark-featured with a thick thatch of iron gray hair and an air of confidence that raised Mari's hackles.

Her father had been quiet and unassuming, a brilliant playwright who had captured Katherine Morency with his gentle wit and loving devotion. He had been everything this man was not.

"No family?" Mari asked.

"There's James. Runs the Astoria mill, I think. He's single, but he couldn't come. His friends...Oh, here they are!" Jasmine elbowed Mari surreptitiously. "Stop frowning!"

As Katherine brought Terry across the sunny garden

to meet his stepdaughters, Mari knew he read the resentment in her eyes, but she made no effort to hide it.

Jasmine, twenty-eight, an attorney practicing in Portland with her husband, smiled warmly and put her pale-gold head to his cheek.

"Hello, Terry," she said. "Welcome to the family."

"And welcome to mine," he returned in a big voice that boomed from his broad chest. He then reached a hand to Althea and asked tentatively, "Marijane?"

"No, I'm Althea," she laughed with a condescending glance at her older sisters. "The baby of the family."

"Ah, the actress," he said, leaning down for her hug. "You're very beautiful."

"Thank you. Someday I'm going to be even better on the stage than Mother was."

Moving on to Mari, he said, "I have to be right this time. Marijane?"

Mari offered Terrence Sullivan her hand. "Jazz and Thea take after Mother," she said quietly, then added, succumbing to an urge to try to discomfit him, "I, on the other hand, resemble my father."

He glanced at the two golden blond heads of the other girls, then back at Mari's short chestnut curls. Althea's eyes were violet-blue and Jasmine's, a wide, clear gray, while hers were velvety brown and boring into him. He took the point of her chin in his hand and turned her face toward Katherine.

"Her coloring is different," he agreed. "But in a way, she's more like you than the others. There's no denying that pug nose."

Katherine's eyes widened in mortification, then closed prayerfully. She had read her daughter's challenge and knew Terry guessed that Mari, like herself, devoted all her efforts to attracting attention away from her button nose.

Keeping a grip on her temper, Mari angled her chin and gently, but firmly, withdrew his hand.

"I definitely *favor* my father," she purred, giving the word more than the genealogical meaning.

"Good," Terry replied amiably, his dark eyes sharpening. "Then we can expect great things from you. Your mother tells me he was a kind and courteous gentleman."

The retort cut her dead, as it was intended to, and Mari withdrew, avoiding contact with her mother and new stepfather until early evening when they prepared to leave for Terrence's home on the northwest tip of Oregon. Terry took Mari aside while Katherine said good-bye to Althea and Jasmine.

"You'll come to see us?" he asked.

"I imagine we'll be getting together for—"

"No, I mean specifically to get acquainted."

"Well…"

"You owe it to your mother."

"Maybe," she conceded.

"Definitely," he corrected firmly. "Good-bye, Mari."

For the last six months Mari had been skillfully sidestepping their invitations for a visit to Oregon. Her night class in tailoring kept her too busy; she'd been fighting a cold; she was babysitting for Althea's little girl, Melissa, for the weekend. . . .

But when Katherine called with the news of the Christmas reunion, Mari considered herself outmaneuvered.

"Isn't it wonderful, Mari!" Katherine enthused.

"I don't know," Mari had replied evasively.

"Mari! How can Christmas not be wonderful? We'll all be together."

"Well…" Mari hedged because that was precisely what concerned her. As she began to fabricate an excuse, Katherine reminded her pointedly, "You couldn't take a vacation last year because your boss was too busy to spare his precious assistant. Well, you should be able to call the tune this year. Terry said to tell you we expect you, and that's final."

"But..."

"You arrange it, darling. We'll help with tickets or gas money, whichever way you'd like to travel. Jazz and David and Thea and Missy are coming. Even James and his son will be here."

"James?"

"Terry's son."

Hm, Mari thought skeptically. The one who couldn't make it to the wedding. He was probably as pleased with the idea of his father marrying as she had been. At least she had had the good manners to appear at the wedding.

"He has a son?" Mari asked. "Jazz said he was single."

"I'll tell you all about it when you get here. Call me as soon as you know when you're coming. Do try for the twentieth, Mari, so we can all spend as much time together as possible."

Mari hung up the phone, reflecting that her mother had certainly gotten bossy since her marriage to Terrence Sullivan.

Still wishing she hadn't bowed to her mother's authoritative tone, Mari followed Scotch Broom Road into the farming area ten miles east of Astoria. Glancing down the gentle slope of hill to her left, she spotted the colorful dotting of cars grouped in front of a white house almost lost to sight in its snowy environment.

Guiding her Volkswagen carefully along the slippery road, Mari pulled under a tree halfway down the hill, hoping to get a view of the house and summon her wits before meeting her family.

The sisters' temperaments had always made get-togethers exciting, but a little bit of a strain, and Mari fully expected the problems of coexistence to be multiplied this time.

Stepping out of the car, her black boots crunching in the snow, she crossed the meadow to find a clear view through a stand of snowy fir trees. Within view of the house, she stopped behind a tall tamarack, jamming her hands into the pockets of her red polyester coat and shrugging into its fake-fur collar. Wishing her knitted gray hat were twice the thickness, she watched the house for signs of activity and spotted Jazz and David's gray Jaguar.

The house was an enormous Victorian surrounded by a deep veranda. Red shutters were slatted with snow and icicles hung from the deeply slanting roof.

"We have a mild climate," Katherine had boasted in one of her letters, and Mari made a mental note to remember to tease her about that. All the way up here, the radio had reported the unusual drop in temperature and the rare, steady snow.

Even though she was a day later than her mother had hoped, Mari noticed that Althea and Melissa still hadn't arrived. Frowning, she wondered what the problem was this time.

There had always been something different about Thea, something selfish in her makeup that was alien to her two sisters, whatever their other differences. She had left home at nineteen to pursue an acting career, had married within several months, had a little girl, then lost her husband a year ago in a motorcycle accident. Mari knew their relationship had deteriorated, but Thea used grief as an excuse for leaving two-year-old Melissa with her at every opportunity, for accepting acting jobs that would take her away for days, sometimes weeks, at a time, and for chasing an Italian director who she told Mari would finally mean security for her and Melissa.

Mari suspected that it wasn't Melissa's welfare Thea was concerned about, but she had stopped trying to second-guess her long ago.

Maybe this reunion would be quieter if Thea decided not to come, Mari reflected; then remembering how Jasmine had behaved at their mother's wedding, she wondered.

The brightest of the sisters, Jasmine had married a

brilliant young attorney the entire family had loved at once. But things seemed to be paling between them, and Jazz had come to the wedding without him. She had refused to discuss his absence and flirted outrageously with the young men present. Jazz was a terrible correspondent, so Mari hadn't heard from her since and wondered a little anxiously if Jazz and David were still together. Well, there was nothing to do but drive down to the house and find out.

Turning to trudge back to her car, Mari stopped frozen. A large black wolf with white markings, barely feet away from her, stared at her for a brief instant with transparent blue eyes, then sprang with a thunderous growl, knocking her to the snow. She heard her own scream vibrate in the air, then halt abruptly as she felt the mind-bending touch of tongue and teeth on her face. Terror gave her new voice, and she screeched again, struggling blindly as her woolly hat fell down over her eyes. Screaming and flailing, she fought the animal's weight, knowing that the house was too far away for her cries to be heard.

Then suddenly there were other sounds: a boy's voice shouting and then a man's sharp command, and miraculously she was free. Still screaming, she struggled to get up, only to find herself pinned again, but this time by what felt like a pair of male hands.

"Easy," the man's voice said quietly but with a firmness that penetrated her panic. "Let's see if you're all right first."

Then Mari felt hands at her face, and as her hat ascended slowly to clear her eyes, she found herself looking into a pair of hazel ones that held concern. As they looked back into hers, their expression changed to amusement.

"Are you all right?" the man asked.

"Of course I'm not all right!" she shrieked at him, reaction giving a strident quality to her usually quiet voice. "I was just attacked by a wolf!"

His black eyebrows rose and wide mobile mouth quirked dangerously. "But I haven't even made a pass," he teased.

"Not you! The..."

She pointed a trembling hand at the wolf, standing apart from them, and stopped, transfixed for the second time this afternoon. There was no wolf. What stood there, tail wagging, tongue lolling, blue eyes watching her interestedly, was an enormous husky.

"Is... is that...?"

"Your wolf? Yes. You'll notice that you're not even scratched. Ta wouldn't hurt a fly."

"But why did she attack me? Or is she a he?"

"She didn't attack you. She spotted you and apparently liked you. She isn't shy about making new friends. She lives up the road and has free run of the neighborhood. Can I give you a hand up?"

There was laughter in those eyes, and Mari, affronted by his amusement over her indignity, ignored the outstretched hand and struggled up on her own.

The man straightened up as she got to her feet, standing a full head taller than she and looking broad as a bear in a brown suede jacket trimmed in sheepskin. Now that the shock of her encounter was past, she began to note a certain familiarity about the dark-featured man.

"You're James, aren't you?" she accused, brushing the snow off her coat.

"Right," he replied, ignoring her tone and reaching out to a boy of eight or nine who had been watching the drama from behind him. "And this is Stephen. Steve, meet your Aunt Marijane."

"How do you know I'm not Althea?" she challenged.

His grin was brutal. "Dad told me that Althea was beautiful and that Marijane had a nose just like Katherine's."

Mari closed her eyes against an encroaching tide of temper, then turned her attention to the boy. "I'm happy to meet you, Stephen," she said, leaning down to stroke the dog that sidled up to him. "I guess I misunderstood Ta's offer of friendship."

"That's okay. She is kinda big and frightening until you get to know her."

Stephen smiled broadly, a fresh-scrubbed, open-faced boy, as blond as his father was dark, and short and stocky in his jeans and red down jacket.

Ta licked Mari's hand, and she tolerated it, unable to dispel the feeling that she had been tasted.

"Where's your car?" Stephen asked with the typical boy's interest in anything on wheels.

Mari pointed to the trees just off the road. "There. I just walked down to have a look around before I drove in."

"Steve." James caught the boy's arm as he started to lope off to inspect the car. "Why don't you tell Gram that Aunt Marijane is on her way and needs a hot bath. Take Ta with you. She looks hungry."

"Okay, Dad. Come on, Ta." The boy ran off without question, the dog running happily after him, and Mari glared up at her stepbrother. "And what if I don't feel like a hot bath?"

"You'll catch pneumonia. Your coat is very pretty, but it's soaked through." He fingered the thin fabric scornfully. "It looks like something a Southern Californian would select for a trip to Oregon."

"It's the warmest coat I own."

"But it isn't padded or lined."

"How do you know?" she asked peevishly. "X-ray vision?"

He chuckled. "I wish. I know because what's under it is outlined very flatteringly." His lazy hazel eyes swept her from top to toe, then he leaned down to retrieve a mitten she had lost in the fracas and handed it to her. "And a good stout lining wouldn't allow that. Don't tell me you're not cold."

"I'm not telling you anything," Mari said feelingly, wriggling her frozen hand into her mitten, trying hard not to tremble. "I see no reason why we have to talk at all. Good day, Mr. Sullivan."

"So you don't like me either?" James asked.

Mari, in the process of walking away, stopped to look at him over her shoulder, raising a chestnut eyebrow. "Either?"

"You don't like my father."

Trying not to react to that, she forced a look of surprise. "That's silly. I hardly know him."

"True, but he seems to feel that you've made the judgment anyway."

"All right. I am resentful," Mari said candidly, taking several paces back toward him. "My father had been gone just a little over a year when Mom married Terrence and he's...he's so different from Dad."

"That doesn't mean that he won't make her as good a husband as your father did. Or a better one."

Unwilling to concede anything, Mari redirected the conversation.

"I noticed you didn't even make it to the wedding. Don't tell me there was no resentment toward my mother on your part."

"My father understood," he replied, a trace of anger in his voice.

"That some other diversion was more important to you than his marriage was?" she taunted.

James closed the few feet remaining between them, and Mari felt a frightened flutter of her pulse at the sudden sharpening in his eyes, and then, as he loomed over her, at the very size of him.

"The day my father married your mother I was making funeral arrangements for Stephen's mother and father—my best friends. They were celebrating their anniversary by driving to Reno for the weekend. Some fool changing lanes on a hill killed them." His voice hardened, and then he frowned at Mari. "Anything else you'd like to judge me on?"

"I'm sorry," she said without hesitation, her cheeks pink with what she knew was deserved embarrassment. "I apologize."

James looked at her consideringly, and she thought for a moment that he was going to throw her apology back in her face. Then he jammed his hands into his pockets and nodded. "All right. But let's settle something here and now."

Mari eyed him warily, unconsciously shifting into a defensive stance, her booted feet set slightly apart, her chin angled. "Settle what?"

"My father is happy...content...for the first time in years because of Katherine," James said, watching her under dark eyebrows that met in a threatening line as he frowned. "There will be natural tensions during this little reunion with the holidays and all our strong personalities coming together for the first time."

"What's your point?" she asked impatiently.

She saw him draw a careful breath and guessed that on the occasions when he didn't take time to do that, he lost a temper that had all indications of being impressive. It pleased her that she had gotten to him.

"My point," he said with deliberation, "is a warning. Don't cause more trouble than we've got already. If you disapprove of the marriage, keep it to yourself."

"I never said I disapproved!" she countered hotly.

"Nevertheless, you've left that impression. And it seems to matter to your mother. So watch your step."

Whatever Mari might have said to that was lost in her mother's excited call. Tall and trim, looking more like a sister than a mother, Katherine sprinted toward her daughter.

"You poor thing!" she exclaimed, holding Mari at arm's length and frowning over her wet clothes before catching her into a fragrant embrace. "Are you all right? Stevie said Ta knocked you down."

"I'm fine," Mari reassured her. "Nothing bruised or broken. Just wet."

"Jasmine is running a bath for you right now and we'll build a fire. We've got heat, of course, but a fire's so much cozier and keeps the draft out downstairs. Come on, darling."

Mari hesitated, pointing up the road. "My car..."

"I'll bring it down for you," James said, holding a hand out toward her. "Keys?"

Unwilling to argue with him in her mother's presence, Mari delved into her coat pocket and dropped the keys into his hand. "Thank you," she said with a decided lack of sincerity.

"No problem, Sis," James winked and turned to stride across the snowy meadow.

"He is the nicest young man," Katherine began, leading Mari back to the house, an arm linked in hers. "No, 'nice' is too insipid a word for someone like him. Maybe 'good' has a little more substance to it. Jim is a *good* man."

"A bit too bossy for me," Mari growled, forgetting herself.

"You don't like him either, do you?" Katherine observed, rather resignedly.

The words "That isn't true!" sprang to Mari's lips, but her mother had always read her like a book.

"Darling, you've always been too honest to lie convincingly or to hide your feelings." Katherine pushed a thick wave of graying blond hair back in a deceptively casual gesture that Mari knew was an attempt to hide disappointment. "Mari, you're not used to this Sullivan breed of man. Your father was so...gentle...so sweet, and that was wonderful because it gave me sweet and beautiful daughters. But"—Katherine lowered her eyes to her hands and added reluctantly— "there were times when I needed someone to lean on and couldn't. Your father was a beautiful person, but not a strong one." She raised her eyes again, revealing a vulnerability Mari had never seen before. "Terry is a veritable rock, Mari. And for the first time in my life, I am secure."

"But..."

"Oh, yes, we had everything. Your father's brilliance made us financially secure, but now I'm secure inside, where it really counts."

Stunned by her mother's revelation, Mari put her arms around her, completely at a loss for words.

"Just give them a chance, darling," Katherine said softly. "Promise me?"

As Mari nodded reluctantly, the front door burst open and Jasmine stood there, elegant in powder-blue sweater and slacks, her golden hair swept back into a severe yet glamorous bun.

"Well, it's about time!" she teased, pulling Mari into the house. "I've been drying dishes alone for five days! You always got out of helping with chores, and it appears you haven't lost the knack."

"Well, you were always so efficient, you made me look sloppy," Mari countered, returning an enthusiastic hug.

"Goodness!" Katherine laughed, shooing her youngest daughter toward the stairs. "Do I have to separate you already? Put the kettle on, Jazz."

"Well, all right." Jasmine turned away with a feigned frown. "But I don't think it's fair. You always loved her best. But then, you had to," Jazz said over her shoulder as she headed for the kitchen. "You had to make it up to her for bequeathing her that nose."

"Okay! I've had it with the nose jokes today!" As Mari took a threatening step toward her sister, Katherine stopped her, turning her toward the stairs instead.

"Really, darling? From whom? Who would dare . . . ?"

"Your 'good man.' James."

"Really?" Katherine looked shocked then her soft red mouth curved into a pleased smile.

Mari watched the smile suspiciously because it remained on her mother's face while she ran in and out of the steamy bathroom with bath oil, powder, a terry robe, and scuffs.

"Where's Thea?" Mari asked, seeking to divert the smile. She slid down into the tub and sighed contentedly.

Katherine's brow furrowed and she turned away from straightening the linen closet and shrugged at

Mari. "I don't know. I was hoping we'd all be together for Christmas and the New Year, but it appears Althea is going to be her usual fly in the ointment."

"Oh, I think she's just been delayed, Mom," Mari said, sorry she had raised the subject. "She'll be here. You won't believe Missy when you see her. Six months have made such a difference. She's talking. Only in two-word sentences, but she's talking."

"Is she?" Katherine sat on a little wicker stool near the tub and smiled. "I haven't seen her since our wedding. She looks like she'll be as beautiful as Althea."

"And as smart as Jasmine," Mari acknowledged.

"She stays with you often, doesn't she?"

Mari, sensing a gentle probing, tried to sound casual. "Yes, she does."

"Why, Mari? I noticed at the wedding that you had Melissa more often than her mother did."

Mari made a project of soaping her arm. "Well, you know how it is with a doting aunt."

"And a casual mother?"

"She doesn't mean to be," Mari tried to explain carefully. "Althea's just...different."

"Yes, I know." Katherine's tone was dry. "It took me a long time to accept the fact that I couldn't change her into something she wasn't. I have two beautiful, warm, loving daughters and that's accomplishment enough for anyone."

"Don't analyze, Mom. Just enjoy. It's going to be a lovely few weeks."

Katherine brightened. "Yes, I think so. I'm eager for you to get to know Terry and Jim better. Speaking of men—what was his name? Kenneth? How is he?"

"Kent," Mari corrected, forcing a light tone. "And I haven't heard from him in three months."

"I thought it was mildly serious."

"Only mildly." Mari casually soaped her other arm. "We were discussing children one day, and when I told him I wouldn't be able to provide him with any, he decided he wasn't serious after all."

"Oh, darling…" Katherine began sympathetically.

"It's all right, Mom," she interposed quickly, pulling out the stopper and rising to slip into the robe Katherine held out. "The more I see of men, the less I think I could live a lifetime with one anyway. There are those like Thea's husband who never grow up and are stupid enough to get themselves killed when they have a wife and child dependent on them. Then there's Dave. He lets Jasmine flirt with every man she sees. And then there are men like James and Terry who would make life a misery of subservience and second-class citizenship for any woman. No, Mom, I don't think marriage is for me."

Katherine eyed her warily with the look of a mother on uncertain, possibly forbidden, ground. "Do you plan a little progressive playing house instead?"

Mari rolled her eyes emphatically. "Risking all the same dangers for the sake of a little 'palimony'? No thanks. I'd rather go it alone."

"But you're a very giving young woman, Mari," her mother protested. "What will you do?"

Slipping into scuffs and belting the robe, Mari glanced at Katherine with a smile intended to put her concern to rest. "Live a very giving life."

Katherine hugged her with concern in her eyes. "I hope so, darling. Of all my girls, you're the one with the most heart."

"And the most nose." That from Jasmine who stood in the open doorway, Mari's suitcase in hand. "Jim thought you'd need this. Come on, Mari. I'll show you to the barracks. Mom, you'd better get down there. The men are bringing in the Christmas tree, and Steve's for cutting a hole in the ceiling if it doesn't fit."

"I told them to cut a small tree!" Katherine groaned, hurrying away.

Shuffling down the corridor after her sister, Mari was led into a large, high-ceilinged bedroom in earthy shades of brown and gold. A pair of twin beds stood against one wall, and a crib meant to accommodate Missy stood opposite.

Mari dropped her bag on one of the beds and snapped it open.

"Dinner's in an hour," Jasmine informed her. "But we don't dress. In this family, if you wear anything but jeans and a sweater, you're overdressed."

"This family? You say it as though we haven't always belonged."

"I mean this Sullivan family. It's a little different from the Westridge one, but I like it." Jasmine opened a dresser drawer and placed the items Mari handed her into it. "What did you think of James?"

Mari felt herself stiffen and couldn't decide if it was aversion to the very sound of the man's name or concern over whether or not he would become Jasmine's current conquest. "Very handsome and very autocratic," she supplied.

Jasmine looked surprised. "Really?"

"Really. Doesn't he seem bossy to you?"

"No. He's been kind and charming to all of us. Mom thinks of him as her own son already."

"And how do you think of him?" Mari asked, closing her empty case.

Jasmine looked back at her in surprise for a moment, apparently wondering if she'd interpreted the nuance correctly. When Mari's gaze didn't waver, she smiled and sat heavily on the foot of the bed. "He's gorgeous! And he doesn't always have his nose buried in a legal brief."

"Jazz . . ."

"Oh, Mari, don't say it, please! I've said it all to myself over and over, but it doesn't change anything." She sighed and leaned back on an elbow. "Dave pretends I'm not here, and I'm tired of it."

"But is this the best way to handle it?"

"Do you think I should see an attorney?" she quipped.

Mari groaned and shook out a pair of jeans and a red sweater. "I think you should see a shrink!"

"When are you going to take the matrimonial plunge?" Jasmine sidestepped.

"Never. You're sure jeans are okay for dinner?"

"You're changing the subject."

"True. But you did it first."

"I'm sorry." Jasmine slipped gracefully off the bed and went across the room to the crib, folding a small crocheted blanket that had been tossed over its raised side. "I'll probably file for divorce after the first of the year. I...I understand his dedication and his drive, but...he doesn't understand mine. And I can't live out my life being ignored."

"Have you talked to him about it? Maybe he doesn't realize..."

"He realizes. We had a fight about having a baby." Jasmine glanced at Mari apologetically and carefully replaced the blanket. "I'm not ready to be a mother. I have my career, too, but I guess he doesn't see that. He's ready to have a child and I'm not. So he's punishing me by pretending I don't exist."

Ironic, Mari thought, that her sister fought against having a child when a houseful of children was all she, Mari, had ever wanted and would never have.

Reading her expression, Jasmine came toward her and took her hands. "I'm sorry. Baby-talk is probably painful to you, isn't it?"

"Not at all," she lied. "But hearing you talk about divorce is. Does he know that's what you have in mind?"

She shrugged. "I haven't spoken the words, but he knows I...that I'm..."

"Fooling around?"

Jasmine smiled. "I'm not really, you know. Oh, I flirt and have had an occasional clandestine lunch or dinner, always being carefully obvious about it so Dave can find out, be outraged, and have a fit. So far, it hasn't worked. But I've never gone beyond that."

"Then why?"

"I don't know. To hurt him back."

"That's unworthy of you. Maybe you can work out

the problem while you're here and both away from home and the office. You'll have him to yourself for two weeks, Jazz. Do something positive.''

"You were always so logical and unimpassioned." Jasmine smiled at Mari and went to the door. "You should have been the attorney. Hurry down. I'll see if I can round up a glass of Terry's spiced wine. It's marvelous!"

Mari stared at the door Jasmine closed behind her and sank wearily onto the bed, her mind amuddle with alarming discoveries. She'd been here barely an hour and so far had learned that her mother had never really felt secure with her father despite twenty-eight years of marriage, that one sister was planning a divorce while another one might not show up at all. And she, had already argued with her stepfather's only son after knowing him a mere five minutes.

Shedding the terry robe, Mari exhaled a breath that fluttered her bangs and began intrepidly to dress.

Chapter Two

Seated between James and David, Mari noted that the atmosphere, if not the elegance, made dinner an event. Despite the jeans and sweaters and bright flannel shirts up and down the table in the rustic, vaulted-ceilinged dining room, a festive mood prevailed. Many happy gatherings came to mind from her childhood and teen years with her father at the head of the table, but they had been as unlike this one as her father and Terry were dissimilar. Her father had presided with quiet wit, leading conversations about the theater, the news, and what was happening in his daughters' lives.

But the pitch of this dinner discussion was positively deafening in its passion and laughter. Even David, who seldom opened up at family gatherings, was engaged in a heated discussion with Terry about pollutants produced by lumber mills and their effects on the environment. The fact that they were at opposite ends of the table didn't appear to dull their vehemence.

"David's looking well these days," Katherine observed, leaning across her empty plate to her eldest daughter. "He's maturing quite handsomely. Not that thirty-five is over the hill."

"He's beginning to act as though he's approaching his dotage," Jasmine replied, angling a disgruntled glance his way. "He seems to think life is passing him by."

"What?" Katherine poured more coffee for her daughters, then refilled her own cup. "With a thriving law practice, a beautiful wife...?"

Mari looked at her sister, who was watching the dark-haired man across the table, and saw sadness in her eyes despite her off-hand criticism. She saw Jasmine look back at her mother and open her mouth as though she had a need to confide further, then apparently thought better of it.

"I guess we all want some things we can't have," Jasmine said instead with a weary philosophical air. She pushed her chair back from the table and excused herself. "I'll go and see how my gingerbread is coming."

As she disappeared into the kitchen, managing somehow to still look glamorous in jeans and a flannel shirt, her mother frowned at her younger daughter.

"Are things that bad between them?"

"Mother!" Mari grimaced at her teasingly. "You live one hundred miles from them and I live a thousand miles away. You should know what's happening better than I."

"I know," Katherine said dryly. "But mothers are always the last to know anything. And besides, everyone always tells you everything. You've been the family adviser since you were twelve years old. You inspire confidences."

Mari sat up straighter and threw back her shoulders. "Yes, the yoke of responsibility..." she began airily.

"Now, don't be smart!" Katherine cut across her teasing by rapping her knuckles with a teaspoon. "I'm serious. We all rely on you, and I think it's time you considered moving closer to home."

"I do live at home," Mari reminded, a gentle scolding in her voice and her eyes, though she hadn't intended it. "You're the one who moved away."

"I know." Katherine chose to ignore the barb. "But home is where one's family is. I would so love to have you living here. I have a lot of time on my own now and we could go shopping..." Katherine's eyes wandered dreamily, and Mari had to laugh. Her mother was a prime candidate for membership in Shoppers Anonymous, should such a group ever form. She was an incurable addict of the favorite feminine pastime, but Mari had not inherited the tendency.

"When we went shopping for clothes for you before the wedding, I was a wreck by lunchtime. There was nothing below my knees but stumps!" Mari's accusation was wrapped in laughter. "Besides, you may be a lady of independent means, but I'm not. Scully's Bookstore in Hollywood could not function without its manager."

"Pooh!" Katherine exclaimed and Mari laughed again, but this time to herself. Her elegant mother was the only woman she knew who could use such a Victorian expression and get away with it. One could almost imagine her snapping open an ivory fan. "You could be replaced in a minute," Katherine went on.

"Thanks a lot!"

"You know what I mean. They don't need you as much as we do, and you could certainly find work in Astoria if you chose to move here."

"The economy is depressed. There are no jobs anywhere."

"Your father has connections."

Mari's eyes flew up to Katherine at that, and the older woman amended quietly, "*Terry* has connections. I'm sorry. Sometimes I forget."

"Even so"—Mari shook her head, making a valiant attempt to ignore that comment—"Thea and Missy are in Los Angeles, and I can't leave."

"Thea has to learn to stand on her own!" Katherine said firmly.

"Thea doesn't and Missy can't." Mari took another sip of coffee, her eyes downcast before her mother could read in them the real gravity of Thea's situation. "I can't leave," she repeated.

"Here it is!" Jasmine emerged from the swinging door with a tray containing a temptingly fragrant gingerbread and plates and forks. "Let's see a show of hands for whipped cream."

While the older girl sliced the cake and distributed it,

Mari turned to pass a plate and found herself looking into Jim's hazel eyes. He looked as though he was awaiting a reply to a question she hadn't heard.

"I beg your pardon?"

"How can you sleep with all this noise?" he grinned. "For the fourth time, would you pass the rolls, please?"

"You've had four already," Mari pointed out, doing as he asked. Quirking an eyebrow, Jim accepted the basket and passed it on to Steve. "Steve's only had three, and he's trying to keep up with me."

"They're delicious, Grandma!" Steve said, buttering the roll he had broken with such obvious anticipation that everyone laughed. "Can you fix them again tomorrow?"

"Of course. But save some room for dessert."

"You'll have to get used to my father being in your mother's life," Jim said when Katherine turned away to talk to Jasmine. He poured Mari another cup of coffee from the hot pot in the middle of the table and sat back to sip his own.

"I didn't say anything, did I?" she asked, immediately defensive, but keeping her voice low.

"You didn't have to. Your eyes looked more injured than words could convey when Katherine referred to him as your father. Why don't you just relax and let yourself like him?"

Annoyed by his criticism, she shrugged with deliberate callousness. "Some people you like and some you don't. It's chemistry."

Jim raised his cup and for a moment stood poised with it halfway to his lips, the lazy quality in his eyes sharpening as he looked at her. "Was that what it was with me, too?"

"Does it matter?"

"Yes, I think it does. I think you see my father as a figure of authority—something you've never really known—and you resent him for that."

"I had a father," Mari reminded him.

He nodded. "Yes, but a very easygoing one, according to Katherine, or you wouldn't be such a rude young woman today, Janie."

"Don't you dare criticize me!" Mari spat under her breath. "And my name is Marijane, or Mari, if words of more than two syllables throw you!"

"Curious," he said, completely undisturbed by her anger. "The name's a lot like you are. Mari brings to mind a cool, serene woman, and Jane makes one think of a vulnerable little girl."

"Well, if that really applies," she pointed out smugly, "you'll notice that everyone else calls me Mari."

He nodded. "You have them fooled, but I can see through you."

Mari speared a piece of gingerbread, trying to appear as though she didn't care what he thought, but secretly hoping to find out what it was he saw. "Next you'll be telling me that you leap tall buildings in a single bound."

"Now you're being smart," Jim admonished.

"And you're being nosy, but that's all right?"

"I'm being interested," Jim corrected. "My father is a fine man. I'd like to see you give him a chance."

"I'll be leaving right after the holidays," Mari pointed out. "I won't be around to be a nuisance, so there's no need to worry."

He held his plate up as Jasmine came around with more whipped cream, then offered Mari's.

"No," she cried and yanked her plate back.

"Don't like whipped cream?" he asked.

"I don't like two hundred more calories on top of the three hundred already on the plate," she explained, then wished she had been quiet when she saw his eyes rove her well-filled red turtleneck visible to him over the tabletop. Then his eyes swung to hers, devilish and lazy. "All your calories seem to have made it to the right places. What are you worried about?"

She blushed alarmingly, and his eyebrow arched as she fidgeted with her fork.

"Modest?" he asked quietly.

"I guess I just didn't expect a compliment from you." She forced a casual tone of voice, wishing the hot color would recede, but he kept watching her and so it persisted.

"What did you expect?"

"More criticism, I suppose. Could we talk about something else?" she asked feebly.

He laughed aloud and put a hand on the back of her chair. "We can talk about doing dishes. I noticed on the schedule Katherine has posted on the door to the kitchen that you and I and Steve are all scheduled to work together tonight."

"I thought you two would like a chance to get acquainted," Katherine said guilelessly, stacking empty dishes. She smiled at Mari who glared back at her, not fooled for a moment. She knew just what her mother had in mind.

"You're scheduled, too, Grandma," Steve said, checking the posted list. "With me and Dad and Aunt Janie."

"Janie!" Mari shrieked at his use of the diminutive, immediately regretting her outburst when she saw the stricken look on the boy's face.

"I'm sorry," he apologized quickly. "Dad calls you..."

"I know. But you call me Aunt Mari," she corrected gently, planting a kiss on his forehead. "I'm sorry. I didn't mean to shout at you. You can even skip the aunt part if you want to."

"No, I like it," he explained, visibly brightening at her forgiveness. "I never had aunts before I came here. Or uncles." He smiled up at David, who was passing with his hands full of dishes.

Dave paused, smiling back, a vague look of longing in his eyes. "You're welcome as a nephew, too, you know that? This family's a little lopsided on women. We need all the help we can get to balance up the male side."

He glanced at Jasmine as he passed her on his way to

the kitchen, a look that spoke volumes, and Jazz colored and looked away.

Terry stood and leaned down to kiss Katherine's hair. "I'm going down to the basement to hunt up the Christmas tree stand. Ask Dave to bring in more wood, will you?"

Jim was leaning over a sinkful of sudsy water, shirt sleeves rolled back over hairy, muscular forearms, when Mari went into the kitchen with the last batch of cups and plates.

Steve had apparently said something smart and a spurt of suds flew from Jim's hand to the boy's nose, delighting him.

Noticing Mari, Steve hurried to relieve her of her burden.

"Well," she praised, "a gentleman."

"Dad told me you gotta help girls," Steve said smiling and opening a drawer for her. "Towels are in here."

Jim looked up from the suds to grin at her. "Sorry. I guess he's just another chauvinist in the making."

"What's that?" Steve asked suspiciously.

"A man who thinks girls are softer," Jim explained, "and should be taken care of."

"A man who thinks women are silly," Mari corrected, "and can't accomplish anything unless they have a man to help them out."

"I don't think that," the boy denied quickly, yet thoughtfully, drying a large dinner plate. "My mom was real smart. Dad used to tell her that all the time. But he took good care of her, too. What's the word for that kind of a man?"

"A saint!" Mari replied. "And there aren't too many of those. Would you open the silverware drawer, Steve? Thanks."

"But Dad"—Steve indicated Jim with a pudgy finger—"I mean this Dad, is a saint, too."

Jim glanced at him dryly over his shoulder. "Thanks, sport."

"You're welcome. 'Cause he thinks girls are smart.

Remember that one, Dad? The one that works on the computer with you at the mill?''

"Steve…''

Ignoring the cautioning quality of Jim's voice, Steve went on, flattered by Mari's attention. "Well, Dad said she was real smart. But one night she came over for dinner and it snowed, and Dad wouldn't let her go home 'cause he said the roads were too slick and she might get hurt. Remember that, Dad?''

"Sure do!'' Jim said emphatically, angling Mari a grin.

"You mean he let her stay the night so she wouldn't get hurt?'' Mari asked with interest.

"Right,'' Steve replied, beaming, his point proven.

Mari bowed her head at Jim in mock admiration and declared gravely, "James Sullivan, you are indeed a saint.''

"How's it going, darlings?'' Katherine hurried into the kitchen, ran to one of the lower drawers and pulled out a hammer.

"I hope you're not planning to help dry with that,'' Mari asked. "Speaking of which, it's about time you showed up. We're almost finished.''

"I'm sorry, dear, but I can't work my turn tonight. Terry's having trouble with one of the screws in the tree stand. It's rusted in place or something. Bye.'' She stopped halfway to the door and turned back with a sly grin. "You aren't fighting, are you?''

Mari looked horrified. "You mean me and Saint James?''

"Who?''

"Janie…'' Jim's voice threatened softly.

In answer to her mother's puzzled expression, Mari, stifling a laugh, shook her head. "No, Mother. We're not fighting.''

"Good.'' Katherine turned away, apparently still puzzled but relieved at least that there was peace. When the door closed behind her, Mari reapplied her towel vigorously to a coffee cup.

"Any pots or pans on your side?" Jim asked blithely, ignoring Mari's earlier comment.

"If there were," she replied airily, "I'd have beaned you with one long before this."

Jim made a low, mocking sound, his laughter-filled eyes slowly appraising her small body, shorter than his by almost a foot and lighter by seventy or eighty pounds.

"Next time we're scheduled together," he said, moving slowly toward her to stop with a mere inch between them, "we'll have to see that you have one handy and go from there."

Refusing to be intimidated by his stance, Mari tipped her head back to look him in the eye and a strange thing happened. She seemed to forget just where the conversation stood. She had said... No, he said... His eyes were more brown than hazel... sort of. There were little green shards of light around the dark pupil and thick, black fringing lashes. There were fine lines at the corners of his eyes, and his eyebrows were rich and dark but finely arched as though they'd been painted by a careful hand.

"You... I..." Mari stammered, awareness coming back to her as the kitchen door swung in. Then Jim, looking over her head at the door, frowned and the spell was broken.

"What is it Katherine?" he asked sharply.

Mari swung around to see her mother in the middle of the room, a piece of paper crushed in her hand. Her face was pale and her mouth was working unsteadily.

"Mom?" A tiny pulse of fear began to beat in Mari's throat. "What happened? Is it Thea?"

Katherine nodded, then shook her head at Mari's gasp and instant pallor. "No, darling, not an accident or anything. It's..." She shook her head and tossed her hair back with a trembling hand. "A taxi just dropped Missy off."

"A taxi?" Mari asked in confusion. "Where is she?"

Katherine gestured beyond the door. "She was
asleep. Jazz is putting her to bed. We have to talk before you see her, Mari. This was in her coat pocket...as if she was a piece of baggage." She handed the
note to Mari, then shook her head sadly. "You'd better
sit. Your sister Thea has struck again."

Mari took the envelope and glanced up at Jim as he
and Steve made to move around her to leave the room.

"No, please stay, Jim, if you don't mind," Katherine said. "We might need you. But, Stevie, would you
go help Grandpa with the tree?"

"Sure, Grandma," he nodded and left as they sat
around the small table in a corner of the kitchen.

Mari scanned the note quickly, felt her heartbeat
quicken, and emitting a little involuntary gasp, went
over it again slowly.

Dear Mom:
      I am addressing this to you because when we
spoke on the phone you said Mari expected to be a
day or two late joining you. If there was any way to
accomplish this without involving you, I would,
but as things are, that's impossible. Mari, I know,
will rise to the occasion, but you will blame yourself, and nothing would be more unjust than that. I
am leaving for Rome today with Giulio and hope
to spend the next year working in his films. At this
point it is impossible for me to bring Missy, and
she is always asking for "Mommy Jane" anyway. I
would like to put her in your care, Mari. If you
would consider her permanent adoption, I would
be grateful. Motherhood has not developed as one
of my talents. If you find that impossible, I would
appreciate it if you could keep her for several
months until we finish the current film, then I'll
try to come home to make arrangements with the
authorities.
      Mom, please don't let this ruin your reunion.
Mari once explained me to myself as someone

"unable to reach out and unable to be touched." I
think she was right. I love all of you as much as I
am able to care for anyone. Please forgive me if
you can; if you can't, then please go on as though I
had never been.

Althea

Mari folded the note, and breathing a ragged sigh that
hurt deep inside, she looked up at her mother.

"Can you?" Katherine asked her gently. The question of Thea was dismissed; what mattered now was
Missy.

Mari thought of the small, dark little girl, so intelligent and loving, and nodded without pause. "Of
course, I can."

"Darling, think!" Katherine covered Mari's hand
with her own and shook it. "Don't let yourself be
pushed. How can you care for and support a small child
all by yourself?"

"Mom, how can I not? She's a little girl who deserves to be loved as you loved us."

When Katherine began to suggest that maybe Jasmine and David or maybe even she and Terry, Mari
shook her head firmly.

"No. Jazz and Dave have demanding careers; you
and Terry have a new marriage and deserve time to
yourselves. Missy knows me and we get along well. It
has to be me. And I'm going to start adoption proceedings immediately, before Thea leaves that address on
the bottom of the note." As Mari stood, ready to seek
out her sister and brother-in-law for legal advice, Katherine pulled her down again.

"Mari, please," she said, with unaccustomed severity. "Having a child all day, every day, never being able
to return her to her mother, will be different from just
having her visit you."

"Last year Missy spent more time with me than she
did with Thea," Mari explained, her dark eyes wide
with emotion. "I've walked the floors with her, cleaned

up after her, hugged her and spanked her. I know life with a child isn't roses, but unlike Thea, that's not what I'm looking for.''

"What *are* you looking for?" Jim, who had read the note, folded it and slipped it back into its envelope, then looked across the table at Mari, his eyes quiet, unrevealing.

"To reach out," she said almost defiantly, daring him to ridicule. "To be touched. And this seems an excellent opportunity."

"Jim, you're a single parent in a similar situation," Katherine turned earnestly to her stepson. "You talk to her."

He grinned, studying the color in Mari's cheeks, the glitter in her eyes. "You want to place me between Janie and her determination?"

Katherine frowned at him exasperatedly, then turned back to her daughter. "Mari, do you know what having a child will do to your social life?"

"I haven't any."

"You'll never have any. Good men, men who'll take an interest in a woman with a child, are few and far between. Those who will marry her are even fewer."

And those who will marry her knowing she'll never bear children are fewer still, Mari thought. Aloud, she said, "Mom, I couldn't care less whether I marry or not."

"That's an unhealthy attitude, Janie," Jim contributed. He had gone to the stove for the coffeepot and opened the cupboard with his free hand, hooking a long finger through three mug handles and bringing them to the table.

"This is no time to tease me."

"I'm not teasing," he said, pouring the coffee. "Every child has the right to expect two parents in his life. I admire your eagerness to take Missy, but I'd hate to see you do it with the idea that it puts paid to any thought you ever had of getting married."

"I never had such a thought."

"You should," he said firmly. "Now more than ever."

"Then why aren't you married?" she asked testily. "Doesn't Steve have a right to a mother?"

"You bet he does," he said without pause, then with a grin, added, "My son needs a mother and Melissa needs a father. Want to get married?"

She raised her eyes in supplication. "I'd be up for murder before we ever got to the honeymoon!"

He shook his head gravely. "That *would* be a shame."

"James!" Katherine said anxiously, her eyes wide and frantic. "Talk to her like an older brother. She won't listen to me. You know more than anyone what it's like to lead a busy life and have the constant responsibility of a young child. Make her see reason. I'm going to find Terry." And she fled the room.

"Don't bother," Mari said firmly, sipping the hot coffee and feeling it slip down to the pit of her stomach where chaos was raging. "My mind is made up."

"All right," he said quietly. He was sitting opposite her, his eyes suddenly sober. "Then consider this. You said before that you had Melissa last year more than her mother had, but was that constantly, every minute, day after day, through colds, sleepless nights, measles and more sleepless nights, upset stomachs and still another sleepless night? It will never stop. There will be no one else to whom you can turn and say, 'Here. It's your turn. I'm tired.' It will always be your turn." He leaned on his elbows, his eyes dark with intensity now. "It's almost impossible to make a child understand that you have a headache or that you've had a bad day and would rather not listen to the rundown on the latest Road Runner cartoon or be the second hand on a game of Space Invaders. You can say, 'Don't bother me unless it's important.' But 'important' to Steve is 'Dad, can I have a banana?'"

Mari nodded knowingly, unable to hold back a smile. "Did anyone try to talk you out of taking Steve?"

He nodded. "My father pointed out all the pitfalls of

parenthood. But I'm blessed with stamina and I inherited his cussedness. I think I'm turning out to be well prepared for the job. And Steve is a genuine jewel. Had I made him myself, I couldn't be more proud of him nor love him more than I do."

She frowned at him. "Then why try to discourage me?"

"Because you'd be a woman alone," he said, watching her in a way that she found very distracting. His eyes were roving her hair and seemed to settle every few moments on her mouth. "I like kids. I wouldn't think twice about marrying a woman with one or more children if I loved her, but your mother is right. To a lot of men, a ready-made family is too much responsibility to start out with."

"Marriage is not the only option for a woman today," she said impatiently. "And despite all you've said about a child needing two parents, I don't think a bad second parent is any better than none at all. No," she said firmly, resolved, "I want my sister to start adoption proceedings immediately, and I'm taking Missy back to L.A. with me."

"Why?"

She looked at him for a moment, puzzled. "I just explained."

"I mean, why go back to L.A.?"

"I live there. I have a job and an apartment there."

Jim nodded and looked at her assessingly. "May I make a suggestion?"

"If I said no, would it stop you?"

He thought a moment, then smiled again. He did have a devastating smile, she noted. "No," he said.

"Then by all means, make a suggestion."

He became very sober again. "A child who has no father could benefit from being close to grandparents. And an uncle and a cousin. And a woman who has for all intents and purposes just 'lost' a daughter could derive comfort from having a grandchild near."

Forced to think about that a minute by the sheer

logic of the statement, Mari was silent, her brow furrowed. "It's not possible," she said, half to herself. "My apartment—"

"There are apartments here," Jim said quietly. "In fact, I own a small house that's standing empty right now."

"My job—"

"Your *father* has connections," he said deliberately, the mocking words snapping her out of her confusion.

She looked into his teasing eyes and felt her annoyance over his remark recede almost immediately. "Why do you love to goad me?" she asked wearily. "We've only known each other about six hours, and you're always after me."

"Certainly Katherine has taught you that men are predatory?" he laughed.

"I don't think you consider me feminine prey for the purpose of catching. You just like to put me in a corner and watch me squirm." She looked a little annoyed and a little hurt, and he reached across the table to give her hand a fraternal pat.

"I'm sorry. That wasn't my intention. It's just that for a mature young woman who's been on her own since college and supporting herself admirably"—he paused to shrug and shake his head as though she were a provocative mystery—"you seem so insulated, so... virginal."

Why she should be stung to the quick when his assessment was so on target, she wasn't sure, but her eyelashes fanned as she dropped them to hide her expression.

She had insulated herself with a cloak of untouchability because it hurt too much to be rejected for an inadequacy over which she had no control. Taking care against it happening again seemed the only protection. And she was still virginal, though twenty-six, because she couldn't imagine being wrapped in the intimate embrace of a man she did not love and could not commit herself to totally, and, so far, she hadn't met him.

"I've done it again, haven't I?" Jim assessed correctly. The hand that had just patted hers reached out to uncurl the fist she had made on the tabletop. He put his fingers in hers then closed hers over them with his thumb. He lowered his head to look into her eyes, but she kept them averted. "I didn't mean to imply that I disapproved."

Somehow that word sparked her temper. Her eyes flew up to his, wide and sparking. "Why should I care if you approve of my virginal status or not?"

He shook his head, his eyes watchful. "I don't know. But you apparently do. And anyway, I'm more concerned about your insulation than your virginity. The one can be treated by the right man, the other can prevent the outside world from ever getting through to you and that could eventually even turn the right man away."

Before she could comment on that statement, the kitchen door swung in and Katherine, Terry, and Jasmine came into the room. That Katherine had been crying was obvious. Jasmine snatched the letter off the table and read it over quickly, making very unladylike comments under her breath. She looked down at her younger sister.

"Are you going to do it?"

"Yes."

"Good. I'll give you the family rate on my services." Then with a curl of her mouth and the slam of her fist on the table, "That—"

"Jazz, please," Katherine interrupted. "Mari, are you sure?"

Terry pulled more chairs around the table and they closed up ranks, Jim moving to sit beside Mari.

"She can do it, Katherine," Jim said, surprising Mari. She looked at him, suspicious of his confidence in her. "And she'll do it well, I'm sure. And, of course, we're all here for support."

"But she'll be so far away!"

"She's considering moving to Astoria," he informed them, kicking her foot gently when her mouth fell open. "The house I own on Sixteenth Street would be perfect, and I'm sure Dad could find her a job."

"That would be wonderful!" Katherine said with such a glow in her eyes that Mari hadn't the heart to correct the false impression.

"I know just the thing," Terry said, his arm around Katherine. "There's a woman I meet in the bakery every morning who owns a small book and gift shop. She was just saying last week that she'd like to have more help."

"But...I...I have to give notice..." she said helplessly.

"Considering the special circumstances," Jasmine offered, "they'll be understanding, certainly."

She imagined they would be since she had always been treated fairly. But things were just moving too quickly for her, and she suspected they were being pushed by her new stepbrother. She glanced over at him and saw him talking to her mother, a look so gentle and charming on his face that it was hard to imagine that was the same man who teased her so and seemed to gain great enjoyment from it. She heaved a ragged sigh, a strange feeling overtaking her. It was as though she was at a crossroads in her life and someone else had climbed into the little motor car in which one followed one's destiny, and was arguing with her over which way to go.

She felt suddenly, overwhelmingly tired. "If you'll all excuse me," she said, getting to her feet, "I think I'll go to bed."

"Mind the stairs, darling," Katherine cautioned. "The light bulb burned out this morning and I didn't replace it yet."

"I'll walk her up," Jim offered, standing also. "It's time I found Steve and got him to bed."

"I can manage," Mari insisted, but he wasn't paying

attention. A gentle touch at her back was pushing her toward the door as a chorus of good nights followed her.

"This is silly," Mari grumbled as Jim led her up the steps.

"I thought it was chivalrous," Jim countered. "No, not that way." His hand caught at her waist as she continued forward when they reached a small landing. "You'll end up in a tall vase of pampas grass. The stairs angle to the left here." It was really dark now, and she was totally dependent on the body beside her for guidance, the hand at her waist to prevent her stumbling.

They reached the top of the stairs, and he steered her to the right where the small glow of a nightlight indicated the room she would share with Missy, was supposed to have shared with Missy and Thea.

"Are you an early riser?" Jim asked when they stopped at the threshold of the bedroom.

"Yes, usually. Why?"

"How about an early morning walk, and you can chew me out for telling the folks you were thinking of moving to Astoria?"

"By the way," she began in an angry whisper. But he put up a large hand to silence her.

"Shh. You'll wake the baby. Tomorrow morning? About seven?"

"Missy might be up, too."

"Bring her along."

"All right." Mari smiled to herself. Jim seemed to have great confidence in himself as a parent. And perhaps he was good at dealing with a sweet-tempered eight-year-old boy. But she had yet to meet a man who wasn't driven wild by the boundless energy of a two-year-old.

After the din of everyone talking at once at the little table in the kitchen, the upstairs hallway seemed deathly quiet. A sudden tension filled the air, and as Jim put a hand to the wall behind Mari, she came joltingly to awareness, all weariness gone. His eyes were on her mouth. "You know," he said casually, "it's very important to our parents that we get along."

She frowned absently, distracted by his nearness. "Yes, I know."

"So far"—his knuckle traced a line along her jaw, and contrary to the laws of physiology, something in her stomach contracted—"we seem to disagree on everything. We have to find some...common ground. I think you were right. There is a certain chemistry at work here."

She looked up into his eyes, willing herself to say something witty or at least intelligent; but the warm, hazel depths seemed to entrance her as they had earlier in the kitchen.

"Don't you agree?" he asked softly.

Her lips parted to reply, but no sound came. She watched in fascination as his head came down, seeing in microscopic detail his finely molded nose, his black, feathery eyelashes, and the small ragged scar over his left eyebrow. Then, as it paused a centimeter away from her lips, she watched his mouth, nicely shaped and smiling even now.

He took her face in his large warm hands and she felt the contact down to her toes. Startled by her reaction, she put both hands to his chest in a defensive gesture, and he paused again, his eyes sharpening.

She had been held and kissed before, and she had enjoyed it, but now she felt on unfamiliar ground. Her breath was trapped in her throat, and she could feel the blood pulsing through her body. This frame in which she had lived for twenty-six years felt suddenly alien to her, reacting in ways she seemed unable to control. And only because there were warm, callused hands on her face and a tall, taut body held her captive against the wall. What would happen, she wondered in concern, if he finally kissed her?

She wasn't sure why that question made her feel so suddenly at risk, but it didn't matter. Her bracing hands now moved over his shoulders, inviting him closer; she had to know.

At first she was very aware of Jim, the soft musky fragrance of his after-shave, the smooth cheek beneath her hand with just a tantalizing prickle of beard, and his mouth, soft and warm, moving over hers with paralyzing effect.

And then she lost awareness of everything but her own reactions. Something seemed to leap from deep inside to meet his mounting fervor, and her fingers were in his hair. Her mouth was moving with his, and her body strained against his, the contact causing a flutter in her limbs.

Then he held her away from him, propping her against the other side of the door frame, facing her.

Missing his warmth, Mari looked at him in soft confusion until she heard footsteps rounding the corner from the stairs to the hallway.

"Dad?" Steve asked.

"Here, son," Jim replied, his voice slightly ragged.

"Grandma said you were looking for me. I was playing with the video game in the basement."

"It's time for bed, Steve."

Steve sighed in disappointment. "All right. Good night."

When Steve's bedroom door closed farther down the hall, Mari heaved a sigh and put a hand to her reeling head.

"I think we've found it," Jim laughed.

"What?" she asked, her voice a whisper.

"The common ground."

"We're supposed to be brother and sister," Mari reminded dryly.

He laughed again. "I think that's definitely out. Your head is obviously spinning, and I'm hearing bells. Those are classic symptoms."

A door opened down the hall, and Steve's voice in an exaggerated whisper declared forlornly, "I can't find my pajamas!"

"Coming!" Jim called back softly. Then he leaned away from the door frame as though reluctant to leave. "See you in the morning?"

"Yes," she agreed, wishing he would touch her again, just a pat on her shoulder, a hand to her face.

But with a casual wave, he went down the hall to the room he shared with Steve.

Chapter Three

After an almost sleepless night Mari awoke to squeals of delight from the crib beside her bed. Reluctantly opening a heavy eye, she looked up to see a pink-sleeper-clad Melissa jumping up and down in the near darkness, two dark, disheveled ponytails bobbing up and down. "Mommy Jane!" she cried in a high-pitched baby babble, plump little hands reaching for her.

Forgetting her exhaustion, Mari sprang out of bed and took Missy out of the crib, returning her surprisingly strong hug.

"Hi, darling!" she whispered. "How are you?"

"Missy fine!" the child whispered back exaggeratedly. "Mommy Jane fine?"

"Yes, Missy. I'm fine. We'll have to be very quiet so we don't wake anyone, okay?"

She put a shushing finger to her lips that Missy copied.

"Good girl. We're going to get all dressed up and meet Uncle Jim for a walk."

"Unnle Jim?" Missy asked, standing still while Mari rummaged through her small bag for a warm top and pants. But coming from Southern California, her wardrobe was in much the same state as Mari's, too thin for the Northwest winter.

"*Uncle* Jim," Mari enunciated carefully, pulling two light sweaters over the baby's head. Tights and a pair of jeans were followed by another sweater and a quilted red coat. Then she sat Missy on her bed and quickly

climbed into jeans and a sweater and her thin red coat.
Reaching for her hat, she realized that Missy had none
and put it on the child's head instead, giggling with her
when it covered her eyes. She cuffed it back, then
pulled Missy along into the corridor, closing the door
quietly behind them.

Glancing at her watch under the soft hall light, she
noted that it was just seven and wondered if Jim was
awake, and if so, if he had slept any better than she had.
The house was silent as they hurried along the hallway
and down the stairs. In the living room the fragrance of
the evergreen assailed Mari's nostrils, and it brought a
little thrill to her spine. Christmas was coming. And
Thea notwithstanding, they were all together, this
strange conglomeration of Sullivans and Westridges.

"Tree!" Missy whispered loudly, pointing as Mari
led her across the living room to the door.

"Yes, sweetheart. We were waiting for you to come
so you could help put all the pretty things on it."

As they reached the door, a figure moved out of the
shadows, and Jim appeared dressed in jeans and a
bright-orange down vest over another flannel shirt.
Covering most of his dark hair was a deep blue woolen
watch cap.

"You made it," he said softly.

"I told you I would."

"Yes, but I heard you thrashing around all night. I
thought you might decide to sleep in."

Yes, and he probably knows the color of my under-
wear, Mari thought grimly, then remembering Missy,
reached down to pull her forward. But the child, who
was usually cautious with strangers, went toward him
on her own, and when he got down on his knees to talk
to her, she didn't draw away.

"This is Uncle Jim, Missy," Mari said. Missy was
studying him with childlike thoroughness, her eyes
roving his face and one little hand reaching out to
touch the shiny snaps on his jacket. She then looked up
at Mari and asked in a loud whisper, "Daddy?"

"No, darling," she said gently. "Uncle Jim."

Missy turned back to the man before her, still having to look up a little into eyes softer than Mari had yet seen them.

"Daddy," she said decisively, then as though that was settled, said it again, apparently liking the sound. "Daddy."

Mari looked at Jim openmouthed, at a loss to explain, but he merely grinned and straightening up, opened the door. "Guess 'Daddy' it is. Let's go."

The early sky was heavy, leaden gray as they stepped outside. Mari took a deep breath of cold, fragrant air and felt it flutter inside her and nudge her awake.

"Horsie!" Missy declared gleefully as Ta came running heavily toward them, her plumy tail wagging excitedly. She leaped on Jim, her paws thudding into his chest. He stroked her black coat roughly, then called her to sit while he introduced Missy.

"This is Ta, Missy. Want to pet her?"

Fearlessly the child put a mittened hand out and gently banged the dog's broad head.

"Stay, Ta!" Jim ordered quietly and the dog, sitting as tall as Missy stood, suffered her attentions with admirable patience.

"Okay. Good girl," he said finally, and the dog galloped away to investigate the snowy bushes up the road.

With Missy between them, Jim and Mari walked slowly up the driveway to the road, completely devoid of traffic at that hour.

Their breath smoked out ahead of them in foggy plumes, and the air was still but for the call of ducks somewhere in the distance. Glancing at Jim out of the corner of her eye, Mari felt a little annoyed that he could trudge along so calmly, head thrown back, drawing deep gulps of this Pacific Northwest morning.

Last night had probably not been as momentous for him as it had been for her. As a handsome man at the peak of his wit and sexual prowess, romantic encounters such as they'd shared last night in the hallway were probably nothing new and certainly not worthy of comment the following day.

But it had definitely been something new for her. So much for her insulation.

"About your announcement that I was thinking of moving to Astoria," she said coolly, anger the result of her thoughts.

Hands jammed in his pockets, he angled her an impenitent grin. "That was rotten, wasn't it? I knew they'd immediately close in on you, and you'd have no alternative but to consider staying."

She stopped in her tracks and stared at him openmouthed. But before she could phrase a protest, he asked with complete change of subject, "Where's your hat?"

"I put it on Missy." She pointed to the child who had stopped to inspect the snowy branches of a tamarack. They stopped, too, and Jim reached into a side pocket of his vest and pulled a green watch cap out of it. He pulled it down over her head, flattening the cold, silky hair to the side of her face. "It's Steve's, but it'll keep you warm."

He watched her tug at it selfconsciously, then reached out to grasp a fistful of the red-brown hair that hung below the hat.

"What a color," he said, studying the spray laying across his hand. "It's like a redwood in the rain. And you must have enough there for two."

"My...my father had a full head of auburn hair," she explained, unsettled by his attention. Missy had started on again, and they moved to follow her.

"You seem to have inherited the best of both your parents."

She frowned up at him, surprised a second time by a compliment from him.

"You have the femininity and feisty charm of your mother and your sister. That's very attractive." He grinned and put a hand out to steady her as they followed Missy off the road, climbing over the snow that had been shoveled to the side. "Too much of that, though, can get on a man's nerves. But there's a blessed quiet in your eyes. I like that."

Unable to speak, Mari searched her mind frantically for something casual to say. But that had been such an intimate observation that she could think of nothing. Then Missy called excitedly, "Daddy!"

"Yes, babe?" he asked, looking up.

She pointed to a small pond off the road where ducks swam, oblivious to the cold. "Birds!" she exclaimed.

"Ducks," he corrected gently. Taking her hand, he led her to the shore of the small pond for a closer look.

"Ducks!" she repeated, a mittened hand pointing, her dark eyes under the cuff of Mari's hat enormous and sparkling. Then she looked at the man squatting beside her and said conversationally, "Quack!"

He gave a shout of laughter and swung the child up in his arms, turning back to the road.

"I think I know where she got the idea that you should be Daddy," Mari said, crunching over the snow beside him. "She has a book about families, intended to teach children about their relationship to others in the family unit. Missy has always been a little preoccupied with the father in it, I suppose because she knows she doesn't have one. I guess in her little mind, you must be the ideal."

"She's going to be a heartbreaker," Jim said, swinging her up onto his shoulders. She squealed excitedly and put her arms out, enjoying the sensation of flight as his strong hands held her tiny ankles.

"Mommy Jane!" she giggled. "Look Missy!"

"Yes, darling," Mari laughed. "Like a bird." Mari heaved a sigh. Well, those two certainly had no trouble relating to one another, she noted. And she had thought that a busy two-year-old might overwhelm him.

"Katherine told me that you manage a bookstore?"

Jim said, peering at her around Missy's denim-clad knee.

"Yes. I went to work there right out of college, and I've been manager for the past two years." She reached down to pick up a snow-covered stick and poked the snowy ground with it as they walked on. "I had hoped to own it one day." She aimed a dark glance at him. "But you're doing your best to scotch that for me."

"There are a couple of bookstores in Astoria."

"You're missing the point."

"No, you are," he said cryptically.

"Meaning?"

"Down, Daddy!" Missy demanded, and Jim stopped to swing Missy over his head and set her on her feet. She ran ahead, following the sound of ducks calling, then stopped, pointing skyward when a flock of them in formation passed overhead under a snow-heavy sky.

Jim laughed and put an arm around Mari's shoulders, pulling her along to follow Missy. "I think you'd like it here. In the winter, as you can see, there's a beautiful view everywhere you look, and in summer, it's every bit as breathtaking. And there's a lot to see and do. We're steeped in history, too. And you should get to know my father."

"I want to live in Southern California where it's warm and familiar and where I've spent my entire life," she said, throwing the stick away. "There can't be more to see and do here than there is there, and we also have a fascinating history. Doesn't that count?"

"But you've seen and done all those things," he said, a smile in his voice. "Don't you want to try something new?"

"I'm not like that," she pouted. "I like things I'm comfortable with."

"And you're not comfortable with me." The remark sat somewhere between a question and a statement, and she wasn't sure how to respond to it. His blatant masculinity made her uncomfortable, his audacity in telling her mother and Terry that she was considering moving to Astoria made her angry, and his constant teasing criticism of her made her furious.

And yet, inconsistent with all that, was a curious rightness she felt when he was near, a new sense of security. She had always been independent and self-sufficient, and though her infertility had made her vulnerable in her relationships, it hadn't diminished her faith in herself as a person. In dealing with men, it was her value as a woman that she doubted.

Jim was the first man she had ever known who made her aware of her femininity. Though she was a fairly respectable five feet five inches, the nine or ten inches he had on her made her feel small, and his attentive courtesies made her feel fragile. Though he teased her mercilessly, she knew he wouldn't if he considered her lacking in intelligence and a kindred spirit.

"I don't understand your attitude," she said, stopping as a light snow began to fall, the road stretching like a flocked white ribbon ahead of them. She was surprised to hear that she had voiced the thought aloud, but he had stopped, too, and she had to continue. "I mean...it's contradictory. You can be very...sweet to me and then tease me ruthlessly. Why?"

He thought a moment, a smile forming slowly, revealing teeth as white as the snow. "I think it's because you're a contradiction. You can be so cool and so mature and then—" He paused and she knew he was remembering last night. She braced herself for the barbed reference, but instead, he took the point of her chin in his hand and looked into her eyes. "Something else becomes visible in your eyes. Way back there, there's both a frightened little girl and a woman with fire in both hands."

He studied her a moment longer, then dropped his hand, and his voice became brisk. "You're a puzzle, Marijane Westridge. And I'm tenacious about things that confuse me. I guess I just haven't figured you out yet, so my reactions to you are contradictory. But one day that will change."

Missy ran back to them, crying, and Jim leaned down to pick her up. "What happened, babe?"

"Went boom!" she sniffed.

He looked to Mari for an interpretation.

She smiled at his confusion, putting aside her own. "She fell down."

"Ah! That two-word sentence structure leaves a lot to the imagination. Okay, we'll head for home and a hot breakfast. That'll make you feel better."

"Hurts," Missy complained woefully, enjoying the new thrill of male solicitude.

He patted her back and spoke sympathetically; and before they had reached the drive leading down to the house, she was quiet, lolling contentedly against his shoulder.

Jim headed for the kitchen while Mari pulled the layers of clothes from Missy, then hurried upstairs, responding to an urgently stated, "Potty, Mommy Jane!"

Mari freshened her lipstick and pulled a brush through the disorder left by Stephen's hat. Finished, she put the brush down, her movement toward the door arrested by something she saw in the mirror. There was fire in her eyes and in her hair; and involuntarily she looked down at her small, slim-fingered hands, remembering Jim's words.

Then, the fanciful moment gone, she growled impatiently at herself and, reaching for Missy's hand, went down the stairs to the living room.

They stepped over Steve at work on the floor with a puzzle, and he looked up at Melissa with a curious smile. "Who's she?" he asked Mari.

"My niece, Melissa," Mari introduced, pulling the child's small fingers back as she reached for a piece of the boy's puzzle.

"Melissa, this is Steve."

"Seevie," she repeated, patting his head, much as she had Ta's.

Steve laughed, smoothing his straight blond hair. "Does that mean she likes me?"

"Definitely. Come on, Missy. Let's go have breakfast."

"No," Melissa whined, pulling against Mari as she tried to move toward the kitchen. "Seevie!" she pleaded, pointing toward the puzzle.

"Darling, you'll just mess it up for him," Mari explained patiently.

"She can stay," Steve shrugged.

Mari looked doubtful. "She'll probably scramble all the pieces for you."

"It's okay." He smiled that open, winning smile. "When you're finished with breakfast, I can fix it again."

Mari squatted down to kiss his cheek. "You're a real treasure, you know that?"

He grinned shyly, his face bright red. "That's what Dad says."

"Well, he's right. If she gets out of hand, you come and get me, all right?"

As Mari walked away, a glance over her shoulder found Missy already reconstructing the puzzle. Pushing through the door into the kitchen, her nostrils were assailed by the homey aroma of bacon and toast.

"Good morning!" she said brightly to the quartet at the table, stopping uncertainly in the middle of the floor when she noted their expressions.

Jasmine had obviously been crying and David looked angry. Discomfort was written on her mother's flushed face and Terry appeared to be making a valiant effort to eat his breakfast as though nothing were wrong.

"How do you like your eggs?" The question came from Jim who stood behind her at the stove. She retraced her steps to look over his shoulder.

"Over easy, please."

"All right," he grinned. "But I'm not promising anything. If you have an aversion to broken yolks, speak now."

"I'll eat it any way I can get it," she responded with a

smile, grateful for his distracting banter. "Want me to make the toast?"

"Good idea."

"How many slices can you eat?"

"Four."

"Four?" she repeated. "At once?"

"Well, four at one meal, but one at a time." He turned six slices of beautifully crisp bacon onto a plate and placed it in the warm oven. "We outdoor types have hearty appetites."

Mari plugged the toaster into the counter beside the stove and wagged a warning finger at him. "Someday that will catch up with you."

Jim patted his flat stomach and eyed her wickedly. "Does that mean you're only attracted to my body?"

Horrified, Mari looked back at the table to see if anyone had caught that remark, but Jasmine was flying past them in tears, pushing her way through the swinging door as Dave snatched his parka from the hook by the back door and disappeared into the snow.

Katherine sagged in her chair and held her cup out as Terry poured another round of coffee.

"Those two are in serious trouble," she said anxiously.

Mari turned back to the toast, not wanting to unwittingly divulge anything Jazz had told her.

"That girl doesn't know if she's an attorney or a woman," Terry said, his tone shot with disgust.

Mari spun around, loyalty rising in her, though her sister's attitude was incompatible with her own. "Can't she be both?" she asked, eyeing her stepfather levelly.

"Not if it interferes with their marriage," Terry responded, returning her steady look.

"What if Mother wanted to act again? Would you deny her that right because it would interfere with your marriage?"

"Our marriage is not in trouble," Terry replied calmly. "Theirs is."

"Then the responsibility to save it is something both of them share." Mari angled her chin as Terry's eyes darkened. "Why should Jazz have to give up her career? Why couldn't Dave give up his?"

"That's absurd!"

"Why?"

"Because he's the breadwinner. And she doesn't have to work."

Mari barely controlled her frustration and took several steps toward him. She sensed Jim moving away from the stove, watchful, as though ready to interfere.

"Jasmine is not 'working.' She's doing something she's wanted to do since we were children, something she's trained for and struggled to accomplish."

Terry, in the Sullivan uniform of jeans and a bright flannel shirt, his iron gray hair silvered by the overhead light, closed the small gap between them. "She has a husband as well as a career." He glowered down at her.

"That's right," Mari agreed intrepidly, "and if she owes him emotional support and physical comfort, then he owes her the same. We are no longer handmaidens, Terry, but equal partners."

A ringing silence met her final declaration, and she glanced around at the three faces watching her, a little embarrassed by her tirade. "Anyway," she mumbled, shuffling a foot, "I don't think we have the right to discuss what she should or shouldn't do. It's her business."

Terry looked down at her a long moment, his expression changing from annoyance to frustration to resignation. He called to Katherine over his shoulder, "Let's go for a walk. This generation is too much for me." Then he added mysteriously, clapping Jim on the shoulder as he passed him, "Watch yourself, son. That little package is trouble."

Mari watched her stepfather walk away, her mother following him after turning to toss her a kiss and a wink.

"I thought I was a goner there for a minute," she

said to Jim with a wry smile. "I half expected him to pick me up by the throat and shake me."

Jim laughed and gestured toward the table. "Sit down. I'll serve."

"The toast!" She gasped, looking toward the bread and toaster she had forgotten.

"I took care of it while you were defending the modern woman. That's one you owe me."

Mari stopped in the act of pushing the pot of jam toward him and glared, sparks rekindled in her eyes. "If you Sullivans would come out of the Dark Ages, you'd find a full partner a lot more help to you than a simpering slave!"

He grinned maddeningly. "I hate to take the wind out of your sails, but I was only kidding. You've got your thumb in the jam."

Growling, Mari scrubbed off the lump of strawberry preserves. Glancing up at him under scowling eyebrows, she found him casually peppering his egg, fighting a betraying tic in his bottom lip. She sighed heavily. "I'm sorry," she admitted reluctantly. "I don't usually get on my soap box about that; it's so reasonable it shouldn't have to be preached. His attitude just rankled me."

He nodded, free to chuckle now that she gave him a halfhearted smile. "And he dared to pick on your sister. Loyalty is admirable in anyone, but it's a prerequisite in a wife... a partner," he added quickly.

"Jasmine's loyal," Mari defended, spreading jam where it belonged. "She's just... at a confusing point in her life."

He looked up to smile at her. "I wasn't talking about Jasmine."

"Who?" she asked, but he returned her a bland look and gestured away her question with a wave of his fork. "Where's Melissa?"

"'Helping' Steve with his puzzle." She rolled her eyes descriptively. "I warned him, but he insisted that she could stay with him. He's an unusually calm and mature little boy."

Jim nodded. "He's been through a lot." He studied his triangle of toast thoughtfully then looked up at her. "You're very good with kids," he said, adding hastily, "Not that I think women should be kept barefoot and pregnant, or anything like that. Or that mothering is all they're good for. Or that their place is in the—"

"Stop it!" she shouted, laughing as she swatted him with her linen napkin. "Enough. You promise not to be patronizing, and I'll promise not to preach."

"Deal," he agreed, his eyes alight with humor.

"Okay," she said. "I like kids." She drew a deep breath to stifle the wince. "I love to cook. I'm pretty good on the sewing machine, and I love to fuss with my hair and to try new makeup. But I can run the most complete and currently stocked bookstore you've ever seen, and I'd put my special order success average up against the major chains. I love it all." She looked at him levelly. "And I can do it all."

Jim smiled gently. "Isn't that preaching?"

She thought a moment, wondering what had made her carry on like that when a simple "I like kids" would have been sufficient. Was it some subconscious desire that he know what she could accomplish as insurance against the day he might learn of her sterility?

"I think it was just an explanation," she said, her expression suddenly sober, her composure shaken by that thought.

"Why?" he asked.

Good question, she thought. But she replied, "You asked."

He looked at her a moment, and she saw the realization in his eyes that she had answered a lot more than he had asked. "So I did," he agreed, studying her analytically, his fork poised over his food. Then he said briskly, "Finish your breakfast. We're putting up the tree tonight. You'll need your strength. Is that coat you had on this morning the warmest thing you own?"

"My mother told me that it rained a lot here but that it seldom snowed," she said, waving a hand toward the frosty window. "I thought sure my California coat would be warm enough."

"It's just a freak cold spell. Happens once in a while. But if you're staying here, you should have a warmer coat than that. And a hat and a good pair of boots."

"I'm not going logging with Terry," she quipped. "I'd just like to stave off pneumonia. Besides, who's staying?"

Ignoring her question, Jim pushed his plate away and went to the stove for the coffeepot. "As soon as the road's clear, I'll take you to Lolly's. It's a chic little shop in Astoria."

Mari couldn't help but smile at hearing this tall, tough man describe a shop as "chic."

"And how did you become familiar with Lolly's?" she teased. "Do all your lady friends receive gifts?"

He smiled, topping up her coffee. "No, but my mother did, and she loved to shop there."

As he replaced the pot and came back to the table, Mari pushed her plate aside and leaned on an elbow, her expression thoughtful.

"What was your mother like?"

He thought a moment and smiled, leaning back in his chair and toying with the handle of his coffee mug. "She was small and blond; a local Finnish girl, as a matter of fact. In temperament she was a lot like you. She was warm and loving and as smart as a whip, but absolute murder if you crossed her. While Dad was building up the mills, he worked long hours and was away a lot, and it was my mother who made decisions and meted out discipline." He chuckled reminiscently. "Even though I was over six feet tall by age fifteen, she wasn't intimidated by me one bit, and I knew enough to respect every word she said."

She could see that in him, the gentleness coupled with an enduring tenacity that would allow nothing to be impossible.

"And had I handpicked your mother as a wife for my father, I couldn't have done a better job." He finished his coffee and smiled again. "She's an all-around genuine person with that extra little zest about her that's put a sparkle in my father that I haven't seen there in years."

Mari nodded, unable to fight a feeling of pettiness because of the antagonism she felt toward Terry.

"I suppose your confrontation this morning hasn't helped your opinion of my father," he guessed. "But I'd appreciate it if you'll remember that his family was and is very important to him. I think he simply can't imagine a woman not wanting one."

"Actually," Mari admitted, after a moment's thought, "he let me speak and he didn't browbeat me. He simply disagreed. I half expected him to stomp all over me, but he didn't."

"Well, that's a place to start," he said, the grave mood evaporating. "According to the dishes schedule, it was supposed to be Jasmine and Dave this morning, but considering..." He grinned and said in his best Bogart voice, "It's you and me, kid."

Chapter Four

The rest of the morning and most of the afternoon was spent hauling boxes of Christmas ornaments up from the basement and decorating the living room.

A chunky garland of juniper hung from the mantel and the stairway, ending in giant red velvet bows at the newels. Colorful pots of holly appeared everywhere, and as the afternoon dimmed into evening, candles were lit on the fireplace, reflecting back into the room from the mirror behind them. With the scent of pine permeating everything, the excitement of Christmas began to build.

Terry was atop the ladder, placing the antique baroque angel on the highest branch, while Katherine and Jasmine directed from below. On Jim's shoulders, Missy placed colorful balls at random, her little face intent on her task.

Mari sat on the loveseat by the fire, stringing popcorn and anxious about the two family members who refused to be involved in the ritual of tree-trimming. Dave's isolation she could understand, but Steve's refusal to join the group around the tree confused her. He sat on the hearth rug with the same puzzle he had worked on most of the day and could not be coaxed away from it.

"Are you all right, Steve?" she asked, leaning forward to touch his shoulder.

He looked around at her, his blue eyes closed against her. "Yes, Aunt Janie."

Surprised by his withdrawal after the bright, open child of last night and this morning, she persisted gently. "Don't you want to help trim the tree?"

"No," he replied quietly.

Probing carefully, she asked, "Are you upset because your father is helping Missy?"

He looked surprised that she should suggest that. "No. I'm just . . . not really interested. I'd rather do this. I'm fine. Honest."

Mari sat back, uneasy, but had no time to contemplate Steve's problem for Jim sat down beside her with a glass of wine. Taking it from him, she found it warm and sniffed the luscious bite of cinnamon.

"Ah. Terry's specialty," she murmured, sipping.

"Right. He's in good form today, too. Hey, Steve." Jim reached a suede boot out to poke the boy's back gently. "They could use some help over there with the tree."

"I'd rather finish this, Dad," he said politely.

Jim frowned at Mari, and she shrugged her shoulders, unable to explain his sudden change in behavior.

"Where's Missy?" she asked.

"She's helping your mother wrap presents in the kitchen."

"Mmm," Mari said vaguely, the warm wine and the fire combining with her sleepless night to make staying awake difficult.

Jim looked down at her appraisingly, his eyes a soft brown in the firelight, going over her heavy eyelids with their blinking lashes and her soft mouth holding back a yawn.

"Naptime?" he asked, setting his glass down on the end table.

She smiled sleepily in self-reproach. "I don't know what's the matter with me." She widened her eyes and tried to sit up, but Jim was settling back in the corner of the loveseat and relieving her of her wineglass.

"What?" She began to protest when he took hold of

her arms, but when he turned her bodily so that she faced him then pulled her gently down to his chest, her protest died. He was warm and comfortingly solid under her woozy head, and when his arms came around to envelop her, she relaxed instantly, the feeling too promising to resist. As though under a spell, she felt him brush the hair back from her face with gentle fingertips, then run his knuckles across her flushed cheekbone.

"Sleep, babe," he said quietly, and almost before he had finished the words, she had complied.

Mari awoke languorously to a delicious feeling of warmth and well-being. Not quite to awareness, she stretched long and sensuously, then curled up again and snuggled into the warmth, burrowing her nose into a pocket of furnacelike heat. Gradually becoming aware of a firm, circular movement at her back that was quickly bringing her out of her drowsy euphoria, Mari opened her eyes and found herself looking into Jim's, the subtle musk of after-shave in her nostrils.

Embarrassed, she moved to draw away, then realized that both her arms were around his neck. Color flooded her already sleep-flushed cheeks as she drew her arms away quickly, but his hands at her back still held her close. Amusement shone in his eyes and she looked away.

"Hi," she said uneasily.

"Hi, yourself," he chuckled, the hand at her back still rubbing lightly, the caressing movement drying her throat, making her heart bump in confusion. "That was quite a nap. We missed dinner."

"We did?" Mari sat up straight, swinging her legs around to face away from Jim, to look about the quiet darkened living room in complete surprise.

"Well, actually, I didn't. Your mother brought me a tray."

"You should have wakened me."

"There was no need. And there's a plate for you in the oven."

"But you missed..."

"I didn't miss a thing," he interrupted. "Come on. Want your dinner?"

Mari shook her head, his attitude leaving her a little breathless. "No, I'm...not hungry. Is Missy in bed? I haven't been much company for her today."

"Yes, she is. And frankly I don't think she missed you. Steve let her help with his puzzle."

Mari nodded, stifling a yawn, resisting an impulse to lean against him once more and go back to sleep. "Where's everybody else?"

"Dave and Jazz are upstairs fighting, I think; your mother and my father are on dishes and being mighty slow about it." He grinned and got to his feet, reaching a hand down to help her to hers. "I think they're necking. Steve's in the basement playing with the video game. Anything else?" An arched eyebrow mocked her nervous chatter.

She blushed guiltily. "No."

"Good. We finished trimming the tree after you dozed off, but it wasn't dark enough to plug in the lights. Let's have a private showing."

Mari stood, and Jim ducked behind the overstuffed chair pulled up to the wall and plugged in the cord. Mari couldn't help the spontaneous "Oh!" whispering from her lips as the tree came to life in all its gaudily beautiful, twelve-foot splendor.

Jim came around to stand beside her. She didn't even wonder at her instinctive inclination toward his side, her arm going around his waist as his came around her shoulder.

"Considering it was done without us," he teased softly, "it's quite a work of art."

Mari leaned her head back to look up at him. He glanced down at her, his hazel eyes ensnaring her.

"You should have wakened me," she repeated, her voice small.

"It was more fun watching you sleep." He leaned down to plant a kiss on her forehead. "And consider what I would do if we were somewhere other than in our parents' living room."

At that moment Katherine and Terry wandered out from the kitchen, a simultaneous gasp of pleasure coming from both of them at the sight of the tree.

Katherine was calling Dave and Jasmine and shouting down the basement stairs for Steve. When they all converged in the living room, there was a long, emotional silence.

Reaching for Steve to pull him near for a better look, Mari saw him stop in his tracks at the sight of the tree, watched his eyes brim with tears, and almost felt herself the painful gulp that held them back. Then he turned away, and snatching his jacket from the rack in the hall, ran into the kitchen.

Mari, turning to Jim, saw him in conversation with his father and knew he was unaware of the pained look on Steve's face. Slipping out quietly, she followed the boy into the kitchen and called his name as he put a hand out to the back door.

"Steve, where are you going?"

"Outside," he replied tersely, the emotion he was trying so hard to hide, heavy in his voice.

"But it's dark. I don't think your father would want you to go out."

"I won't go far."

Mari came up behind him and tried to turn him toward her, but he resisted. "Steve, what's the matter?" she asked gently.

"Nothing," he replied stiffly. "Please, Aunt Janie. I won't go far and I won't be gone long."

"I can't let you go. It's cold and dark, and—"

Steve reached out and yanked the door open and would have run out into the night when Jim's voice stopped him. "Steve!"

Mari turned with him, surprised by Jim's presence and a little startled by the look on his face. Apparently all he had heard was her refusal to let the boy leave and his apparent disobedience. But now that Steve had turned toward her, Mari saw it all written in his young face; all the pain he had thought was behind him had suddenly erupted because of the memories brought back by a Christmas tree.

"What's gotten into you?" Jim said sharply.

"I just want to go out for a few minutes, Dad." His attempt at bravery tugged at Mari's heart, and she had to swallow before she could find her voice.

"Aunt Janie said no," Jim reminded, "as I would have had you asked me."

"I'll just be a minute," he whispered, eyes brimming dangerously, despite his effort to fight it.

"Why is it so important?" Jim asked, impatience in his voice at Steve's uncharacteristic stubbornness.

Unwilling to say, Steve shook his head and made a helpless movement with his small hands.

"I think I know," Mari said quietly, going past Steve to push the door closed. A gust of fragrant, snowy air swooped around them as she pushed the boy gently toward the middle of the room where his father stood. She tugged his jacket off and, tossing it onto a kitchen chair, leaned down to him and took his face in her hands, making him look at her. His brimming eyes were wary as he said tremulously, "Please, Aunt Janie!"

"Darling, if you want to cry, it's all right," she said. "You miss your Mom and Dad, don't you?"

He looked at her in stunned surprise for an instant, then a sob burst from him and he fell against her, painful sounds in his throat. Holding him close, Mari stroked his rough boy's hair and rested her cheek on it.

"Grief is nothing to be ashamed of, Steve. Christmas is a hard time for everyone who has lost someone. It brings back so many memories that emotion is a very natural thing, and you don't have to be brave and try to hide it."

He wept for a few moments; then quieting, he pulled away enough to look guiltily at his father. "Are you mad?" he asked uncertainly.

Jim came to enfold them both in his arms. "Of

course I'm not mad," he said, squeezing the boy to him. "But if I was, it would be because you didn't tell me how you felt."

"You've done everything for me," Steve explained in a strained voice, his arm reaching around Jim's flat waist. "I...I was afraid you'd think...I...didn't care about you."

Jim groaned and tugged playfully at Steve's hair. "Remember when we first talked about your coming to live with me? I told you I didn't want to replace your parents; we both loved them too much for that. We can have a good relationship, but what you had with your Mom and Dad no one can take from you. It'll always be with you, and I wouldn't want it otherwise. But"—he paused, and the hand in Steve's hair relaxed to stroke it gently—"when your grief makes you feel lost and alone, I want you to come to me, all right?"

"Okay, Dad. I'm sorry." Steve shook his head and took a deep breath. "When I saw the Christmas tree...I got...all..."

"I know."

"And I thought after the first few months...it wasn't going to happen anymore."

"You never get over someone you love and who has loved you," Mari said. "They stay with you always. Sometimes it feels good and sometimes it hurts. That's just the way it is."

"Mostly now," Steve said thoughtfully, "it feels good. But today...it hurt." He looked up at Jim and smiled. "But not anymore."

The kitchen door swung open, admitting a pink-sleeper-clad Missy, rubbing at her eyes with tiny fists.

"Missy!" Mari exclaimed, hurrying over to scoop her up. "What are you doing out of bed?"

"Hungry!" she said forcefully, then noticing Jim and Steve, she pointed excitedly. "Seevie! Daddy!" and reached small arms toward the man, giggling.

"You're hungry, huh?" Jim said, taking her from Mari.

"Me, too, Dad," Steve agreed.

"So am I," Mari added, putting a hand to her now empty stomach.

"Could you make pancakes, Dad?" Steve asked.

"Oh, Steve ..." he began to protest.

But that was one word that was part of Missy's vocabulary. "Pan-cakes! Pan-cakes!"

Jim looked heavenward in supplication. "Why me?"

"Because you're a saint, James," Mari said, fighting a grin. "I love pancakes, too. And I'm sure after all this time in the oven, whatever Mom saved for me is no longer edible."

Frowning, he glanced at his watch. "It's almost nine o'clock!"

"Dad makes the best pancakes in the whole world," Steve said enthusiastically. "When Grandpa visits us, we always have them."

"Not at nine o'clock," Jim said.

"A gourmand's stomach is not regulated by a clock," Mari contributed, siding with Steve, her eyes wide and innocent under Jim's feigned glare. "Or are you afraid they won't be as good as Steve says they are?"

Accepting the challenge, Jim put Missy down and turned to the stove, pulling Mari with him.

As the aroma began to fill the kitchen and drift into the other rooms of the house, Terry wandered in, sniffing the air.

"I thought I smelled pancakes." He looked over Jim's shoulder at the batter bubbling lacily on the griddle. "Can you spare a few of those?"

"Depends on how hungry Mari is," Jim said, expertly flipping the golden pancakes. "Steve's good for a dozen."

"I'm starved!" Mari said impishly. "You'd better make another batch."

He looked down at her threateningly.

"That is if you want any," Mari added intrepidly, returning his glare with a bland look of nonchalance.

Jim looked up at his father who shrugged. "Don't

look at me. I don't know how to deal with this generation's women. But it appears to me if you're hoping to have any pancakes, you'd better make another batch.''

The swinging door opened and Dave walked in. "What's cooking?" he asked, rubbing his stomach. "And can I have some?"

"Why don't we call the neighbors over?" Jim asked with an exaggerated gesture of exasperation.

"Good idea, I'll..." Mari started toward the phone to be hauled back by a firm grip on her upper arm. She fought hard to stifle a laugh but lost.

"Young lady," Jim said, his eyes gleaming wickedly, "you're pushing your luck. Now will you keep your eye on these while I mix another batch?"

It was not so much a question as a threat, and Mari took the pancake turner from him, trying desperately not to giggle.

Terry, Dave, and Steve had been served when Jasmine walked in sniffing the air. "What smells so good?" she asked.

Unable to suppress it any longer, Mari burst into uproarious laughter and went to the refrigerator for the ingredients required for yet another batch.

By the time Steve and Terry had seconds, it was nearly ten o'clock before Jim and Mari sat down to eat. Jasmine and Dave had begun the dishes, and Mari noted gratefully that though they weren't talking, they weren't quarreling either.

Mari took a bite of buttery, syrupy pancake and emitted an enthusiastic sound of approval.

"Good?" Jim asked.

"Delicious!" she praised. "Definitely worth waiting for."

He gave her a lingering smile. "That's true of a lot of things."

"Jim." Terry spoke from the doorway. "The mill's on the phone. They've got a problem."

"Don't tell me," he sighed exaggeratedly, pushing away from the table. "They want pancakes."

Terry laughed, slapping Jim on the back as the younger man passed through into the living room to take the call. Seeing Mari stare after his son in puzzlement, Terry went to sit across from her with the coffeepot and a cup.

"What is it?" he asked.

"Mom said Jim was on vacation," Mari replied.

Terry smiled, a look that combined pride and respect in his dark eyes. "He's supposed to be, but he keeps in close touch. Jim *is* the mill right now. We've got computers and follow a lot of modern procedures that I don't understand. But he knows it all, he's not afraid to get his hands dirty, and he's damn good. More coffee?"

"Please." Mari held out her cup, intrigued by what she was learning about Jim.

"A high-rollin' outfit up the road from us tried to hire him away from me last year at twice the pay and half the responsibility, but he stuck with me. That says a lot for him."

"It says a lot for you, I'd say," Mari suggested, pushing the sugar bowl his way. "You'd be gratified to hear him talk about you."

Terry nodded, embarrassed. "Yeah, well, it's mutual. With more feeling than words on my part." Then he went on to refute his statement by asking, "I don't suppose he's told you about his stint in Vietnam?"

Mari shook her head in complete surprise. "No. I didn't know he'd served."

"He was part of a small attack force on a special mission fifteen miles beyond the perimeter. Only five of them made it back, and one of them Jim carried all the way with a bullet in his own shoulder. He was decorated by the President."

Mari sat speechless as he went on. "When Steve's parents were killed, Jim called me to tell me he was taking the boy. I wasn't surprised. There's his mother's generosity in everything he does."

Jim pushed through the kitchen door as Terry finished in an undertone, smiling as he stood, "But don't tell him I told you. He hates it when I brag about him."

There were tears standing in Mari's eyes when Jim joined her at the table. He reached down to pull her out of her chair, a dark frown between his eyes. "What's the matter? Did you two quarrel again?"

"No," she said quickly, at a loss to explain what was really wrong because she simply didn't understand it. "We...it...was kind of an emotional conversation."

"About what?"

She lowered her lashes, fighting confusion. "You."

He was silent for a moment, his hands moving up to cup her face and raise it to his. His expression was half serious and half amused. "It isn't very flattering that the mention of my name takes you to the brink of tears."

"He told me about Vietnam," she said.

He groaned and shook his head. "A lot of guys did the same thing. Only I was lucky enough to come home. Look..." He pulled her after him toward the living room. "You and I have been assigned a very important duty by your mother."

"What's that?" she asked, trying to shake off this emotional mood, trying to forget that she now had modest hero to add to all the other attributes he possessed that attracted her to him.

"We have to hang the mistletoe." He said it with a straight face but his eyes were dancing, and suddenly she was caught up in his irrepressible sense of humor.

"And you're bringing me along to climb the ladder." She feigned strained forbearance.

"All you have to do is hold the ladder. I'll climb it."

"Do you have to go to the mill?" Mari asked as he moved the ladder from near the tree to the archway between the living room and the dining room.

"It can wait until tomorrow. You don't get casual with Astoria roads at night when there's snow on the ground. Terry and Katherine were stranded in town all night just last week." At the top of the ladder, he pointed to the dining room table. "I think I left the mistletoe there. And there's a package of tacks in that box of stuff right next to it."

Mari got the required items and took them to the foot of the ladder. Jim reached a long arm down for them, and in a moment a jaunty sprig of mistletoe on a red ribbon swung from the dark molding of the threshold.

"Is it centered?" he asked.

She stepped back to look. "Perfectly," she said, then added airily, "Well, good night." And she began to walk toward the stairs, laughing when he caught her and dragged her back to the mistletoe.

"No, you don't. You don't do a job without testing it to make sure it works." He smiled down at her, his eyes changing from laughter to something that made her bones melt. The curve left his lips and she felt his hand under her hair as his mouth came down to meet hers. Last night's kiss, though completely effective, had been explorative, tentative. But this one had the mark of possession about it, as though they both knew that something had ignited between them and that they would never be entirely separate beings again.

Spiraling away in ever-diminishing circles, Mari clung to him, her body straining against his. There was fire in her lungs and in her limbs, and a paralyzing languor stole over her. She had the sensation of being lifted; then they were sitting in the big chair by the fireplace. It wasn't until she felt the warmth of his hand against her bare midriff that she pushed against him. Jim released her instantly and leaned against the back of the chair.

"What is it?" he asked.

She drew a deep breath and sat up in his lap feeling drugged.

"This is our parents' living room and everyone is still awake," she cautioned in a whisper.

He frowned good-naturedly. "Want to go upstairs?"

"Yes," she smiled. "But, no."

Jim sat up in the chair, steadying her as he did so.

"Well, your clarity of expression leaves a little something to be desired."

She punched his shoulder. "You know what I mean."

"Yes, I do," he grimaced. "Once again morality rears its ugly head." He reached up a large hand to smooth her disheveled hair. "I'm going into Astoria to the mill tomorrow. Want to come in with me and I'll leave you in town to shop?"

A day in his company was appealing and she consented readily. "Yes, I'd like that."

"I'll be leaving at eight-thirty." Jim got to his feet, steadying Mari to hers as he did so. Holding her before him, his hands on her shoulders, he leaned down to kiss her gently. "Get some sleep."

Upstairs in the darkness of the room she shared with Missy, Mari considered her position in relation to Jim, and a little niggle of fear began to stir in the pit of her stomach. A lifetime spent with a man had never seemed an appealing prospect before, but now scenes flashed through her mind of Jim laughing, building a fire, of him with Missy on his shoulders. She felt such a loss at the realization that she could not allow a serious relationship to develop between them. Whatever it was about her that attracted him, she was sure he would no longer want her once he knew about her sterility.

Pulling the blankets up to her chin, Mari swallowed a pointed lump in her throat and thought that she hadn't felt this resentful since she had awakened from a drugged sleep nine years ago to find her mother in tears at her bedside and had listened while she told her tearfully, haltingly, what the surgeon had had to do.

Chapter Five

Mari awoke to a frame of mind that was more philosophical than it had been the night before, if not more cheerful. Though she could not allow herself to love Jim, she could still enjoy his friendship, and the trip he had suggested to Astoria might be a healthy diversion.

But her positive approach to the day was almost destroyed by the sight of him seated at the breakfast table in a light blue turtleneck. The color made his hair blacker, his complexion ruddier, and thoroughly confused the brown in his eyes so that there was blue there, too. Her heart reacted with a leap, and she had to force herself to walk easily into the room and smile a casual good morning.

At her entrance he put down his cup and stood. "If I'm going to make it to the mill on time we'll have to leave now." He smiled apologetically. "But I'll get you some breakfast at the Danish Maid."

"I'm ready," she said, crossing over to hug Missy sitting beside Katherine in a high chair. In red sleepers, her pony tails askew, she was heart-warming, and Mari hugged her a moment longer.

"I heard her singing when I came down to fix breakfast, so I brought her with me," Katherine explained, smiling fondly at her daughter. "I like your sweater. It isn't fair that time is making you prettier and me older."

"Mom!" Mari scolded. "As though you aren't as beautiful today as you ever were. Can we bring you anything from town?"

"A few more rolls of wrapping paper and your safe return." She glanced a little worriedly at Jim. "You're sure the roads are safe today?"

"So the highway department said. We'll be fine. Don't worry, I won't let anything happen to Janie," Jim grinned. "I'd be more concerned about Dad and the other three delinquents sledding down the hill out back."

Katherine rolled her eyes. "Your father is hopeless. He seems to think forcing Jazz and David together on a sled will solve their problems. Poor Steve probably isn't even getting a turn on his own sled."

"If being forced together got them talking, it couldn't hurt." Jim took his jacket from the hook and turned to Mari. "Ready?"

She hugged Missy again and then her mother. "Bye. I'll get your gift wrap. And don't worry about us."

"Worrying is what mothers are for," Katherine said.

Seeing Mari leave, Missy began to whimper, and Mari, plagued with guilt, turned back to her.

"You go on," Katherine said firmly. "You need a day to yourself. We'll be fine."

"Don't cry, darling," Mari coaxed. "I'll bring you a present, okay?"

The tears halted and a tentative smile formed. "Duck!" Missy said emphatically, apparently selecting the form her gift should take.

Mari smiled at Jim as they walked out to the car. "How do you feel about carrying a duck back home on your upholstery?"

"If you think a plush one would do," he said, opening the passenger-side door on a battered blue pick-up, "I know just where to get one."

The road was fairly clear, except for several patches along the way where the roadside trees stood tall and shoulder to shoulder, blotting out the sunlight. There Jim slowed to a crawl as he explained that a thin layer of black ice could linger all day long, given the right conditions.

"Black ice?" Mari asked, unfamiliar with the term.

Checking the rearview mirror before speeding up on a clear stretch of road, he explained, "The name comes, I think, because the ice is virtually invisible on the black pavement. The snow melts during the day, leaving a layer of water that freezes as the sun goes down, forming ice. Same thing happens when the rain freezes at night."

"Sounds treacherous."

"It is. Fortunately it isn't usually cold that long here for the condition to persist."

Watching the stark green-and-white scenery, Mari noticed a small bridge up ahead and was delighted by what she saw as they crossed it.

"Houseboats!" she exclaimed. "Doesn't that look like the life?"

Jim grinned. "I guess it would to a good sailor. Personally I prefer terra firma."

"In a seafaring town like this?" she asked, surprised.

"Yep," he affirmed, unashamed. "I'm a man of the woods, not the water." Then he slanted her a dry glance. "I get seasick."

"Well," she said smiling as though having made a great discovery, "it's nice to know that you have a weakness."

He stared at the road ahead, braking carefully as they came upon a series of winding turns. "I have more than one," he said, and though he didn't look her way, she knew what he implied.

The rest of the journey into town required care and concentration, and there was no more conversation until Jim pulled into a parking spot in the downtown area.

"I thought loggers and fishermen got up early," Mari commented, wondering why, at almost nine A.M. two days before Christmas, the main street was still almost deserted.

"They do," Jim said, "but you won't find them downtown. However, the gossip booth should be full in the bakery."

"The what?" she asked, taking his hand as she leapt down from the truck.

"The gossip booth. The last table in back." He opened the bakery door and an aromatic whiff met Mari's nostrils. Suddenly she forgot every calorie count she had ever learned and hesitated on the threshold. "I won't be strong enough to resist," she warned.

"I didn't bring you here for you to resist," he laughed. "Come on in. Most of the downtown merchants pass through here in the morning at one time or other. Some real life-and-death discussions are held here. Come on," he said, a hand at her back pushing her inside. "You've got to try an applejack and a cream cheese Danish."

"Both?" she protested, then immediately considered adding a third item when she saw the tempting array. One side of the small bakery contained four booths and the other a row of display cases filled with a variety of pastries and breads.

She groaned aloud. "We'd better go with what you suggested," she said defeatedly. "I'd never be able to make a decision."

"Hi, Dorothy!" Jim greeted the friendly middle-aged woman in bakery whites covered by a festive cobbler apron. He ordered an applejack and a cream cheese Danish pastry and coffee for Mari and a large box of assorted doughnuts to take on to the mill.

The woman, apparently in tune with all her customers, asked about Steve and how the reunion was going.

"Beautifully," Jim replied, receiving his change. "I'd like to introduce my little sister." He glanced at Mari with a grin. "Marijane Westridge meet Dorothy Schoen. Dorothy, I'd like to leave her in your capable hands. She needs a warm jacket, and I thought she might find one at Lolly's. Would you introduce her?" Then he looked down at Mari, his smile warm. "I'll meet you right in front of Dorothy's window at two o'clock, all right?"

She nodded and he was off, the box of doughnuts under his arm. For the next hour Mari, tucked into the deep corner of the gossip booth that accommodated three people on each side and sometimes at peak moments, four, learned more about Astoria than any book could have told her. Problems were discussed heatedly, the condition of the economy was frowned over, and the latest joke was passed on. She was warmly invited to visit every shop represented in the booth and at opening time moved out with Lolly, an attractive gray-haired woman with a bright smile and a shrewd eye on Mari's figure.

Lolly's assistant Jan was a tall girl with sandy-blond hair and tireless enthusiasm for helping Mari find just the right thing. She nodded approval when Mari finally selected a navy hooded jacket with a wool lining in red-and-blue plaid and deep slash pockets. Lolly produced a blue-and-white woolen hat with matching mittens and scarf, and Mari kept the outfit on for her exploration of downtown Astoria.

In the middle of the sidewalk, looking up and down the main street with its turn-of-the-century buildings with modernized storefronts, Mari felt a curious stirring of excitement. Compared to Southern California where she had lived all her life, Astoria was small, but there was nothing sleepy about it. With a smile, she headed toward a sign declaring "Young World" and reflected that nothing could lie dormant in a town where everyone was as lively as those who occupied the gossip booth in the Danish Maid.

A display of plush animals in the window of Young World looked promising, and Mari ventured in to find a beautiful stuffed mallard duckling, the perfect gift to take home to Missy.

Charming children's clothes caused her to linger more than an hour, and she finally emerged with a bright red parka for Missy and a candy-striped woolen hat and mittens.

Heading in the opposite direction, Mari window-shopped her way down another block, when a book-store sign across the street caught her eye, and she remembered Terry's remark about a girl he met in the bakery who owned a bookstore.

Morning traffic was lively, so it took her several min-utes to cross and finally shoulder her way into the shop. She was greeted almost immediately by a small girl in jeans and a rainbow-striped smock. The badge on her collar read "Wanda."

"Hi!" the girl said and smiled. "Want to set those down?"

Gratefully Mari dropped her cumbersome packages in a corner near the counter and refused the girl's offer of help, preferring to browse.

"I work in a bookstore in Los Angeles," she ex-plained, stuffing her hands into her warm pockets, "and it's always fun to see what other shops are do-ing."

"Los Angeles," Wanda repeated, her eyes widening. "I imagine we've got a few less books here than you're used to dealing with."

Checking up and down the single wall of books, Mari nodded, noting that despite the limited number, the selection was fairly thorough. "That's true. But there have been times when I've wished we were this size so that I didn't have to juggle ten people's schedules and send out fifty special orders a day."

Wanda grimaced. "You're right. Well, have a look around. If you need help, Toni and I are working in the children's section in the back. Just give a holler."

Mari perused the books, then meandered down the greeting card aisle, selecting several friendship cards for the people she worked with back home. She frowned for a moment, the tenuousness of her present position darkening her mood, but she shook off the thought, refusing to let anything spoil this day.

Coming upon a display of Christmas gift wrap, Mari made several selections for her mother and added rib-bon and tape, then wandered back to the children's book section where the women were stacking new titles.

"Are you finding what you need?" Mari turned in surprise at hearing the broad New York accent in an area full of casual drawls. She was confronted by a small dark-haired girl, whom she assumed was Toni, holding an armload of books. Mari exclaimed, pointing at the girl's burden, "Hardy Boys! That's just what I was looking for. I have a special young man on my list." The stack tottered dangerously, and Mari dropped her purse to help the girl place them on the shelf.

"What's a New Yorker doing way out here?" Mari asked.

"Running a bookstore," Toni smiled. "Wanda was telling me that you manage a shop in Los Angeles."

They talked until Mari glanced at her watch and realized that she had five minutes to get back to the bakery to meet Jim.

"I don't suppose," she began uncertainly after she had purchased several books, "that you'll be needing help after the holidays?" She wasn't sure why she asked the question. She was still uncertain about whether to go back to Los Angeles or stay in Astoria, but this was such a charming little shop, and if she would want to work anywhere in Astoria, it would be here.

Toni's eyes widened. "As a matter of fact, Wanda will be leaving me for several months in January. Her husband is a photographer and he's gotten a special assignment for a publisher of pictorials. They're going to the Bahamas." The dark girl rolled her eyes descriptively. "I should be so lucky. Leave me your name and number, and I'll get in touch with you. We've just moved into a new home, and I could use some time with my family and time to get things in order."

Mari jotted her name and her mother's phone number. "I don't have a permanent address yet, but my mother will know how to reach me."

"Great!" Toni waved Mari off. "Merry Christmas!"

Downtown was now as crowded as any street in Los Angeles, and gripping her packages, Mari dodged distracted shoppers and congested traffic to race across Commercial Street and reach the bakery just as Jim approached it from the other direction. His dark hair was ruffled and the tip of his strong nose was red with the cold. Her heart leapt at the sight of him.

"What are you smiling about?" he asked, smiling back. "The merchants you dealt with must be smiling! We'd better put those packages in the truck before going to lunch. We're parked around the corner."

"It's been a lovely morning," Mari said in answer to his question, relinquishing her bundles into his arms. Then she added sheepishly, "Do you think we could take some applejacks with us when we go home?"

"Addicted?" he grinned. "Welcome to the club." They had reached the truck and he transferred the parcels to one hand to unlock the door to put them inside. "Lunch is serious business. What are you in the mood for?"

"Hot soup," she said without pause.

"Okay." With a casual hand at the base of her neck, he directed her down the street toward the river. "Incidentally, I like your coat. Warmer now?"

"Much."

"Well," he said lightly, catching her hand as they ran across a street without traffic signals, dodging cars and trucks and ladies with strollers. Safely on the other side, he continued. "Does that mean you plan to stay in Astoria?" When she said nothing he prodded, "Certainly a poor working girl doesn't make that investment without thoughts for the future?"

"It certainly is a beautiful place," Mari said heavily, that threat to her happy mood invading her thoughts. They were right at the river now, crossing the planks of a pier that reached out into the water, a large weathered wooden structure on their left, apparently where they were headed. Jim still held Mari's hand, and she pulled him toward a walkway that ran around the building, wanting a closer look at an enormous rusty freighter that was moving downriver toward the open sea.

"I wonder where he's going?" Mari asked dreamily, leaning her arms on the railing. "Are those logs he's carrying?"

"Yes. They're probably being taken to Japan," Jim guessed. As he spoke, Mari noticed a figure moving up a ladder that hung over the side of the large ship.

"What's he doing?" she demanded, straightening away from the railing.

"The ship is taking on a bar pilot," Jim explained, smiling at her concern. "The Columbia River Bar is one of the worst hazards to navigation in the world. Scores of ships have been wrecked in this area. It takes a real expert to get them through without mishap."

"If he's so valuable," Mari offered worriedly, "you'd think they'd find a safer way to get him on and off."

Jim laughed loudly and pulling her to him, kissed her forehead. "I'm sure he'd appreciate your concern. Come on. Let's get you some chowder."

The wooden structure Mari had noticed housed a little shopping mall called Pier 11. She moved instinctively toward the shops on a raised boardwalk to their left, but Jim pulled her back to him, gesturing to the restaurant on the right.

"I've been dreaming about the Feedstore since I went to work at the computer this morning, and it's been the only thing that kept me going. You can shop after."

Decorated in what Mari personally thought of as maritime elegance, the Feedstore was a wall of windows on the river, and everything else, even the beautiful tables and elegant captain's chairs, paled in interest.

Jim was quiet, letting Mari observe, and it wasn't until he finally shook her arm that she realized the waitress had arrived and she hadn't even looked at the menu.

"Clam chowder and a sandwich?" Jim suggested, his eyes indulgent. She had to turn away from that look

or fall under his spell. And that would be too dangerous.

"Not after all I've eaten already," she said in horror.
"Just a bowl of chowder, please. And a cup of coffee."

Jim, who had chosen to select from the salad bar,
disappeared to return with a plate piled high with a variety of greens and vegetables and two dinner rolls.

They ate and talked companionably until the lunchtime crowd began to thin and Jim glanced at his watch.
"If you want to check the shops before we head home,
we'd better move out. It'll be dark in a couple of
hours."

While they ate, the sky had clouded over again, and
Mari saw Jim give it a thoughtful glance before leading
her to the cashier.

The shops were full of unusual gifts Mari had never
seen before, even in Los Angeles; and she went slowly
from shop to shop, Jim apparently content to wander
along behind her. It was hours later and she had
another armload of packages when she turned to find
him glancing at his watch.

"I'm sorry," she said breathlessly. "I keep forgetting
the time. I'm ready to go." Then she added anxiously
as he took her packages and started toward the mall's
exit, "But let's not forget the applejacks."

He grinned. "I'm going to convert you to a logger
yet."

It was dusk when they emerged from the covered
structure, and snow had been falling for some time,
judging from the thickness of the snowy carpet.

"Oh, Jim, I'm sorry," Mari said. "It'll be bad getting
home, won't it?"

"No, we'll manage," he said calmly. "And anyway,
it's my fault. I should have been watching the time, but
I was distracted by you."

She looked down at herself, almost nothing visible
but her nose, and laughed. "In this outfit?"

"Your body is charming," he conceded, "but you
have other attributes that are even more lethal. But

let's not talk about it. We'll end up arguing and it's been too nice a day."

With a bakery box added to all the other things Mari had purchased that day tucked under the canopy on the back of the truck, they started for home. The streets were virtually empty of cars now, except for the occasional vehicle that had been stranded in town and was now fishtailing its way up one of the notorious Astoria hills, tires failing in the snow.

Mari tensed at the sight, and Jim reached out a hand to pat her knee. "Don't worry," he said. "I've driven some logging roads a mule would think twice about. You're safe. But you'd better buckle up."

"I know," she replied, her implicit trust in him standing boldly in her eyes. "I was hoping that he would make it, not afraid that we wouldn't."

He glanced back at her a moment as though she had surprised him, then put both hands on the wheel for night had now fallen and the road ahead was dark.

They had reached the hill that Mari remembered from the morning was about a halfway mark between town and home. She was just about to remark that they hadn't seen another car on the road since leaving Astoria, when two headlights became visible on the other side of the highway. She watched them, simply because there was nothing else to see in the darkness, wondering idly where the car was going in these conditions, when it became apparent that the driver was either drunk or that the vehicle was out of control.

But then it was too late to determine which, because it was bearing down on them. At the same moment that Mari cried out, Jim muttered an explicit oath and turned sharply, the oncoming headlights blinding them as the lurching car missed them by less than an inch. Jim's truck plunged off the road into the darkness.

Her eyes closed, her hands covering her face, Mari heard the strain of tires on ice, the snap of frosty bushes and low branches being run over and felt herself thrown against the confining seat belt harness as the truck bounced over the embankment and slammed down onto the dark pasture, bouncing again until coming to a suddenly silent halt.

There was an instant's deafening stillness, then Jim was tearing at her seat belt, pulling her hands away from her face.

"Are you all right?" he demanded.

She looked up into the two bright points of light in the darkness, which were his eyes, and was still too shocked to answer.

"Janie!" His voice sounded frantic and his hands were on the brink of snapping hers.

"I'm okay!" she gasped quickly, willing her heart to stop thumping, her breathing to relax. "Are you all right?"

"Are you sure?" he insisted, ignoring her question. He was fidgeting with the glove compartment and something fell out onto Mari's lap. Then there was a blinding light in her eyes, which ran over her face, then her body, and down her legs. Jim snapped the flashlight off. "You didn't hit your head?"

"No." Thinking back on the bouncing as they went off the road, Mari shuddered. "But I hate to think of what could have happened if you hadn't reminded me about the seat belt."

"Well, we were lucky, so don't think about it. Sit tight. I'm going to look around and see how bad it is."

He went slowly around the truck with the flashlight, lingering in the front and bending down to inspect the tires. Mari was not surprised when he jumped back inside and told her that the two front tires were blown.

"What does that mean?" she asked calmly. "About us, I mean."

"It means we have to sit out the night," Jim replied as calmly as she had asked. "But we've got a sleeping bag and a CB."

"And half a dozen applejacks," she said, trying to

sound light, but her voice erupted high and squeaky instead.

Jim reached for the radio. "You aren't going to panic on me, are you?" he asked.

"I might," she replied in a small voice.

She heard his chuckle in the dark. "As long as I know what to expect."

He called Terry on the CB, and even persistent static couldn't conceal the anxiety in the older man's voice. "Are you all right? What happened?"

"We're safe," Jim assured him quickly. "But we're off the road halfway up Fern Hill. We blew both front tires."

Terry's voice was sharp. "I'm coming right now."

"No!" Jim shouted back. "The hill is bad and right now there's no visibility. We've got a sleeping bag. We'll be fine. But you could pick us up tomorrow morning about seven o'clock on your side of the hill."

"Let me call for a service truck," Terry suggested.

"No," Jim replied again. "I really don't think it could make it in these conditions. We'd only get the truck stuck. Janie and I are all right, and we've got all we need for a comfortable night." He glanced at her and grinned. "Well, semicomfortable. We'll walk down the hill in the morning and meet you, all right?"

"If you're sure." Terry sounded reluctant to agree.

"I'm sure. Tell Katherine not to worry. Oh, and don't forget a thermos of coffee tomorrow."

"I'll even lace it."

Jim replaced the transceiver and turned to Mari. "Are you holding up okay?"

"So far," she lied, a tremor in her voice refuting the statement. "What time is it?"

Raising his wrist, Jim checked the illuminated dial. "Six fifteen. But what difference does it make?"

She shrugged. "I don't know. I just ... wondered."

He sighed and turned in his seat to look at her. "You were trying to find out how long you have to cope with being confined in this enclosed space with me, is that it?''

When she refused to answer, he hooked an arm over the steering wheel and said, his voice grave, "Maybe the dark is a good place to discuss this. Why is it that you're attracted to me, yet don't want to be with me? You behave as though you're afraid of me, and yet I can't remember having done anything to hurt you."

Mari stared at his shadowy features in the dark, feeling trapped. How could she explain that she was worrying about their confinement because she trusted her emotions less than she trusted his and that she couldn't let anything develop between them because it could only result in grief for both of them?

"You're imagining things," she said feebly.

"No, I don't think I am."

"I was dividing the hours left until morning by the number of applejacks," she said with an artificial laugh. "I can have one every other hour, but you'll have to wait for the thermos of coffee."

He was not amused by her evasion, and without saying another word, he slid open the window that connected the cab to the canopy and reached a long arm in to pull out a rolled-up sleeping bag.

"That's the biggest sleeping bag I've ever seen!" Mari remarked, hoping to change the subject. She didn't realize she was only worsening it.

"It's a double," Jim said in a hard tone of voice, yanking apart the bows that kept it rolled. Then he reached into the back again and pulled out the sack of applejacks, dropping them in her lap. A tangible tension sat between them on the seat.

"Here," he said. "Have at it."

Defiantly she pulled one out of the bag and ate it with an attempt at maintaining an air of separateness from the whole situation, as though she were taking refreshment while watching it happen to someone else. Then the illusion was shattered when Jim got into the bag, angled his length sideways, and held his arms out to her, indicating that she, too, should climb in.

"I'd rather not," she said casually. "My new coat is very warm. I'll be fine."

"It'll go below zero tonight, and sitting here with nothing to keep the blood moving, you're going to get uncomfortably cold. Now stop being such a priss and get in."

"Thank you," she said icily. "I'll be fine."

"Suit yourself." He settled into the corner of the cab, leaned his head back against the window, and closed his eyes.

Angry at everything: herself, him, the impossible situation, Mari got as far to the other side of the cab as she could and tried to find a comfortable position. She shifted several times, sure that crossing or uncrossing her legs would help her, that leaning her head back or hunching down into the collar of her coat would make her feel warmer. She folded her arms, then jammed her hands into her pockets; tucked her legs under her, then stretched them out; but nothing seemed to help. The front seat of a pickup truck was simply not meant for spending the night, particularly when the other half of it was occupied by a hostile party.

She knew that blaming Jim for the sudden cold war between them wasn't really fair, but the problem went too deep to think sensibly; he was there and without him there would be no problem. That was damning enough.

While shopping this afternoon, when she had tried to convince herself that she could look on Jim as a friend and nothing more, she had seriously considered moving to Astoria. But now, knowing that something existed between them that neither of them would ever be free of, she began to realize how impossible it would be to live near him. To see him regularly, to visit her mother and know that he could be there, to work at the bookstore and know that he could walk in at any moment would make life a misery, and she was simply not strong enough to deal with that.

Whether or not it was the best thing for Missy, she had to go back to Los Angeles. Her job was there and her friends would be supportive.

Having reached that decision, she felt considerably better and leaning her head against the window, dozed into a light sleep.

When she awoke, her nose was frozen, her fingers and toes were numb, and despite her new coat, she had never been colder in her life. Her teeth were chattering, and she was loathe to move for fear of disturbing the little pocket of almost-warmth that her unmoving body created. But the choice seemed to be the risk of stirring a breeze or cramping into permanent paralysis. She finally chose to move the leg she had been sitting on and gasped when it protested painfully. She glanced at the sleeping bag longingly out of the corner of her eye. Jim had it pulled up to his chin and he was breathing evenly as though asleep.

"I promise not to say 'I told you so,'" he said quietly, startling her into sitting up. "It's much warmer in here." He unzipped the bag and held it open invitingly.

Pride frozen, Mari slipped off her shoes and wriggled into the bag as Jim helped her. The only way their two bodies would fit on the narrow seat was to lean hers against his, and he did so, zipping the bag up over her shoulders.

"Comfortable?" he asked.

"Yes," she said, embarrassed by her capitulation. "But you won't be with me leaning on you all night."

"Nonsense," he said gallantly. "There's been many a lonely night when I've wished I had company in this bag."

"Do you camp out often?" she asked nervously, conversation seeming to hold at bay the intimacy of the quiet night. Snow now drifted around the car in large puffy flakes, and there was not a sound but that of her voice in the white world.

"Every other weekend or so when the weather's warmer. Steve enjoys it." He paused a moment, then added in a different tone of voice, "Speaking of which, I haven't thanked you for last night. I thought I understood him about as well as a man can understand a child, and I didn't see that grief in him at all."

"That's all right." She shrugged off the compliment. "It was right there in his eyes when he finally looked at me. He's so open, it's hard for him to hide anything. And I suppose, having lost someone I loved very much not that long ago, I could identify with how he felt. That special Christmas feeling that invades when the tree goes up seems to call back to mind every beautiful moment you've ever known and everyone you've ever loved."

Jim was quiet for a moment, then he asked softly into the silence, "Can you tell me about your father?"

She shrugged, unconsciously relaxing against Jim's chest. "It would be hard. I could tell you that he was not much taller than mother and that he was a successful playwright with red hair and freckles. But what he was inside is hard to describe. We all loved him, but I don't think anyone else in the family really understood him." She grimaced, remembering her mother's remark about his weakness. "There were dreams in his eyes, and I don't think he ever quite came out of them. By some genetic quirk, I understand that. Jasmine inherited the clarity of his thought patterns. I've seen her lay out a case in a courtroom in a way that makes every man there forget how she looks and admire instead how she thinks. Althea has his fine sense of drama; in spite of everything..." She paused to sigh. "She's a fine actress. But I fell heir to his dreams." She paused again, smiling at the darkness. "I can't put them on paper as he did, but I love to read them and live them. At fifteen I lived at Tara for a full three weeks, though it only took me one to read the book. Then it was Manderley, then Drogheda." Her smile became a laugh. "If

I had my way, I'd screen book buyers of my favorite titles for sensitivity and nobility. But I'd be fired."

Jim laughed too. "Maybe you'd get a raise for your innovative approach."

"I doubt it. But my father would understand. He always understood. Mom often got upset with me and sometimes punished me for neglecting chores or doing them quickly and sloppily, but Dad would look at me with understanding and sometimes pity. There was always a half-finished novel waiting for me; just like he always had a half-formulated plot that needed work or maybe just thought." She sighed heavily now, the smile gone. The words came from deep inside her into the quiet darkness, and she was surprised that she said it aloud. "I really miss him. Last year at least we were home for Christmas."

Jim hugged her briefly and gently chafed her arm. "You are home."

When she would have quarreled with that, he silenced her as he often did by diverting the conversation. "Any other men in your life?"

In the fraction of a second it took her to reply, her mind swiftly registered all the reasons why it would be to her advantage to let him think she had left a serious relationship in Los Angeles. It would be easier being near him if he thought she was pining for someone else.

"Yes," she replied.

"Serious?" he asked.

She paused. "Yes."

There was a moment's silence and expecting more questions, Mari's mind raced ahead, considering answers. She was surprised when Jim said instead, "We'd better get some sleep."

She relaxed, thinking the conversation over. Then he asked unexpectedly, "Is that why you can't decide whether or not to leave LA and move to Astoria?"

She had decided, but she didn't want to argue that now. Besides, he was beginning to sound testy. "Partly," she evaded.

He sighed heavily, settling her against him, pulling the thick front of the sleeping bag up a little higher. "I'm sure when you've had time to think about it, you'll make the right decision, whether to go back to him or to stay here. But for now, sleep."

Well, she congratulated herself dryly, she had backed out of that argument nicely. Now all she had to do was lie in his arms until morning, hearing the rhythm of his heartbeat under her ear, feeling the warmth and strength of him against her, wishing against all that was real that she had a right to stay there forever.

"What time is it?" she asked again.

He pulled his wrist up and held the pale green dial to her eyes.

"Eight thirty!" she said with such disappointment that time had passed so slowly.

"Time flies when you're having fun," Jim said coolly, then added, an underlying trace of anger in his voice, "Go to sleep, Janie."

She made a genuine effort but found it impossible to slow her senses enough to reach a restful state. She seemed suddenly to be all nerve endings, frayed and protesting Jim's nearness.

She wriggled against him in the small space afforded her, trying vainly to put a little distance between them.

"Stiff?" Jim asked, helping her shift.

"A little," she admitted. This was going to be impossible, she thought, real panic surfacing. Even the touch of his hands through her coat was disturbing. What on earth had happened to the cool, untouchable young woman she used to be?

"What would make you more comfortable?" he asked.

"I could get out of the bag," she suggested, suddenly more anxious to face the cold than one more minute in his arms.

"Besides that." He sounded impatient.

"There's so little room," she whined in a manner so uncharacteristic that it startled both of them, and she pushed against him, panic growing. "I'll just climb right out . . ."

Both arms clamped around her, and he bit out angrily, his mouth at her ear, "Listen to me! It is freezing. We are both staying in the bag. Just find a comfortable position and stop moving!"

She subsided against him. "I'm sorry," she whispered, on the brink of tears.

"Forget it!" he snapped.

Everything seemed amplified as she lay there, bound in his arms: the sound of her breathing, the sound of his, her heartbeat, her nervous swallowing. Tension hung in the air, almost visible, and she moved against him as though trying to turn away from it.

"Jane, for God's sake!" he shouted. "Stop moving!"

"I want out!" she screamed, unable to bear the confinement a moment longer. She scrambled away from him, but he turned, pinning her between himself and the back of the seat. She knew what was going to happen and both wanted and dreaded it. "Jim . . ." she pleaded, pushing futilely against his chest, but she was no match for him, and when his mouth finally came down on hers, her meager strength had been expended.

Though the kiss began punishingly, it soon altered, affected by that subtle something that always came alive when he touched her. She responded hungrily, the emotional knot in which she had been tied since the wreck, suddenly and violently undone. She pulled her mittens off and put her fingers inside the collar of his sweater. She felt him react and held him closer, sliding her hand down over his back to his lean waist.

He had opened her coat, and his hand ran over her sweater-clad breasts to her waist, reaching inside to touch bare skin where her sweater had pulled out of her jeans.

Then, as though some movie director had shouted "Cut! Print," Jim stopped and sat up, pulling her with him and pulling the bag back around them.

"There!" he said in that brisk, controlled tone she was becoming familiar with. "That's what you were afraid would happen and it's done. Over with. You don't have to lie awake worrying about it anymore. Now maybe we can get some sleep!"

She could not have been more shocked had he opened the door and tossed her out in the snow.

"You did that . . ." she began haltingly.

"Deliberately? Yes. but it's nothing you have to keep from your friend in Los Angeles. Nothing irreversible happened."

No, she thought bitterly, *nothing "irreversible" could happen, not to me. But there is this irreversible need for you that becomes stronger and more desperate every time you kiss me. You haven't done much to alleviate that.*

Defeated, despairing, Mari relaxed under the arms that pulled her back against him and decided to allow the world to move on around her. Like the swirling snow beyond the windshield, her problems were too persistent, yet too intangible, to fight.

Chapter Six

When Mari awoke, sunlight streaming through the windshield of the truck, she was alone in the sleeping bag. Sitting up, she stretched cramped limbs and looked around for Jim. But there was nothing around but snowy fir trees and a white pasture running up to a snow-covered hill.

Her heart picked up an erratic beat, and the frightening thought that he had left without her crossed her mind. Pushing the passenger-side door open, she leaped out of the truck, her boots crunching into the snow.

"Jim!" she shouted, a trace of fear audible in her voice.

"What?" he asked instantly, appearing from behind the truck. He had the back open and was putting her smaller packages into a backpack and tying the larger ones together with a length of cord. He surveyed her worried expression and grinned. "Did you think I'd left you?"

Last night's angry mood seemed to have been replaced by his customary friendly harassment, but she still remembered his deliberate cruelty and could not smile back.

"It had occurred to me that you might," she nodded.

He studied her stiff countenance one more minute, then heaved the pack over one shoulder and picked the large bundle up in the other hand. "I wouldn't do that," he said, smiling again despite her frown. "We've got to keep you safe for old what's-his-name. What is his name?"

Unsure what he was talking about, she looked puzzled for a moment, but when his expression changed to confusion, she remembered the remark he had misunderstood last night and her decision not to correct him. She recovered and replied, "Kent Walters," giving him the name of the young man she had broken up with several months before.

"What does he do?" Jim slammed the back of the truck closed and locked it.

"He's a publisher's rep," she said truthfully. "I met him at work."

"How is he going to feel about Melissa?"

She could not keep the irony out of her voice when she replied, again truthfully, "He wants children."

"Can't beat that." There was irony in Jim's voice, too. He locked the door on the driver's side, then walked around to the other door. Reaching in, he handed out the bag of applejacks, then locked the passenger side. He turned to Mari. "Are you ready?" he asked. His eyes were clear and challenging, and she knew there was more to the question than the meaning of the words.

She looked back at him and angled her chin. "I'm ready."

Terry was precisely where Jim had asked him to be when they crested the hill at 7:00 A.M. When Jim handed Mari into the sleek new truck, Terry reached a hand out to help her, then pulled her to him and hugged her.

"Are you all right?" he asked, studying the grim look about her eyes.

She forced a smile. "I'm fine. How's Mom? Was she very upset?"

"She tried to be but I wouldn't let her." Terry grinned at his son. "I told her if my son was in charge of her daughter, nothing would go wrong."

"You were almost right," Jim said dryly, pulling the door closed after him. "Steve okay?"

"He tried to be tough, but I think he was worried about you. Incidentally, the coffee's behind your seat, Jim, and there's spiced wine brewing at home. I hope you're hungry." He slid them a side glance while pulling onto the road. "Katherine is laying on a feast that would take a crew of choker setters to polish off."

Forgetting her antagonism, Mari frowned at him. "Choker setters?"

"Choker setting is where a logger usually learns his trade," he explained. "He attaches a cable to a felled log by which it's hauled up to be loaded on a truck. He has to know which way it will move when it's hauled and be agile and quick. It's probably the lowest paid job in the woods and is usually filled by young men, and they usually have very good appetites."

"Ah!" she nodded. "Thank you," as Jim handed her a cup of coffee.

"Is the truck badly damaged?" Terry asked.

"No." Jim took a swig of the steaming coffee and closed his eyes, enjoying it. "Nothing permanent. I'll call Tom when we get home to have it towed. You have no idea how good this tastes."

"Cold night?" Terry asked sympathetically.

"Cold night!" Jim affirmed with such feeling that Mari glanced at Terry to see if he noticed more to the remark than mere words. But he was watching the road, apparently unaware of innuendoes.

Katherine, Jasmine, David, and the children ran out of the house as the truck pulled into the driveway. Jim, helping Mari down, turned just in time to receive Steve's body, slamming into him as though he'd been shot from a cannon.

"Hi, Dad!" he said, joy and relief in his eyes as he smiled up at his father.

Jim hugged him fiercely. "Hi, Steve! How are you? Did you finish the puzzle?"

"Almost. But I was worried about you, and I couldn't get the pieces to fit anymore."

"Well, you can try it again after breakfast. You did save me something to eat?"

"We've been waiting for you two to arrive!" Katherine declared, ushering everyone into the house. Mari, carrying Melissa who had a stranglehold on her neck, noted that her sister and brother-in-law went into the house hand in hand.

"What's with them?" Mari whispered to her mother.

"I'm not sure," Katherine whispered back, smiling widely. "But Jazz was up most of the night, worried about you. Somehow I think a lot of things came to a head for her last night, and she got sort of hysterical." She shook her head, the smile becoming a frown. "She was very unlike herself. Anyway, I couldn't do anything with her, but Dave took her rather forcefully into his arms and made her quiet down. I left them, but I heard them talking most of the night. I guess they talked out their problems and found each other again."

Cheered by that news, Mari followed her mother inside to the breakfast table. Terry had not exaggerated when he said that Katherine had planned a feast. The table was set with flowers, and plate after plate of tempting dishes passed through Mari's hands. There were eggs, bacon, sausage, potatoes, toast, and fruit and a large coffee cake Jasmine had baked that morning.

The festive atmosphere and the good news about Jazz and David lifted Mari's spirits, and she was able to smile at Jim when he watched pointedly as she cut a second piece of coffee cake.

"Practicing to be a choker setter?" he asked.

"No," she replied, glancing teasingly at her sister. "I don't want Jazz's feelings to be hurt, so I don't think we should leave any."

"How noble."

"When are we gonna open presents?" Steve asked, too excited to eat.

"You didn't get any," Jim said with a straight face. "Didn't I tell you?"

"There are seven under the tree for me already!" he said, his eyes wide and bright.

"How many do I have?" Jim asked.

"You didn't get any," Steve replied with a conspiratorial wink at Mari. "Didn't I tell you?"

Jim took the boy's head in the crook of his arm and tapped it gently with his knuckles while Steve laughed helplessly.

Mari turned away from their camaraderie not wanting to be reminded of how easy it would be to love them both.

Missy's duck was a big hit, and she napped with it while Mari soaked in a tub filled with hot water and her mother's rose-scented bath beads. Jim, too, had escaped the breakfast table to shower, and Mari could still see him in her mind's eye, tall and lean, walking up the stairs with an arm around Steve's shoulders, talking quietly.

It was beginning to upset her that her mind seemed always filled with him; images of his face, remembered words, moments when he had touched her, recorded with electronic accuracy in her memory's store. Though she had decided that she couldn't love him, shouldn't love him, she seemed powerless to dispel him from her thoughts.

Disgusted with herself, she immersed her head, shampooed briskly while the scented water drained, then rinsed and shampooed again. Turban-style, she wrapped a towel around her wet hair and reached to the bathroom hook for the terry robe that always hung there. It was missing. She stared at the vacant spot for a moment, realizing that she had no change of clothes, having handed her jeans and sweater out the door to Jasmine who had been gathering a load of laundry. As everyone was downstairs, she thought she could wrap a bath towel around herself and run the length of the hall to her room.

The way the fates had been dealing with her lately, she was not entirely surprised to find Jim buttoning a

blue-and-white flannel shirt as he walked down the
hallway toward the stairs. She had just run out of the
bathroom and turned up the corridor, her bare legs
flashing, one hand holding the place where she had
folded the bath towel in on itself, the other at her top-
pling turban.

She stopped frozen, in the middle of the hall, as Jim
deliberately slowed his pace. He came toward her, a
wicked smile forming, and she stood immobile, her
eyes closed in resignation.

"I like your outfit," he said lazily.

A blush rose to her turban as he moved around her,
his eyes lingering on the length of leg below the towel,
then moving up to the knot she held for dear life.
"Very fetching."

"I'm cold," she said defensively.

"No, you're not," he admonished. "The furnace
has even the hallway warm as toast."

"Then I'm tired," she said, staring down at the carpet.

"I doubt that, too," he said softly, reaching out to
untwist the towel on her head. "You slept on me for a
full nine hours."

"What are you doing?" she demanded, too late to
stop him, sure that she would look like Medusa once
the towel was completely unwound.

Ignoring her question, Jim smiled at her mockingly,
placing the towel back over her hair then rubbing it
briskly.

"Ow!" she objected to his rough handling, reaching
up a hand to stop him, but too worried about the knot
in her towel to resist him for long. She finally stood still
under his hands while he continued toweling her hair.
The carpet was warm under her feet, and her hot blush
was now so complete that she was in no danger of being
cold.

He finally stopped, bunching the towel around her
neck, maintaining the ends in his hands. A storm was
building in his eyes, but she couldn't look away, drawn

toward them like a piece of debris in the vortex of a hurricane. When his lips came down, she rose on tiptoe to meet them, all the longing of last night alive in her arms as they wound around his neck. She parted her lips and he invaded.

The towel began to slip, and Mari tried to wedge a space between them to reach for it; but Jim had a handful of her half-dried hair and held her to him, the points of her breasts against the soft flannel of his shirt.

Then without drawing his lips from her, one hand molded her hip, holding her against him while the other cupped her breast, teasing it with a callused but gentle thumb. She gasped at the exquisite sensation, her body stilled against him, afraid to fracture the delicious moment.

Then the ground went out from under her, and she wondered for a moment if she had fainted. But she was still aware of Jim's lips and that sweet caress at her breast. She hadn't fainted; she was being carried. Panic tried to surface, but she was dropped on a silky spread covering a hard mattress. Jim tore off his flannel shirt, and as he came down to cover her with his body, his eyes were flaming.

Panic died the moment his mouth covered hers again, and the only struggling she did was to strain closer. Bombarded by the sensation of touch, she trembled against the tickle of his chest hair, his cold belt buckle against her waist, the rough denim of his jeans against the bare soles of her feet. Jim rolled over, taking her with him. She lay full length along his body, her own pulsating with so many new feelings, she wondered with a corner of her mind not occupied with ecstasy if she could be the same woman who had emerged from the bathroom only moments ago.

Jim's torturous fingers were tracing a tantalizing line from the small of her back, over her bottom, to follow the line of her thigh to the back of her knee. She gasped a little moan of pleasure and was surprised when Jim covered her mouth with his hand. He tensed, holding her still.. Then she heard the call.

"Mari!" It was her mother's voice.

She came abruptly to awareness as two thoughts registered. She was lying naked on Jim's bed—on Jim!—and though the door was closed, she had left her betraying towels somewhere in the hall.

Panic did surface this time, but Jim rolled her onto her back and put his finger to her lips with a wicked smile.

He rose and opened the door, holding it wide enough that no one would guess it concealed anything—or anyone.

"Katherine?" he asked.

"Oh, Jim," Mari heard her mother's breathless voice reply. "I'm sorry if I spoiled your nap. Have you seen Mari?"

"When I came upstairs, she was still at the table."

"Her boss is on the phone. I guess I'll just have to take a message. But where could she be? I was sure I saw her come upstairs." There was a pause, then Katherine's voice said, as though there was a mystery building, "Those are Mari's towels on the floor!"

Mari covered herself with the far end of the spread and drew it up over her eyes, clenching them shut.

"Are they?" Jim replied casually. "Sorry. I didn't know that they were Mari's, and I used them. I must have dropped them when I came out of the shower. I had an armload of clothes. I'll try to be tidier."

"Nonsense. I'll just toss them in the hamper. If you see Mari, tell her I have a message from her boss about a missing invoice. He'd like her to call him back this afternoon. I can't imagine anything being that urgent on Christmas Eve, but he apparently thought it was. Go back to your nap, dear. Sorry I bothered you."

"No problem."

Mari heard the bedroom door close and the spread was pulled away from her face. Jim was suppressing laughter with great difficulty. "Your boss called about a missing invoice..."

"I heard!" Mari hissed, resisting his efforts to pull the cover down further. "What are you doing?"

He had lain back down beside her and stretched an arm across her blanketed form. He shrugged. "Your mother told me to go back to my nap..."

Mari pushed at him, only succeeding in dropping the spread and affording him the view she'd been trying so hard to deny him.

"You weren't napping!" she snapped, her eyes in velvet brown turmoil.

"Neither were you, my love," he said softly, supporting his head on an elbow. His expression was suddenly serious. "What are we going to do about it?"

She looked at him warily. "What do you mean?"

"Isn't it obvious? Something's developing here, Janie. Something we're going to have to make a decision about."

"Why?" she asked peevishly.

"Because I'd like it to continue," he said, frowning at her, "but not by hiding you in my room. What are you angry about?"

"You!" she replied hotly; then, realizing that didn't make sense when she'd been as interested in what was developing as he was, she amended with, "Nothing!" That made no sense either so she finally admitted bleakly, "I don't know."

He studied her thoughtfully, a finger tracing the line of her collarbone just visible over the cover clutched to her breasts. "I think I do."

When she glared at him, refusing to ask the obvious question, he volunteered, "I've gotten through the insulation, haven't I? You care about me."

"It's only been a few days," she said lamely, using the argument she'd been using unsuccessfully on herself every quiet moment she'd had since she'd arrived.

"That's irrelevant, and you know it. I'm in love with you, Janie."

"I'm not in love with you!" she denied in frustration, trying to wrap the spread around her body but finding it unwieldy and much too big. She turned to him, her cheeks hot with embarrassment and anger. "If you were a gentleman, you'd find me something to put on!"

He considered her for a moment, her dark hair in wild disarray around pink cheeks and eyes ready to ignite; and his face softened.

"All right. You can wear my robe if you'll agree to a date."

She looked at him in dismay. "A date?"

"Yes. You know, dinner, dancing?"

She closed her eyes and shook her head. "We have just spent the night in the same sleeping bag, tumbled in bed, and I am wearing nothing but this blamed spread, and you want to take me on a date?"

"Right."

"James…"

"Those are the terms. Or you can try to get all the way down the hall in your lovely alabaster skin. What's it to be?" There was an unholy light in his eyes, and she finally closed her own and nodded out of sheer weariness.

"Whatever you say. Just get me something to wear."

His blue terry robe skirted her ankles, and he cuffed the sleeves back three times while she clutched the lapels together and glared at his bare chest. "I do not love you," she felt compelled to say one more time.

Jim tilted her chin up and shook it gently between his thumb and forefinger. "That's not what your eyes say. And that's definitely not what your body just said."

"That was just…chemistry," she mumbled, her face reddening at the memory.

"Bull," he replied softly. "That was magic."

She left the room in tears, aware of his frown following her along the hall.

When Mari walked down the stairs to the living room that evening in a simple teal-blue and silver dress, silver loops at her ears, and her hair caught back in an elegant bun at the nape of her neck, she walked sedately and with an air of mystery. It was not an affectation.

When she had spoken to her employer on the telephone that morning, she had explained the situation with Missy and told him that she thought it in the child's best interest to remain with her family in Astoria. She had reacted contrary to all her carefully made decisions and had so surprised herself that now, many hours later, there was still uncertainty in her eyes.

She held Missy by the hand, the child dressed in a red velvet dress with a white pinafore, her dark hair caught back with a white bow.

Everyone had changed into more formal dress for the Christmas Eve festivities, and the sight of Jim in a three-piece gray suit made her swallow with an effort. She knew without a doubt that her decision had been influenced more by wanting to be close to him than by wanting Missy close to her grandparents.

Jim stood with Steve and Terry at the dining table, which was now laden with special Christmas fare buffet-style, and she would have gone toward the kitchen on the pretext of seeing if her mother needed help. But Missy had spotted Jim and with a cry of "Daddy!" ran toward him.

"Daddy?" Terry asked, handing Mari a glass of spiced wine.

Jim shrugged, lifting the child up. "Seems I remind her of a character in a book." He looked from the child to Mari, his eyes roving her dress and flicking over her hair before settling on her face. "You look like an angel," he said.

Trying not to look embarrassed, she inclined her head in thanks.

"This is angel season. Can Missy stay with you while I see if Mom needs help?"

At his knowing nod she went to the kitchen where

Katherine and Jasmine were arranging raw vegetables around a creamy dip. They were giggling together and Mari smiled.

"Okay, what are you up to?" she asked, advancing toward them. "Who's been in the punch?"

"Neither of us," Jasmine denied, her gray eyes sparkling. She wore red wool, her hair brushed down in a silvery blond veil to her shoulders. "It isn't alcoholic spirits but simply high spirits. We were remembering the Christmas when we were little and we had mumps. Remember?"

Mari giggled, the picture returning as though it had been yesterday. "Mom put up a tree in our bedroom and Dad played Santa, climbing in through our window."

"And landing on the tree and knocking the whole thing over." Katherine shook her head, tears standing in her eyes though a smile rested there, too. How mysterious love was, Mari thought, watching her mother dry her eyes and go back to her task. She had loved her husband completely, Mari was sure of that, yet Terry was now her whole world and she seemed as content as it was possible for a woman to be. And still, something clung to her from her first love, enough to bring tears to her eyes.

"Okay, that's it. Jazz, you bring the dip, and Mari, can you manage the coffee service?"

"I think so." Mari picked up the silver tray with the ornate pot and sugar and creamer and started cautiously for the door Jasmine held open. Halfway to the table, Terry intercepted her and, with a warm smile, relieved her of her burden.

"Thank you," she said, studying his face a moment longer because of the thoughts she had just entertained, comparing him with her father.

He wore a deep-blue sport coat over gray slacks and a crisp white shirt. His thick thatch of gray hair was slicked back into order, and his dark eyes were bright, his vitality even more pronounced tonight than usual.

"You still haven't decided about me, have you?" he asked, a fraction of a smile teasing her.

"Mother loves you very much," she evaded. "That's all I need."

"But you'll never accept me as a stand-in father?"

"That isn't it at all," she said, unwilling to reveal the trend her thoughts had taken for fear of hurting him.

"Then what is it?"

Mari looked around her, saw Jim watching over Missy and Steve as they scrambled around on their knees, checking the tags on the presents under the tree. Jasmine and David were standing under the mistletoe, and her mother had run back to the kitchen for some forgotten item.

"We're quite alone," he prompted, grinning. "Let me have it."

"It's . . . well, it's really none of my business," she admitted ruefully. "It's just something I was thinking about . . . about Mom and my father and you and . . . and Jim's mother."

A line appeared between Terry's eyes, and he watched her, waiting for her to go on.

"I guess what I don't understand . . ." She hesitated, feeling very uncomfortable. "Is . . . that you could both have been so in love the first time . . . and still be so in love again." With that finally out, she sighed and said with a shrug, "I told you it was none of my business."

"No, that's all right." Terry put a hand to her shoulder and gave it a curiously paternal squeeze. "That tells me something about you, something I've wondered about. Something that is also none of *my* business."

He gave her an underbrowed glance as though expecting her to stop him from going on, but instead she waited, curious.

"My son is in love with you."

She shifted uncomfortably, and he put that hand out again as though to stop her escape. "I'm not making a recommendation on that one way or the other, but I know you're unsure, and I thought it might have been because you loved someone else. But anyone who has been in love would understand about your mother and me.'' He paused, watching Katherine come into the dining room with a basket of rolls and run back to the kitchen again, the eyes that followed her so shamelessly full of love. ''Love has such power,'' he said, turning back to Mari, ''that loving someone and losing them doesn't diminish your ability to love but intensifies it. You've heard that saying that 'Love isn't love until you give it away'? Well, you never know how true that is until you're without someone with whom to share it. I did think I would die when Jeanine died, but the love we shared was still alive in me and, believe it or not, still growing. It had to be given. It had to be shared.'' He smiled reflectively. ''And then your mother walked into my life as though God Himself had sent her.'' He shook his head, apparently unable to believe his good fortune. ''I have been so blessed. And I'd like to see Jim love and be loved as I've been. I don't know anyone more deserving of that than he is.''

Mari opened her mouth to speak, but a helpless shrug and a wordless shake of her head were all she could manage. ''I know. It's been such a short time,'' Terry said with a grave smile. ''But he's known you in his mind for years. You didn't have a name or a face, but he's been in love with the idea of a woman like you for a long time. He's the settled type. He needs a home and a family to be complete, but he was waiting for just the right woman to share it with.''

''But is that me?'' Mari asked, that chaotic spot in the pit of her stomach beginning to tremble.

''I think it is,'' Terry smiled at her indulgently. ''You're your mother all over, and you could make him happy as hell.''

Katherine emerged from the kitchen with a ham on a platter, calling for Terry to carve. Mari looked beyond him to her flushed and glowing mother, then smiled up at her stepfather.

"Whatever happens, you've made Mom very happy, and I love you for that." With a pointed lump in her throat, she reached up on tiptoe to plant a kiss on his cheek. "Merry Christmas, Terry."

Replete from the buffet, Mari sat on the floor between Jim and Missy in the circle gathered around the tree. Terry passed out presents, and Melissa bounced with excitement. Steve, tearing open a package from his father, looked at the printed cover of the box and gasped. When he opened it and the contents contained exactly what the box had promised, he ran to Jim and threw his arms around him.

"A video game! Thanks, Dad!"

"You're welcome, Steve. The way you've been using Grandma and Grandpa's, it seemed a matter of getting you one or moving you in here."

Steve hugged him again. "Not a chance. It's me and you forever."

"Right!"

"Steve, here's another," Terry said, and Steve scurried back to his pile of packages.

Mari's mound was growing, and Jim indicated a small box wrapped in red foil on the top. "Open that one," he suggested, pulling at the bow on a large box in his lap.

Examining the tag, Mari found that it was from Jim and Steve. She looked at the man curiously, then delved inside. It was a circular scrimshaw pendant with a rose inscribed on it.

"This is a little different from the usual scrimshaw," Jim said, coming around her to help her fasten it, his hands at her neck causing a ripple of feeling down her back. "My friend who did this works on elk bone."

Mari held the intricate carving up and noted the tiny initials "J.H." in the inscribed circle that bordered the rose. It was exquisite, and she blushed with pleasure.

"Thank you," she whispered. Then to distract those glowing brown eyes from her, she put her gift to him in his hands. It was a sumptuous pictorial book entitled *Timber Country* that she had picked up on their trip to Astoria.

Jim's large hand around her neck pulled her closer and kissed her lightly, the experience almost more heady than a passionate embrace would have been.

"Thank you," he said, his eyes on her hair. "I've got quite a logging library, but nothing like this. You know, there's something very seductive about you with your hair up."

"Oh?" she asked, surprised by the remark. "I didn't think you'd like it. Kent..." Something flickered in his eyes when she said the name, but it was gone instantly, and she wondered if she had imagined it. "Kent said it made me look schoolmarmish."

He smiled, shaking his head. "You could never look schoolmarmish. If anything, you look even more appealing than when it's down because"—he paused to fiddle with a tendril at her temple—"it looks like it's begging to be undone."

She leaned closer and whispered, "But that would never suit my insulated, virginal image."

He studied her closely, his brown eyes warm and roving. "Tonight you don't look very insulated. And I saw you kiss my father."

"I've decided that I like him after all," she said airily. "What's wrong with that?"

"Nothing," he replied, then gave her a level look. "Then do I get another chance, too?"

"It's Christmas," she replied, looking away from him because what she read in his eyes warmed her blood, and she was still confused. "Anything could happen."

After everyone's gifts had been opened and admired, Jasmine and David put the sleepy children to bed while Terry and Katherine and Mari and Jim drove into Astoria for Midnight Mass at St. Mary's.

On the way out of church, Mari was introduced to the small, smiling priest in white-and-gold vestments.

His warm handshake dispelled the middle-of-the-night chill.

"I'm delighted to meet you, young lady. Does this mean something, Jim? Katherine?"

"Mari is my daughter," Katherine explained. "She's spending the holidays with us."

"Oh?" the priest said, retaining Mari's hand. Then he glanced again at Jim, his eyes shrewd. "Anything you want to add to that?"

Jim smiled but replied quietly, "Not yet."

"Well," the priest grinned, "I'd like to be in on it when it happens."

"You bet," Jim assured him.

In the back of Terry's sinfully comfortable Cadillac, Mari wrapped her arms around herself and shivered. Jim instantly drew her to him in the corner and wrapped his long arms around her.

"Why did he ask that?" She looked up at him in the light from the downtown area as they sped along the main street home. Terry and Katherine were singing to Christmas carols on the car radio.

"What?"

"If you had anything else to add?" Mari reminded him.

"Oh," he laughed. "Father O'Shea? He's been a priest so long he sees things without having to be told."

"But it isn't there!" she said, sitting away from him to look into his face. It was in shadow but his eyes were bright.

"You only think it isn't," he said gently, "for some reason known only to you. It's there, Janie."

She sank back against him with a sigh. "What'll I do?"

He was silent for so long, she was beginning to think he hadn't heard the question. Then he replied casually, "Well, maybe if the matter were given time, a solution would become clear to both of us. Preferably the same solution."

"You mean if I stayed," she said.

"Yes," he replied. "I mentioned before that I have a house vacant close to town. And I don't think finding you a job would be a problem."

"I've already found one," she said too quickly, and when he looked down at her in surprise, she explained haltingly, "I...I mean, I was talking to a girl...in... the bookstore..."

"Toni?" he asked.

"Yes. She said she might need someone after the holidays." Then a thought occurred to her. "But I don't know what I'd do with Missy. I don't want to plague Mom with babysitting."

"You could probably use my babysitter," he said. "Steve goes to Janet Hudson's after school until I pick him up about five. She's an accredited day-care home, and she's always got hordes of kids around."

Mari tried to hold back a smile but failed.

"All right," Jim said resignedly. "Out with it."

"It's just that..." she laughed. "Your domesticity surprises me. You're so..." She made an indescribable gesture with her hands and he grimaced.

"Really? Is it as uncomplimentary as it looks?"

"Male, I guess is what I mean," she struggled to explain. "But then, because of Steve, you come out with things that surprise me."

"They say that continual surprise is a good sign in a relationship," He kissed her forehead. "It lends a certain endurance. What do you think Walters will say when you tell him you've decided to stay on in Astoria for a while?"

She was silent for a moment then decided to treat the question lightly. "He'll become suicidal, I imagine."

"What about your old job?"

"They're sending on my severance pay tomorrow," she said and tried to look innocent when he looked down at her condemningly.

"Just when did you decide to stay? And why didn't you tell me?"

"It was just today. I was talking to Missy about going

back to Los Angeles, and she started to cry. I decided we'd better stay near some familiar faces for a while." It was a lie, but it sounded convincing to her. Then she added, "I thought you'd be pleased to hear about my check coming. Now I can give you first and last month and a cleaning deposit."

"Someday," he said, leaning his head against the back of the seat, "when I understand you better, I'm going to beat you."

"I'm safe then. Because when you understand me better, you'll realize that I always hit back."

"My father warned me that you were a dangerous little package."

"I remember. You should have listened."

Something Jim had said yesterday occurred to her, and she thought a moment before asking, realizing that she didn't have the right. But curiosity was too strong.

"Was *she* there when you had to go to the mill yesterday?"

"She?"

"The programmer," Mari prompted. "The one who's responsible for your sainthood."

"Oh," he laughed, his shoulder moving against hers in the intimate darkness. "Yes. She's always there."

"What's her name?"

"Why?"

"Just curious."

"Julia Kramer," he obliged. "And she looks a little like Brooke Shields."

There was a moment's silence, then Mari taunted, "Isn't that a little young for you?"

"Yes," he agreed blandly, his glance at her recognizing the barb. "That's why I'm after you. Older women are more my thing."

The purse slinging and laughter in the back seat disturbed the passengers in the front, and Terry turned the radio off and looked in the rearview mirror with a grin. "Come on, you two. We just got Jazz and David patched up."

"Let them fight, dear," Katherine said, smiling at them over her shoulder. "Sibling rivalry is healthy."

"I don't think they think of themselves as siblings," Terry said, laughter in his voice. "God, what a family!"

When they returned home, they found that everyone had gone to bed and a plate of cookies and a glass of milk had been left on the dining table for Santa. Terry and Katherine said good night and Jim, too, had disappeared.

Mari turned all the living room lights off and sat on the floor in front of the tree, her heart heavy. She knew that she was playing a dangerous game with Jim, but she seemed powerless to stop herself. She wanted him so much, and staying in Astoria, letting him hold her and kiss her and make plans for a future they might share, was playing with fire.

But this was a time of miracles, wasn't it? she thought desperately. Couldn't it be possible that he could accept her sterility and her reluctance to share that secret with him? That, given more time for their relationship to develop, he would come to love her so much that that wouldn't matter?

Suddenly the scene she had played with Kent in the living room of her apartment replayed in her mind, and she closed her eyes against it, wincing. It had hurt so much. She knew she couldn't bear that kind of pain again.

"Janie?"

Jim's quiet voice startled her, and she looked up from her puddle of blue-and-silver silk on the carpet, tears standing in her eyes. He frowned and sat on the floor beside her, one knee bent behind her back.

"Why are you crying?"

She wiped at her eyes with the back of her hand, noting that it trembled. "I'm always...emotional at Christmas," she fibbed. "I miss my father and I feel badly about Thea..."

He nodded with understanding. "I know. But for a

minute, stop thinking about everyone else and think about you." He put an arm around her and held her near him, his voice a stroking sound in her ear. "I know something is haunting you, and I know you don't want to share it with me, whatever it is."

Her eyes flew up to his, and a tear spilled over before she could stop it.

"Let me finish," he said gently, offering her his handkerchief. "I can't decide if something or someone has hurt you, or if you're simply afraid that someone might, but I want to offer you insurance against it. I love you, Janie, and I'd like to stand between you and whatever would hurt you. Take this."

He held out a small box wrapped in gold paper with a jeweler's insignia on it. She started back against his arm, knowing instinctively what it contained. "You don't love Walters," he went on. "If you did, you wouldn't have decided to stay. But you care for me; I know you do. There's something between us that, given time, will make us invincible. Take it, Janie. Open it."

With fingers that trembled so badly that the arm around her reached in to help, she uncovered the jeweler's box, snapped it open, and sat looking at a small gold band with a rosette of diamonds trapped between two emerald leaves.

She gasped, tears falling freely now, because the ring was beautiful, because his declaration had been what every girl must dream of, and because she was consumed with guilt because she should refuse him and had not the courage to do so.

Instead, she turned in his arms crying, "Yes, yes, yes!"

Chapter Seven

No one seemed particularly surprised by Mari and Jim's engagement. Katherine and Terry were delighted but were quick to say that they had seen it coming, and Jasmine and David, who Mari thought had been too wrapped up in each other the last few days to have noticed anything outside of their warm little circle, nodded calmly.

"I think you're making a good move, Mari," Jasmine said, hugging her. "Have you set a date?"

"No," Mari replied a little nervously. "Nothing concrete yet."

Jasmine looked into her eyes and Mari looked away.

"You will invite us back from Portland for the wedding?" Dave asked, putting his arm around her. He squeezed her gently, then released her.

"Of course. But it might be a few months yet."

"Why so long?" Jasmine frowned. She had just finished drying breakfast dishes and was hanging up the dish towel.

"Well, there's no rush," Mari went to the stove and poured a cup of coffee, wishing desperately that her sister would drop the subject. But Jasmine was a successful attorney because she knew how to reach the truth.

"I'm going to get gas and have the car looked over," Dave announced, kissing the top of Jasmine's head. "See you in about an hour."

As soon as he was out of the door, Jazz joined Mari

with a cup of coffee and said directly, "You haven't told Jim, have you?"

"Told him what?" Mari hedged.

"Mari, this is Jazz," the older girl said firmly. "You know what."

Mari sighed, giving her sister a level glance. "No, I haven't. The right moment hasn't come up. But I will."

"Being unable to have a baby is not that tragic, Mari." Jasmine leaned toward her earnestly, her silvery hair haloed by the overhead light. "You're so intense about it, but it might not even be that important to him. After all, he has Steve and you have Melissa."

Mari gave her sister a dry smile. "He'd love to have more children. He's the type who could handle seven or eight and love every minute."

"But he loves you. We can all see it. That can change what he wants."

"But do I have the right to deprive him?" Mari expressed a thought that had kept her awake most of the night.

"Tell him," Jazz said simply. "And find out."

"And what about you and David?" Mari diverted the conversation. "Is everything all right now?"

"Not entirely," Jazz admitted, lowering her eyes to her cup where a long index finger traced the rim. "We still aren't agreed on a baby, but we are agreed not to hurt each other with it. I think we just needed to talk it out and hadn't taken the trouble before."

Reaching out to pat her sister's hand, Mari smiled brightly. "Well, that's wonderful. And if you can solve your problems, there's hope for me, too, isn't there?"

The older girl nodded, smiling back, but when Mari lowered her eyes to sip her coffee, a flicker of worry crossed Jasmine's expression.

Jazz and David left for Portland three days later as the family waved them off from the porch. Katherine was tearful and Terry held her to him, caressing her arm.

"They're only a hundred miles away," he consoled.

"And now that Mari will be here, I think we'll see more of Jazz and David. How about a trip to the Long Beach Peninsula? Would that cheer you up?"

Katherine had written Mari several times about that little pencil of land that jutted from the Washington coast just across the river where many little specialty stores were a shopper's heaven.

"Oh, oh, Terry," Mari teased. "Cut up your credit cards. Mom will go wild."

"I was thinking we could take Steve and Missy with us," Terry grinned. "That would keep her too busy to even withdraw her purse. You two would be welcome, of course, but you must be ready for a day to yourselves."

Mari looked up at Jim because it seemed so natural now to consult him on many decisions. He wasn't stifling her with their engagement; in fact, quite the contrary. He seemed to be giving her as much space as she needed. Yet every time she thought his name, he was there beside her for whatever she required.

"That does sound inviting," Jim admitted, smiling at his father. "But you two are still newlyweds, and we've all invaded your turf. Wouldn't you like a little privacy?"

"No, we've both been looking forward to having you all here," Katherine insisted. "And if we're going to uphold our titles as grandparents, we have to get some serious spoiling in. You two consider yourselves free today, and we'll take the kids with us."

Mari looked at her mother doubtfully. "Are you sure?"

"If we could come home to your special spaghetti," she assured Mari, "the arrangements would be perfect."

Mari glanced at Jim, and at his consenting nod she laughed. "All right. You're on. But don't blame us if you need psychiatric counseling before the day's over."

Watching their parents and the children drive off,

Mari leaned into Jim who had put an arm around her shoulders. "I feel guilty," she said.

"You should." He squeezed her, his eyes alight with laughter. "For a fiancé I'm not getting nearly enough attention. I'd like to see that rectified today."

"Indeed, m'lord." Mari swept out from under his arm and curtsied. Her jeans and sweatshirt diminished the effect, she was sure, but the sweep of her arms was very regal. She was lighthearted at the thought of a full day in Jim's company without the responsibility of children. And she felt surprisingly comfortable in her role of fiancée; at least for the moment it made her feel loved and cosseted and didn't require her to divulge her secret. Her eyes sparkled and she felt just a little wicked. She scooped up a handful of snow that hadn't melted in the shade of the porch and shaped it threateningly in her hands. "And what kind of attention would his lordship like? A cool hand upon his brow perhaps?" She approached him and walked slowly around him, staying carefully out of reach. He stood, arms folded across his chest, watching her with lazy eyes. "A snowy softness against his skin? The cool kiss of..."

Distracted by her own monologue, she missed his lightning swift movement that snatched her arm, grabbed the fistful of snow from her, and dropped it down the front of her shirt.

"Jim!" she shrieked, then "Oh!" and "Oh!" as the snow melted against the warmth of her body and icy water dripped into her bra. She shook the offending object out of the bottom of her sweatshirt, uncomfortably aware of a tautening in her breasts at the icy contact.

"That was not a saintly thing to do!" she accused, turning away from him, her face reddening, grateful she wore a sweatshirt and not a T-shirt.

"You were being devilish," he countered, coming around her to look down into her flushed face. "That

was not the kind of attention I was talking about."
Hands on his hips, he surveyed her with glowing eyes,
challenging her. "I was hoping for a certain...ardent
softness in your attitude toward me."

"Ah..." she replied, as though finally understanding. "Well, your lordship must be more specific in future to avoid such...misunderstandings."

With that she locked her fingers behind his head and
brought it down to her, rising on tiptoe to meet his lips.
They flamed instantly, a hot brand on her mouth, at
her ear, tracing her ivory neck to her high neckline.

He drew away, looking in disgust at her sweatshirt.
"I don't suppose you'd like to slip into something less
concealing and spend the day at home?"

His voice sounded strained, and her own breath was
like a fire in her lungs. This combustion between them
seemed to happen more quickly and with more intensity each time he kissed her. It never failed to amaze
her, and now she stood looking at him, rocked by the
trembling in her limbs. But she had to think. She had to
maintain her sanity.

She smiled and felt the imprint of his lips in the curv-
ing softness of hers. "You promised to take me to Fort
Catsup," she reminded.

"Clat-sop!" he corrected, enunciating. "It's a tribe
of Indians."

"That's it. And I'd like to go today. I deserve a little
attention, too, don't you think?" At his glittery leer
she amended quickly, "Not that kind. And I'd like
lunch first, please. And a glass of wine and perhaps a
light dessert."

"You won't have room for spaghetti," he warned.

"If we get enough exercise—" she began seriously,
then realizing how that sounded, looked up into his
bland smile with a grimace.

"I was trying to provide that," he said innocently.

"You, m'lord, have a one-track mind," she accused,
laughing.

"Only since you walked into my life, my lady," he

replied, opening the front door. "We'd better get this show on the road before it's too late. Change your shirt and I'll get my car keys."

It was a bright sunny day and, accustomed to smoggy Los Angeles, Mari stared voraciously at the brightness of color against color: the deep evergreen against the jeweled blue sky, the yellow of a little house in a grove of towering green, the crisp red and white and black of a tugboat on a slate-blue river shot with sunlight. Staring out the restaurant window at the tugboat, Mari experienced a feeling of rightness, a sense of falling in with some complex design.

"You're smiling," Jim observed.

Mari turned away from the window to see him leaning on elbows folded on the table. In a red Pendleton shirt his dark good looks were almost more than she could bear. Her heart began to race just looking at him.

"I was thinking that being in Oregon is like walking into technicolor after living in a world of black and white. I haven't thought about a palm tree all day."

Jim smiled, putting a glass of Chablis to his lips. "The real test will be if you still love it if it rains tomorrow and every day after that until June."

"Every day?" she frowned.

"Perhaps not all day," he conceded, setting his wine down and leaning back as the waitress placed a chef's salad in front of each of them. "But at least some of every day. Then every once in a while there's a day like today, and you know why you're living here."

"I guess I'll find out," she said doubtfully.

"Actually there's nothing quite as cozy and intimate as rain on the roof," Jim said, passing her the basket of rolls. "It's like music to love by."

She carefully buttered a roll, deliberately keeping her eyes on her task. The thought of being loved by him, of loving him back, was a fire in her chest, and she was sure there were sparks in her eyes. But the thought of loving him always reminded her that there was something she hadn't told him. And he was so perceptive, she was afraid he would read it in her eyes.

"Look at me, Janie," he ordered quietly.

She finished buttering with a final swish of her knife and, replacing it on the side of her plate, looked up at him with studied nonchalance. But he wasn't fooled and she saw that instantly.

He frowned, more puzzled than angry. "Why are you afraid to let me see that you care?"

She frowned back at him as though she didn't understand, inwardly cursing herself for her transparency. "Isn't agreeing to marry you proof that I'm not afraid to show you I care?"

He smiled wryly. "I think that was just bowing to the inevitable. We're like a pine tree and a bolt of lightning together."

Mari eyed him in exasperation, hoping frantically to divert the conversation. "You make me sound like an arsonist or a careless camper. I'm just a poor working girl who came to Astoria to spend a couple of weeks, and look what happened."

He considered her, fork poised over his salad. "Are you sorry?"

She didn't really have to think about that. Marrying Jim meant she had to confront her sterility, a part of herself she hated but could not escape. But if the alternative to that was never having known Jim, then the reply was easy. "No!" she said.

He looked at her for a long moment, then went comfortably back to his lunch. "Good," he said. "Do you want to check out the house today?"

Puzzled for a moment, she asked, "What house?"

"My house," he replied, then corrected, "or your house, for the time being. You can see what you'll need and we can get it for you before our merry little band disperses after New Year's Day."

"I'll have to send for my things."

"I've already done that," he said.

"When?" she demanded, looking up at him with wide, indignant eyes. "Why?"

"Day before yesterday," he answered calmly. "And because I thought you'd appreciate the help. The mill has a truck coming from Los Angeles with supplies next week. Your landlady will have everything ready, and our truck will pick it up. Whatever you would have done would have been more complicated than that... and slower. You didn't even think of it 'til today." His smile challenged her to argue.

She was torn between resenting his high-handed taking over of her affairs and relief that she need no longer worry about it.

"Thank you," she said finally, relief winning. "Will we have time? We'll have to stop at the market to pick up some things for dinner."

"How much preparation time do you need?"

"About an hour."

He looked surprised. "I thought great spaghetti sauce cooked for many hours," he challenged with a grin.

"Working girl spaghetti does not," she retorted. "It comes out of a jar, and my own special touches make it magnificent." She was about to state teasingly that if he wanted sauce that was cooked all day, he might want to reconsider his proposal, but he was wearing a look that turned her spine to oatmeal.

Jim took her hand from where it lay next to her wineglass on the table and brought its palm to his lips. The kiss was feather light, and she felt it to her toes. "Your touch does magnificent things to me, too," he growled softly. "I wish we had stayed home."

"James, behave yourself," she pleaded, looking furtively around her and finding interested eyes looking back. "Everyone is watching us."

"Then don't get defensive," he returned, grinning as he let her go. "When your color's high and your eyes flare, you test my self-control. Finish your lunch so we can get out of here."

"You promised me dessert," she reminded.

"Janie..." he warned.

"Are you going to be this hard to get along with after

we're married?'' she asked, studying him over hands steepled under her chin.

"Are you?" he countered.

"Probably."

"On second thought," he said, looking over his shoulder for the waitress, "maybe you should have dessert. It might sweeten you up."

At the visitors' center at the fort they watched a film about Lewis and Clark's two-year trek to Oregon, then home again, and viewed artifacts in the small museum. Following a bark-dust trail to the fort itself, they wandered through the replica of the fort's primitive and confining accommodations.

"Being a book nut," Jim observed, "you don't have to be told about the scout's wife Sacagawea and how valuable a member of their party she was."

"No, the novel about her was a best-seller in Hollywood, too. For someone who went on the trip only incidentally, just accompanying Charbonneau, she saved their skins more than once with her knowledge of medicinal herbs and Indian ways and language." She angled him a saucy grin. "Pays to have a woman along who knows her stuff."

Laughing, Jim hooked an arm around her neck and led her along another trail that signs indicated would lead them to the canoe landing. The trail was narrow and sun-dappled, tall evergreens on both sides reaching for the sky, their lower branches forming a canopy over their heads. Their fragrance was elemental and intoxicating, and Mari breathed deeply, feeling the peace of the place fill her lungs and her being.

As they approached the river, the trail muddied, and Jim led her carefully around it to a patch of grass crowded by bushes. Holding her before him at the water's edge with two solid arms around her, he was silent while she took in the view.

The silvery Lewis and Clark River moved smoothly north toward the Columbia, shimmering as though embroidered with sunlight, and disappeared quite a way beyond them into waiting arms of green. A log raft bound to old pilings moved gently on its surface. Across the river were more deep green pines against the bright blue sky, dotted now with tufts of cottony clouds. A small plane passed overhead sounding like an angry insect, and Mari looked up, leaning back against Jim's shoulder to watch it pass.

"If you stand here long enough," she observed dreamily, "you could almost forget what century it is."

"Mm," he agreed, tightening his grip on her, his cheek against hers. "That's part of the charm of Astoria. You can live in the present, but everywhere you turn there are memories of the past and, if you choose to, you can get lost in them. Like now." He planted a kiss on her temple. "I'd like to take you back to Charbonneau and Sacagawea's cabin and make love to you."

She turned in his arms, clasping hers around his waist Her smile was full of her love for him and her pleasure in this day. "But what would the visitors to the fort think?"

His eyes looked deeply into hers, his expression frustrated. "When you look at me like that, I could almost say I wouldn't care what they thought. Have you considered setting a wedding date?"

Suddenly the sun dimmed for her and guilt wound around her as though it were a blanket dropped on her shoulders. Before she married him, she had to tell him she was sterile, and she wasn't ready to do that. She was afraid to risk losing the closeness with him she had known today.

"No," she said quietly, pushing against his confining arms. He let her go, a frown forming between his eyes.

"What is it, Janie?" he asked, watching as she looked around herself helplessly for a means of escape. Behind her was the river, before her was Jim; to the left of her were thick bushes, and to the right a muddy track on which she might slip if she had to leap around him to reach it. She was about to try it when he caught her arm.

"You'll either end up in the drink or in the mud," he said impatiently. With one long stride he was across the mud, reaching long arms back for her to pull her across. He retained both hands he held and looked down at her, obviously surprised by her reaction.

"What is it?" he asked again.

"Nothing!" she insisted. "Really. Nothing."

"Is it Walters?" he asked.

She frowned up at him, surprised for a moment, then remembering her ploy replied, "No. It isn't Kent."

"Then what?"

Hating herself, she looked at him, her expression deliberately closed. "Nothing," she said with what she hoped was finality.

He studied her averted eyes for a long moment, then sighed heavily. "All right. Do you still want to see the house, or have you changed your mind about that, too?"

"Yes, I'd like to see it," she replied quietly, not correcting his implication that she had changed her mind about their engagement.

A group of young people talked and laughed their way along the trail toward them, and Jim gestured her toward the trail that led to the parking area. They walked back to the car side by side, never touching.

What Jim had referred to as a small house turned out to be a spacious two-bedroom with a separate dining room and a good-sized kitchen. The lot was small, but if Jim's predictions were accurate and it would soon be raining nonstop anyway, a place outdoors for Melissa to play was not a problem. On a residential street within walking distance from the downtown area, the house seemed tailor-made for her present needs.

Mari looked around her and thought that her furniture would fit in perfectly. There was a dishwasher in the kitchen and a washer and dryer in a small service porch by the back door.

"You've thought of everything," she said, her voice echoing hollowly in the empty living room.

"I'm a good landlord." He walked toward her from across the room. "The last tenants were here for two years until the Coast Guard transferred them east. What do you think?"

"I'll take it, of course." Mari started to pull her checkbook out of her purse, and he stopped her, pushing her hand back inside until she had dropped the book.

"Let's not worry about that now," he said, an edge to his voice.

"But business is business," Mari insisted.

"Mari," he said, closing his eyes for an instant, exasperation very evident in him, "you're going to marry me."

"I know," she said in a small voice, "but it might not be...I mean, we aren't..."

"You mean you're hoping to put it off as long as possible, and in the meantime you don't want to be indebted to me for anything. Is that it? It gives you an opening, a way out."

He had read her mind precisely, and she felt her color rise as she turned away from him, looking through the open dining room drapes down the hill to the river. Three blocks of brightly painted houses stretched before her.

"I have that right, haven't I? Isn't that what engagements are for?"

She heard him sigh, then felt him walk up behind her, only a breath away. "Technically I guess you're right. But I think the time is supposed to be spent in looking for a way to hold a relationship together rather than in finding ways to make a hasty exit."

She turned around to look into somber hazel eyes. His face was set in hard lines, and she knew he was losing patience with her.

"That isn't what I'm doing," she said earnestly. "Honest."

He looked back at her for a long moment, his expression softening a fraction. But he didn't smile. "I wish I could be sure of that," he said. Then, with apparent effort to reestablish normal conversation between them, he added, "The truck should be here New Year's Eve. I'll bring you over to direct the unloading. Then you'll be ready to move in on the second if you like."

"That's fine," she agreed.

At the market they purchased the makings for spaghetti sauce, Italian sausage, a bottle of Chianti, and a candy bar for each of the children.

"Don't I get one?" Mari asked, smiling up at him winningly, trying to pierce the wall of reserve that had risen around him at the rental house.

He looked down at her, his expression unchanging. "You haven't been good," he said. Just as he had her convinced that he was serious, a flicker of laughter showed in his eyes.

"I'm never good," she laughed, relieved to see his good humor restored. "You can't make that a condition for anything!"

"I keep forgetting." He tossed another candy bar in the shopping cart and headed for the checkout stand.

When they got home, while Jim put the bag of groceries on the kitchen table, Mari noticed a note on the refrigerator. Removing the magnet that held it in place, she read while shrugging out of her jacket, "Steve is playing next door and has strict instructions to be home before dark. Missy is napping and so are we. Love, Mom and Dad."

Jim grinned across the room at Mari, and she understood instantly that napping for Mom and Dad probably translated to something entirely different.

"You're blushing," Jim chuckled, coming to pull her jacket the rest of the way off. "They're not dead, you know. Just... mature."

"I'm not blushing," she said with dignity, pulling at the turtleneck of her blue sweater. "I'm just warm." She delved into a lower cupboard to hide her face while ostensibly pulling out the skillet. Ignoring Jim who lounged against the counter watching her move about, she got onions and celery sauteing and snatched up the large jar of off-the-shelf sauce. She handed it to him without looking up from stirring the contents of the skillet. "Would you open that, please?"

With a flick of his wrist, he opened the jar and handed it back to her, watching as she stirred it into the fry pan. On a back burner she put the sausages, their spicy aroma quickly filling the kitchen.

"Is that what strikes terror into your heart every time the word 'marriage' comes up?"

"What?" she asked innocently without raising her eyes.

"The thought of going to bed with me?" he asked candidly, his voice soft in the quiet kitchen.

She glanced at him then, hoping that a seductive smile would help her bluff her way out of this conversation. "Do I act as though I'm afraid when you kiss me?"

"No, you don't. And that's what's so confusing. I know you care for me. I know you enjoy being kissed. But something's in the way."

It would be so simple to say it now, she thought, her heart quickening as she tried to summon the courage. He was in a gentle mood and just might understand. It would be such a relief to have the words spoken.

She set the wooden spoon on the edge of the pan and ran her hands down her apron in a stalling gesture, searching her mind desperately for the words.

Then the back door flew open, and Steve appeared on the threshold, blood streaming from his nose.

"Dad!" he called, his voice panicky, but Jim was already there, a handkerchief pressed to the boy's face, an arm around his shoulders leading him toward the sink.

Mari had the water running and took the square of linen from him to run it under the faucet.

"I was sledding..." Steve explained, shrinking back against Jim's arm as Mari wiped blood away in order to assess the damage. "I...got a low branch in...in my face."

"The trick, son," Jim said gently, "is to sled where there are no trees."

"Then we'd...we'd have to move to LA with Aunt...ouch!...Aunt Janie," he quipped, "instead of her...moving in...with us."

"Oh, we've got nice thorny palm trees there, Steve." Mari rinsed the handkerchief again and caught a weak trickle of blood from his nose. "They could really redecorate your face for you. If we had snow, of course, which we don't."

Jim leaned down to study the boy's face.

"I think you've been lucky, Steve," Jim said, his long fingers probing gently. His cheek was bruised, but Steve's slim freckled nose appeared unbroken.

"Doesn't look like you've done any serious damage. How do you feel? Want to lie down for a little while?"

"Not if the spaghetti's ready," he said, apparently horrified at the prospect of an unscheduled nap.

Jim straightened up and grinned at Mari. "I think he'll live."

"Darling, you've got to take a little better care of yourself," Mari said, leaning down to press a kiss to his bruise.

"That's right," Jim seconded. "Fathers can handle this kind of trauma day after day, but mothers get upset about it. And now that you're going to have one, you have to think about that."

"Okay."

"Okay. Go put your feet up and watch television until dinner's ready."

As the boy disappeared, Mari turned away from Jim and back to the sauce, because his remark had brought back to mind the subject they had been about to dis-

Harlequin reaches
into the hearts and minds
of women across America
to bring you

Harlequin American Romance.™

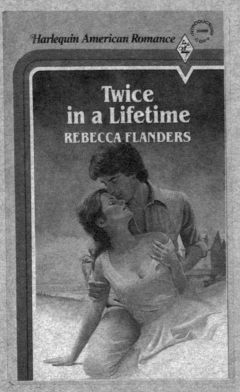

Enter a uniquely American world of romance with

Harlequin American Romance.™

Harlequin American Romance novels are the first romances to explore today's new love relationships. These compelling romance novels reach into the hearts and minds of women across America... probing into the most intimate moments of romance, love and desire.

You'll follow romantic heroines and irresistible men as they boldly face confusing choices. Career first, love later? Love without marriage? Long-distance relationships? All the experiences that make love real are captured in the tender, loving pages of *Harlequin American Romance* novels.

What makes American women so different when it comes to love? Find out with this special *Harlequin American Romance* offer!

Send for your FREE introductory book and tote bag now.

Get this Book and Tote Bag
FREE!

MAIL TO:
Harlequin Reader Service
2504 West Southern Avenue
Tempe, Arizona 85282

YES! I want to discover *Harlequin American Romance*.
Send me FREE and without obligation, "Twice in a Life-time" and my FREE tote bag. If you do not hear from me after I have examined my FREE book, please send me the 4 new *Harlequin American Romance* novels each month as soon as they come off the presses. I understand that I will be billed only $2.25 per book (total $9.00). There are no shipping or handling charges. There is no minimum number of books that I have to purchase. In fact, I may cancel this arrangement at any time. "Twice in a Life-time" and the tote bag are mine to keep as FREE gifts even if I do not buy any additional books.

154 CIA NAYB

Name	(Please Print)	

Address		Apt. No.

City	State/Prov.	Zip/Postal Code

Signature (If under 18, parent or guardian must sign.)

This offer is limited to one order per household and not valid to present subscribers. We reserve the right to exercise discretion in granting membership. If price changes are necessary you will be notified. Offer expires April 30, 1985.

PRINTED IN U.S.A.

AR1PT384

EXPERIENCE
Harlequin American Romance™
with this special introductory FREE book and
FREE tote bag offer.

**SEE EXCITING
DETAILS INSIDE**

Send no money.
Mail this card today.

cuss. Her courage had fled with the distraction of Steve's injury, and she prayed for a respite.

There was silence for a moment, then Jim went to the silverware drawer and began to set the table, apparently aware also that the moment was lost.

Chapter Eight

Mari spent New Year's Eve day supervising the moving of her furniture and possessions into her new home. Katherine kept the children, and Jim, Terry, and the young man who had driven the truck from Los Angeles hauled piece after piece into the house while Mari tried to establish order in the kitchen.

It was noon before she produced a tray with four mugs of steaming coffee and wandered into the living room in search of her crew.

Jim was sitting alone in the middle of the floor looking through a photo album her mother had kept of her.

"Where is everyone?" she asked, setting the tray down and offering him a cup. "And where did you get *that*?"

"Gus took the truck back to the mill, and Dad went for a pizza, and I found this when I was checking the contents of a box that looked a little mangled. Everything was okay, but when I discovered what this was, I had to have a closer look." Jim smiled up at her, pulling off his woolen cap and leaning back against a stack of boxes. "You were a cute little kid, Miss Westridge."

She knelt beside him to look over his shoulder at her eighth-grade graduation picture. She wore a short curly bob and a lacy white dress that fell just above a pair of knobby knees.

"My shoes were killing me!" she recalled, leaning on his shoulder to point at the high-heeled shoes. "They were my first pair of heels."

"But your smile is something else!" he said. "You look like you've got the world by the tail."

He turned several more pages, and there were pictures of her in her high school drill team costume, skinny and shapeless in a bathing suit, heavily made up and lavishly gowned as Juliet in the drama club's production of *Romeo and Juliet*.

The final page held her senior picture, and Jim paused to study it. It was a very formal pose, and she recalled having argued with Katherine about what to wear and how to fix her hair.

She had had her surgery just two months before and had been living under a cloud of depression. Her mother had insisted that the dark sweater she had chosen be changed for the ruffly white blouse in the picture and had brushed down the hair she had swept back severely.

"Something happened between Juliet and graduation," Jim said, closing the book to look at her. "It's in your eyes. And it's there now. Even a little deeper than it was before."

The sound of Terry's truck pulling into the drive filtered into the room followed by the metallic slam of the door. Jim shook his head resignedly and leaned over to kiss the frown line between her eyes.

"You're saved again, my love." He stroked an errant strand of hair behind her ear, his eyes grave. "But maybe one day you'll decide that I can be trusted."

The pizza consumed, Terry and Jim helped Mari with the boxes she wanted taken to the basement, then Terry pulled on his jacket.

"Are you two coming home before you go out tonight?" he asked.

"Yes, we'll have to change. Sure you and Katherine don't want to come with us?" Jim ignored Mari's surprised expression and walked Terry to the door.

"No, New Year's Eve is for you youngsters," he said, his fine physique and the bright sparkle in his eyes belying the fact that he was thirty years older than his son.

Jim slapped him on the back affectionately. "You're not kidding me. I know why you're staying home."

"It's time you caught on." Terry grinned, then waved at Mari. "Hope everything is in good shape. See you later this afternoon. And don't worry about tonight. We'll keep the kids for you."

"Won't that cramp your style?" Jim teased.

"We'll put them to bed early. See you later."

When Jim closed the door behind his father, Mari looked at him condemningly. "You're doing things without asking me again."

"What?"

"Where are we going tonight, and why didn't you ask me first?"

"We're going to the Thunderbird for dinner and to see the New Year in. And I did ask you." He smiled. "Remember the day you promised me a date?"

Recalling the episode when he had caught her in only a towel, Mari closed her eyes and frowned ruefully. "How could I forget?"

"Well, I'm collecting tonight. Did you call about having the phone connected?"

She nodded. "They'll be here on the fourth or fifth."

"Okay." He turned to the boxes behind them. "Where would you like these?"

"The smaller one in the bedroom, the large one in the basement," she replied, picking up their plates and the empty pizza box.

"How's the kitchen coming?"

"Very well. My kitchen in Hollywood was about half this size. Steve will be pleased. Lots of counter space is conducive to making cookies."

"Good. We'll expect them the day after you move in," he teased, hefting the smaller box. "Can you be finished in an hour?"

"I think so," she nodded.

"All right. I'm going to put these away for you, then run out to the mill to check on things. I'll be back in an hour."

Mari had gone back to the kitchen and was preparing a shopping list when she heard the crash. Something had fallen down the basement stairs and, by the sound, hit every step along the way. Her heart jolted in her breast as she ran for the basement door, shouting, "Jim? Jim!"

She was halfway down the dark stairway before she was stopped, viselike fingers gripping her upper arm from behind.

"I'm here!" he shouted over her heavy, panicky breaths. "That was a toolbox I was using for a doorstop that fell. Come on up here before you fall down."

He hauled her back up the stairs after him, and when they emerged into the light, he frowned at her pallor. "Are you all right?"

She gave his arm a vicious punch, and though it didn't even rock him, it gave her great satisfaction.

"I thought you'd fallen!" she accused.

He enveloped her in long, strong arms, pressing her hot face against the soft flannel of his shirt. His head rested on her hair, and she felt his lips at her temple.

"I'm all right," he assured her. "But your concern is flattering."

"I don't want to lose you." She was horrified to hear herself say it aloud. She said it silently everytime she looked at him lately, but considering her reluctance to set a wedding date, he probably thought she was playing with him.

But his voice and his manner were gentle. "You won't, babe. You've got me for the duration."

However long that would be once he knew, she thought despondently. She wedged a space between them and looked up into his face. There was amusement and tenderness there.

"I'm sorry," she said with a sigh. "I guess I'm tired."

"This Christmas vacation hasn't been your classic relaxing two weeks for any of us. It'll almost be a relief to get back to work. Will you be all right if I leave you for a little while?"

"I'll be fine," she said, then having a thought about the plans he proposed, frowned. "I haven't anything very formal to wear."

"I like the blue and silver thing you had on Christmas Eve," he said, smiling in memory. "Would you wear it again?"

"If you don't mind seeing it again," she said uncertainly.

"As long as you're in it, you can wear it every day. Bye, Janie. See you in an hour or so."

Leaning against the window and watching his truck pull away, Mari knew she should either tell Jim about her sterility tonight and get the New Year off on the right foot, or she should leave quietly now before he returned and hide out somewhere until she could get back to Los Angeles.

But she knew she would do neither. Going back to LA was no longer an option because all her earthly possessions were now in this little house in Astoria. And she had given up her job there.

Telling him was the only choice left that would give her any peace of mind, but she simply hadn't the courage. She could no longer live day to day without his presence in her life. She, who had been so withdrawn, so insulated, was now dependent upon his smile, his laughter, his touch, to simply get by.

She went back to her shopping list, reflecting that life would certainly be much simpler had she been able to convince her mother that she had been too busy to come to Astoria for the Christmas holidays.

Swags of greenery hung with Christmas balls decorated the restaurant's elegant dining room. Beyond a wall of windows overlooking a marina, the lights on scores of small fishing boats decorated the night.

As Jim walked in pushing Mari gently before him in the wake of the hostess, the people at several tables called to him and he waved. At one of them, a young man made reference to his visit to the mill that afternoon, and Mari presumed that the people seated there were men and women he worked with.

When they were seated, a tall, dark-haired girl, wispy slim in a white crepe sheath, came over to their table accompanied by a man about Jim's age, shorter and with sandy-blond hair.

Jim smiled warmly and stood, pulling the girl to him by her bare shoulders and kissing her cheek. Mari knew without being told that this was Julia Kramer. The man, apparently a totally infatuated boyfriend, watched the operation with an approving smile, feeling none of the consuming jealousy that had come upon Mari the moment Jim touched the other girl. But she forced a smile when Jim introduced them.

"Mari, I'd like you to meet Julia Kramer and Peter Morton. Julia, Peter, this is my fiancée, Marijane Westridge."

Julia eyed Mari thoroughly for a full twenty seconds before putting out a long, sinuous hand. Her eyes were challenging and her smile less than warm. "I'm pleased to meet you Marijane. We were all thrilled to hear that *someone* had finally cornered James."

The way it was said, Mari got the distinct impression that the "someone" was indeed a disappointment, particularly when the vision in white had once tried to corner him herself and apparently failed.

Vicious, primitive feelings were rising in Mari, and she fought to control them, alarmed because jealousy was usually so foreign to her nature.

When the couple sat down at the table to join them, Mari knew she was in for a long evening. Because the other three worked together, she was virtually excluded from the conversation, though Jim did try several times to draw her in. She ignored his gesture and replied in monosyllables or so tersely that by the time their drinks arrived, Jim was frowning at her. With so little to say, she had more time to brood and to sip the delicious piña colada he had ordered for her and was on her third when he suggested with a dark look that they order dinner.

Another couple joined them, and because the young woman seemed unaware of Jim after giving him a friendly greeting, Mari was able to talk to her without wanting to scratch her eyes out. The woman had two small children she was eager to brag about, and she and Mari divorced themselves from the rest of the table. While mill talk carried on round them, Mari listened with mixed gratitude and pain to stories of clever remarks and indications of budding genius.

It hurt to listen to the woman carry on and watch her beam about her children, but it was less painful than watching the beautiful computer programmer devouring Jim with her eyes and his seeming to enjoy it. That Peter could be so unaware of his girlfriend's behavior confounded Mari.

She was finally forced out of her conversation with the young mother, when the young father asked his wife to dance. Mari looked up to discover that she and Jim sat alone at the table.

He was leaning back in his chair, his features dark and dangerous against the crisp white shirt. His dark suit was such a change from the jeans and flannel shirts she was accustomed to seeing on him that he looked like a stranger. The anger on his face was something new, too, and she wasn't sure how to react to it. His mood was a little frightening, yet she refused to betray that feeling because her behavior was his fault and not her own.

She looked around at the empty chairs, then fixed him with a saucy smile and asked, "Julia appears to be dancing with someone else. Want to dance with me?"

His expression darkened further, and for a moment he didn't move. Then he pushed his chair back and stood, walking around the table to offer her his hand.

She took it and followed him to the dance floor where a small band played a mellow popular tune.

His anger was evident in the way he held her, rigidly, hurtfully. Mari leaned her head against his chin and said airily, "Well, darling, you can't expect me to be pleased about your flirting with another woman."

"Julia and I have worked closely together for a year and we're friends," Jim said stiffly. "What you're seeing is in your own mind, probably because you're not used to drinking."

She laughed lightly, the sound brittle against the muted music. "Is that why she glared at me when you introduced us?"

"If she glared at you," Jim said, his voice quiet but tight and his hand at her waist biting into her, "it's because you looked so hostile. She just reacted to bad vibrations. What in the hell is the matter with you tonight?"

"With me?" she asked hotly, her attempt at lightness vanishing. "We're supposed to be getting married, and you two are undressing each other with your eyes!"

"Oh, we are getting married?" he asked. "I was beginning to think you were having second thoughts about that."

"I'm not!" she whispered harshly. "But apparently you are! Well, don't let Peter stand in your way. I'm sure all you'd have to do is crook your little finger and Julia would come running."

"You'd like that, wouldn't you?"

"What?"

"An excuse to back out." He ground the words out, crushing her closer to him. "Well, you can forget it. We're both committed, and there's no way I'm going to let you welch on me."

"Oh, really?" she asked, stopping still in his arms. "If you think I'll sit idly by while you marry me and keep her on the side, you're crazy!"

"I think you've gone crazy," he said disgustedly, moving again with the music, his grip on her so firm she had the choice to move with him or be dragged. "Stop making a scene. These people are my friends, and I refuse to treat them to an exhibition of your bad manners on New Year's Eve!"

"But an exhibition of yours was all right?" she asked, looking up at him. There was thunder on his brow, but she refused to be intimidated. "Haven't you heard that there is no longer a double standard in man/woman relationships? If you can do it, so can I, but if I can't, then neither can you."

"I can do it," he said with a sardonic grin, "but I had the impression you didn't want to, at least not yet."

She growled, "You know what I mean!"

"No, I don't," he returned quietly. "And I don't think you do either. Now we're going back to the table and I'd like to see you refuse anything more to drink and be a little more congenial. Julia is a friend and nothing more."

With a withering glare Mari turned away from him and walked back to their table where the other four were already seated and chatting. The cocktail waitress returned, and Mari ordered another piña colada, smiling defiance across the table at Jim. He ignored her and asked Julia to dance.

Furious beyond reason, Mari downed her drink and thought reluctantly that they moved well together, how tall and glamorous the girl was next to Jim's elegantly garbed muscle. Julia leaned her head back and laughed, and Mari ordered another drink, stabbed to the heart.

When she got up to dance with Peter, his grip was fraternal, not at all what Mari had hoped for under the circumstances. She leaned her head against his shoulder, hoping to inspire a reaction. But apparently only Julia could make him react.

When they returned, they found Jim and Julia seated side by side, huddled into a tête-à-tête that made Mari see red. The only alternative to tears was anger.

"I'd like to go home!" she said icily.

Jim looked up at her, temper banked in his eyes. "It's quarter to twelve."

"Oh, yes," Mari said sweetly. "'Auld Lang Syne' and all that. Well, right after then?"

"With pleasure," Jim said, rising to pull her back with him to the dance floor. "Actually I'm quite anxious to take you home."

"Do I detect a threat, James?" she asked, smiling to show him that she was not afraid.

"More like a reckoning," he said. "Now, be quiet and let's see the new year in peacefully."

They danced until the midnight countdown, then on the stroke of twelve, when everyone else turned into a loved one's arms, Mari turned away from Jim, headed for the table and her wrap.

But she didn't get far. A tensile yank landed her back up against him, and a steely grip held her captive. One final glance before he kissed her told her not to make a scene, but she had lost all desire to, thinking greedily of his mouth on hers, his hands on her back, stroking down over her hip. When they finally stood apart, everyone else was dancing, and it was Jim who firmed his jaw and said archly, "Let's go home."

"I'd like to stay and dance," she said perversely, suddenly a little afraid of being alone in the dark night with this man whose touch made her lose control and reason.

"We're leaving," he said, the tone of his voice brooking no argument. Back at the table, he leaned down to kiss Julia on the cheek and to shake Peter's hand.

"I've enjoyed meeting you," Julia said to Mari.

"It's been ... something ... meeting you, too, Julia," Mari returned, her smile and manner artificial.

"Good night," Jim said, pushing Mari ahead of him. "And Happy New Year, you two. See you Monday."

It was a starless night, and Mari inhaled deeply of the damp fresh air as they walked to the car.

"More snow?" she asked, looking up at the shadow clouds against the dark sky.

"Rain," he said tersely, opening the car door on the passenger side. Before closing it again, he rolled down the window.

"I'll freeze to death," she complained.

"But you'll sober up," he said, slamming the door on her indignant gasp.

"I am not drunk!" she insisted as he got in beside her and turned on the ignition.

"Then how do you explain such uncharacteristic bad manners?" he asked, glancing judiciously at her as he backed out of the parking space and pulled onto the road. "You were not yourself tonight. It's just not like you to be intentionally rude."

"*I* was rude?" she shouted, thinking, as she heard her own voice yanked away from her by the wind generated by the speeding car and her open window, that she did not sound like herself either. But how dare he accuse her of rudeness. "You were the one pawing Julia, and she was the one making bedroom eyes at you! If I appeared rude, it was because I wasn't anxious to become friendly with someone who was trying to steal my fiancé."

"Janie!" he barked angrily. "For the last time—that did not happen! Julia and I are friends, good friends, but *just* friends. Either more alcohol than you're accustomed to made you hallucinate or ..."

He paused and she prodded angrily. "Or what?"

He pulled off the highway onto a dark little road leading onto a short pier. To the right of them was an old ship with large white letters declaring it the *Columbia* and next to it an empty moorage.

Jim stopped at the point where the pier went out into the water and turned off the motor. He turned in his seat to face her, his left arm slung over the steering wheel, his face illuminated by a powerful light on the pier.

"Or you're jealous," he said.

She looked at him one surprised moment, then turned away before he could see the truth in her eyes. "That's absurd!"

Her reply hung in the air between them. When the silence stretched on, she knew he considered her reply too false to even deny.

"What's that ship?" she asked, trying to divert him.

"Janie..." he began impatiently.

"Do you want to start the New Year fighting?" she asked. Laying the blame on him was becoming a tactic she used more and more often.

He drew a breath as though preparing to say something, then shook his head and leaned it back against his window.

"That's the lightship *Columbia*," he said, his voice sounding rehearsed. "It was stationed off the bar as a guide to navigation in 1950. A couple of years ago it was decommissioned and acquired by the museum. That's beyond us in the dark and full of remnants and relics of local shipwrecks." He pointed to the empty slip. "The Coast Guard cutter *Yocona* usually sits there, but she's out to sea right now." He paused, then straightened up, and though she was peering out the window, trying to appear absorbed in what he had told her, she knew he was looking at her. "Do you want to start the New Year keeping secrets?" he asked quietly.

Here it was, the face-to-face confrontation, and she couldn't handle it tonight. After five drinks and the ego blow of finally meeting Julia and seeing how lovely she was and how Jim was attracted to her, she was so unsure of herself as to be close to panic. Why would Jim ever want her, Mari, when he could have that beautiful younger woman?

He was probably convinced that a more mature woman would be a better mother to Steve and might even make fewer demands on him than Julia would. But she felt sure that his knowledge of her own infertility would cancel all her other pluses, and she couldn't bear to lose him. It occurred to her for the first time that if she did marry him without telling him, he might come to love her enough that it wouldn't matter. Now, that seemed her only hope.

Mari looked at him in the darkness and said softly, "Didn't you say that a little mystery in a relationship only enhanced it?"

"Darling," he said gently, his manner softening, a warm hand shaping the side of her face, "I know something is hurting you more and more every day, by all appearances. It's not a gentle, harmless, little mystery. It's a painful secret."

"You're imagining it," she said, trying to work a ploy. "Just as I imagined your relationship with Julia being more than platonic, maybe? I think we're both living on our nerve endings. You were right this afternoon when you said it hasn't been a very restful vacation."

Jim was silent for a moment, and Mari watched a light flick on and off far out on the river, her insides trembling.

"Is this where I'm supposed to say 'Of course. That's it, sweetheart. We're both jittery'?" He stopped and she heard a sigh escape him. "You're trying to work me, Janie. I'm not imagining anything."

Frustrated that her plan hadn't worked, Mari turned on him, anger flashing from her eyes. "And I'm not imagining anything either, am I? There's something between you and Julia."

"Yes, there is," he snapped back. "A computer. We're the only two in the place who understand it, and that gives us a special kinship. But for the fourth and final time, that's all there is to it. You can't use her to put me off either."

"You mean to tell me that that beautiful young thing spent the night with you and nothing happened?" she persisted.

"I have an eight-year-old son, remember?"

"Eight-year-olds do not stay up all night. Certainly there was a time when conditions were right?"

"Had I cared for her that way, that would have been entirely possible. But I didn't. And I don't."

Mari snorted. "Ha! I didn't think the modern American male was all that discerning. I thought modern morality decreed that you took your fun where you found it."

There was a pause, as though he were reining in his temper. "Is that the philosophy you espouse?"

"No!" she shouted.

"Well, why should I be all that different? The fact that I was born a male of the species doesn't mean that I lust after every woman indiscriminately or that I'd be ready to hit the sack with anything in skirts. Women don't have the market cornered on sensitivity, I don't care what the current sex report says." He turned in his seat, his movements swift and angry. "And if you're such a fan of the modern morality, why are you still a virgin?"

"Because I'm fastidious," she said in a small voice.

"Well, unpopular as it may be, that makes two of us. Do you or do you not want to marry me?"

Surprised by the suddenness of the question, she searched his face in the shadows. His jaw was firmed and angry, and she knew that if she said no now, it would be over, and her secret would no longer be a problem. She wouldn't have to tell him because it wouldn't matter any more.

She would be Marijane Westridge, a girl on her own, just as she had been before this fateful visit. But she recognized with a feeling of inevitability that that wouldn't do anymore. Life without Jim would simply be existence, and he had made her want so much more than that.

"Yes," she said softly. "I do."

There was another pause, as though he were steadying his voice. "All right," he said. "When?"

She had known that question was coming next, and she tried to sound matter-of-fact. "I'd like to see about my job. To get Missy adjusted to her...her new life..."

"All right," he said again, facing the dark river, his profile like a carefully cut silhouette against the window. "I won't push you for a date, and I won't mention your secret again." Then he turned to her, the full force of his feelings in the eyes that probed into hers. "But I don't want any half measures between us. I love you totally, and that's what I want back from you. You can take your secret to the grave as long as it doesn't get between us or hurt Steve in any way. Agreed?"

He turned the key in the ignition and when she didn't answer, looked at her again. "Well?"

Enveloped in misery, she nodded. "Agreed."

They drove home in silence.

Watching the darkness fly past the window, Mari wondered why, when he had struck a compromise that was perfect from her point of view, she should be so completely unhappy. Glancing over at his set profile, she knew that it was because she had left him no choice and that nothing would ever be the same again. They would still love each other, he with his gift for totality and she with her fears and doubts, but that fragile little tie that had always been between them had been severed and something important was lost.

The porch light had been left on for them, and Mari stepped aside as Jim turned the key in the lock. He let her pass before him, and she heard the door click locked as he closed it. The living room was dark, and she moved cautiously to the stairs where a ray of light was visible from the landing. The fragrance of the Christmas tree caught her nostrils, and sadness enveloped her, tears springing to her eyes. Before she could blink them back, they were falling.

Jim, with his radar sensitivity, caught her arm and pulled her to the kitchen where a door could be closed between them and the upstairs bedrooms. He flipped the light on, revealing the spotless, quiet kitchen and Mari's tear-streaked face.

He sighed exasperatedly and looking down at her as more tears fell, put his hands on his hips, his jacket thrown back behind his hands. "Janie, what more do you want from me?"

The anger from earlier this evening was gone, and she saw only frustration and confusion in his eyes.

"Would you just hold me for a minute?" she asked in a strained voice.

He looked for a moment as though that was the last request he expected, but he opened his arms and she went into them. As he enveloped her, holding her gently, she wrapped her arms around his middle and clung to him, small broken sobs coming painfully from deep inside. He brushed the hair back from her damp face and kissed her forehead, shushing her as though she were Melissa.

"It'll be all right, Janie," he said again and again. "It'll be all right."

She finally pushed away from him and forced a smile. "Do you really want to marry *me*?"

"That was never in question," he said, his smile fractional.

"Isn't it now?" she asked.

"No," he replied without stopping to think. "Since the day I pulled Ta off of you, I haven't been able to see my life without you in it."

"Maybe you should hire me as your housekeeper or something," she teased, trying to reestablish the light mood that worked so well between them.

He smiled again, a little more enthusiastically this time. "That's not quite the role I had in mind."

So grateful to see his smile, Mari sobered and said earnestly, "I hope I can be everything you want in me."

"You are everything I want," he said firmly.

She shook her head. "You are a saint."

He grinned wryly. "I think it's virtually impossible

for anyone who has ever been a logger to be canonized.''

"Father O'Shea seems pretty fond of you."

"I let him win at tennis." He cupped her face in his hands and kissed her lightly. "It's late, babe. And I have to be at the mill early tomorrow." He turned her toward the door with a gentle shove. "Get some sleep. Some day we'll have ten kids and forget that we ever had a rocky beginning."

She made it through the swinging door without reacting to that lightly spoken remark, then ran the length of the stairs and down the hall to her room, her hand stifling the sob.

Chapter Nine

A guarded peace existed between Jim and Mari for the next few weeks. She settled into the little house, enjoying the time for private thought after the busy holidays. She was working three days a week at the bookstore and had found a place for Melissa at the babysitter Jim used for Steve.

Janet Hudson was a lively young woman surrounded by children and apparently unflappable. Her home was bright and cheerful, and the living room rug and coffee table were always cluttered with children's projects.

Mari saw little of Jim during that time, though he called every evening to check on her. His vacation over, he seemed to spend every waking hour at the mill. She guessed also that he was being true to his promise not to press her about setting a date for their wedding. The easiest way to insure that the subject didn't arise was to avoid being together. It made no sense, but it was working. And it seemed to be giving Mari a certain rational distance from the situation that allowed her to evaluate it calmly.

She planned to spend the next few months gaining experience on her job and helping Melissa adjust to life in Astoria, an accomplishment already well under way. She, herself, seemed to be recapturing some of the poise and logical thinking that had fled because of Jim's constant nearness, and that could only have a positive effect on every phase of her life.

When the time came that she could share her secret

with Jim, she would be established enough to make a life for herself and Melissa if he was unable to deal with it. Remembering his gentleness in the kitchen on New Year's Eve made the possibility of life without him an abhorrent prospect. But remembering, too, how Jim and Julia had looked at each other, how quickly she knew the woman would run to him if he beckoned, she knew it was a possibility she had to consider.

As Jim had predicted, the rain had returned, and every day was a repetition of the day before, at least from a climatic point of view. Walking to work down Fifteenth Street, one of Astoria's many hills, Mari watched the leaden gray sky meet the deep gray of the river as rain fell in an incessant sheet. She had invested in rain gear for herself and Melissa, and they wore their bright slickers every day.

It amused Mari that her customers in the store always commented on the rain, when she thought it would have become so much a part of their lives as to be beyond notice. But for the lively older ladies who were a large part of the store's clientele, nothing escaped attention.

"Colder today!" one would comment. Or "The wind is from the east. Bad storm coming." And the inevitable "Raining hard enough for you?"

In Los Angeles everyone ran for cover when it rained, but here the main street teemed with activity, colorful umbrellas brightening the rainy afternoons.

But in her cozy little house, with Missy asleep upstairs, Mari paced away the rainy evenings, feeling something out of joint or missing in her life. She suspected what it was and avoided analyzing it too closely.

February brought more rain and a disruption in Mari's stabilizing world. Her old Volkswagen had developed an ailment too expensive to permit its instant repair. She was able to take Missy to the babysitter and to get to work on foot, but hauling groceries home up the hill in the rain was a problem.

Shortly after the car was immobilized, Mari woke up

to fix breakfast one morning and noticed that the house was colder than usual. She checked the thermostat, and though it was set at sixty-five degrees, the temperature registering was only sixty. By the time she and Melissa returned home that night, it was fifty degrees. She tried to call the oil company, forgetting that she was no longer in Los Angeles where all services were available to one every hour of the day or night.

The next morning, Saturday, the house was so cold, she knew she had to take action. Dressing Melissa warmly, Mari walked down to the supermarket for fabricated logs to burn in the small living room fireplace. It was raining and they were drenched by the time they returned home, Mari's arms aching from the heavy logs.

She was on her knees before the fireplace, her damp hair hugging her neck, when she heard a knock at the door. Missy ran to it before Mari could get to her feet, and the child giggled delightedly when Jim reached down to scoop her up. Steve followed his father into the house, and Mari sat back on her heels as they walked toward her.

"What's the matter?" Jim asked, frowning.

"Cold!" Missy replied, hugging her arms in an exaggerated shiver.

"The furnace won't go on," Mari got to her feet, brushing her jeans off as she stood. "I tried to call the oil company but no one answered."

Jim put Missy down and disappeared into the basement. Asking Steve to watch the child, Mari followed him down, getting on her knees beside him as he checked the lines from the motor to the furnace.

"How did you get so wet?" he asked, letting a line drain a moment, then capping it again.

"I walked to the market for logs," she said defensively, wondering why he sounded so annoyed.

"Why didn't you drive?"

She sighed impatiently. "My car is broken down."

"When did that happen?" He was now outright angry and stood, towering over her.

"About a week ago," she replied calmly.

"And how long has the furnace been out?" he asked tightly. "It's cold enough in here to have been more than one day."

"About two," she replied in the same tight tone. "I noticed it yesterday morning. I assure you I did not decommission my car nor break your precious furnace specifically to annoy you."

He glared at her for a moment, then drew a deep breath. "I have been calling you every evening to find out how things are going for you and whether or not you need anything. Why didn't you tell me your car was broken down and that the furnace wasn't working?" He reached out to lift a hank of her wet hair. "You could have caught pneumonia."

"I'd have called you when I felt the rumble in my second lung," she quipped and regretted it instantly. His eyes sparked and he raised his hand. She flinched, thinking for a startled moment he was going to shake her with it, but instead he pointed to the stairs. "Go upstairs and turn the thermostat way up," he barked, sounding as though he was at the end of his tether.

She complied, heard the motor go on, and hurried back to the top of the stairs, hoping to hear the sound of oil catching flame, but nothing happened.

After another attempt Jim came back upstairs and went to the kitchen phone. After a brief conversation with a friend who apparently understood such things and promised to come right over, he hung up and asked Mari to fix a pot of coffee.

"Anything else I should know about?" he asked, leaning against the counter as she filled the pot with water and spooned the fragrant coffee into the basket. She slammed the lid on and flashed at him.

"No. And considering the way you're taking this, I wouldn't tell you if there was."

"I am not angry because you are having problems," he enunciated carefully. "I am angry because you would prefer to freeze to death before calling me for help."

"You've been busy at the mill," she said placatingly, turning away from him to pull mugs out of the cupboard. She also put a pan of water on to heat to make cocoa for the children.

"That's not why you didn't call," he returned. "Suffering was preferable to having to accept my help."

"Now you're reading minds?" Mari asked tartly.

"It doesn't take a clairvoyant." He moved aside when she reached behind him for a hot pad.

"Jim." She clutched the potholder in both hands and fought to remain calm, a corner of her mind not occupied with this argument thinking that they hadn't been together two minutes when this quarrel erupted. Could there ever be a peaceful relationship between them?

"I have been on my own for three years," she tried to explain. "I am accustomed to having to cope with things by myself. I am a capable person."

"Janie, had you been capable of handling *this*, we wouldn't be standing here fighting in a room that's ten degrees colder than it is outside!" He closed his eyes to summon patience and went on more quietly. "And an independent attitude works well when one is independent. But you are no longer alone. I am here to help and support you. Why is that so difficult to accept?"

"You want to run my life!" she accused, groundlessly, she knew.

"I don't want to run your life, but I would like to be part of it." He folded his arms across his chest and his voice softened. "Your eyes invite me closer, and you let me come, as long as my reactions are only physical. But the minute I try to touch the Marijane that lives inside you, you push me away. You won't share anything with me that would require a"—he paused—"a meeting of souls, so to speak."

Mari sighed wearily and turned to the stove, adjusting the burner as the coffee began to perk. "How many times can we have this same argument?"

"Problems have a way of hanging around until they're solved," Jim said, straightening away from the counter. "But I promised I wouldn't keep harping on it and I won't. Excuse me. That's Jake's truck."

Jim went into the living room at the sound of a motor in the driveway, and Mari turned back to the task of making hot chocolate for the children. She frowned guiltily as she worked because she knew his complaints were justified. But at the moment she was powerless to change things.

The children were having cinnamon toast and cocoa when Jim returned to the kitchen half an hour later. As he came in the door, the sound of a truck departing followed him through. He looked thoughtful.

"Couldn't fix it?" Mari guessed.

"It's something in the switch," Jim explained. "He has to send for the part. The order won't be filled until Monday at the earliest, and it might be Wednesday before it gets here."

Mari shrugged, wondering why he seemed to think the situation so grave. "I've got the fireplace."

He drew a steadying breath and said calmly. "The fireplace will heat roughly halfway across the living room. Melissa is drenched." He pointed to the little girl, her hair hanging lank and wet about her face, her warm coat and hat still on as she ate her breakfast, unaware that she was being discussed. "Has been drenched for more than an hour. You'll both be sick if you stay here."

Mari looked at Melissa and grudgingly admitted that he had a point. Even in her coat, she was almost as cold as they had been the night they spent in Jim's truck.

"I'll call Mom," Mari said with a sudden half-smile. "I don't think she'll mind the company for a few days."

Jim reached out to stop her as she moved toward the phone. "Katherine and my father left for a few days on the peninsula this morning. That's what I came over to tell you. She tried to call you, but that must have been when you were out for the logs.''

Undaunted, Mari shrugged. "Well, then I'm sure they won't mind if Missy and I camp out at their place till they come home.''

"Your car isn't working, remember?''

Impatient now, she cocked her head up at him. "Is that your subtle way of telling me that you won't drive us there?''

"No,'' he said quietly. "It's my subtle way of telling you that I don't like the idea of you and Melissa stuck outside of town without transportation. The phone service and electricity are always iffy out there during bad weather.''

"Then what is the solution?'' she asked stiffly.

"The two of you will have to move in with Steve and me for a few days.'' He said the words matter-of-factly, and she could tell by his eyes that he was waiting for her to explode. She decided to disappoint him.

"All right,'' she replied. "I'll pack a few things for us.'' And she left the room before he could say any more. Upstairs, she put night things and several changes of clothes into a bag for herself, then went to Melissa's room and did the same. Her hands were trembling, but she forced all thoughts of what the next few days could mean to the back of her mind and tried to concentrate on the task at hand. He was right, of course. It would be best for Melissa if they were in town. What being that close to him could do to her did not bear considering.

Getting an empty box from the basement, she took the perishable groceries she had purchased the day before and handed the box to Jim.

"These will spoil,'' she said. "We may as well take them along.''

Spying the chocolate chips she had also tossed in, Steve exclaimed delightedly, "Can we make cookies this afternoon? And can I help, Aunt Janie?''

"Of course.'' She looked at the man beside her. "Do

you have everything else I'll need? Eggs, flour, sugar?"

"And baking powder and vanilla," he nodded knowledgeably.

She frowned in mild surprise. "You can bake cookies?"

He shrugged and slanted her a captivating grin over his shoulder as he headed for the door. "No, but Steve and I have tried so many times I've got the ingredients memorized. It'll be a thrill to watch a pro in action. Steve, can you take the smaller bag?" That, as he picked up the large suitcase she had put by the door, carefully balancing the box with the toe of his boot.

"Sure, Dad."

"Going?" Missy wanted to know.

"To Uncle Jim's house," Mari said, a feeling of going down for the third time settling over her.

"Duck!" the child cried woefully.

"He's in the grocery box," Mari reassured her. "Daddy... Uncle Jim has it." She bit her lip over the slip and avoided Jim's eyes while handing Missy up to him. Steve had put the small bag in the back and retrieved Missy's duck. He tossed it up before jumping up himself and closing the door behind him.

Jim's eyes went to Steve's door, saw that it was locked, then ran over his other passengers with a warm, possessive look. Mari was resisting its warming effect on her, but he smiled and she lost the struggle.

"This is a good-looking family," he said.

Mari looked from Steve with his fair-skinned, yet very boyish, good looks to small, delicate Melissa in her lap, her bright brown eyes peering out from under her woolly hat.

"Yes, it is," she agreed.

His eyes lingered on her a moment, indicating that he included her in the compliment, but she looked away, unable to deal with that. He gave her knee a pat then turned the key in the ignition.

Jim was silent until they reached a road on the outskirts of town and followed it about half a mile to a restored Victorian set in a grove of naked maples. A spacious front lawn was parted by a paved walkway. 'We're home," he said, pulling into the drive.

"How lovely!" Mari said, handing Melissa to him as he came around the truck to help her down. 'It's so big."

"It was in my mother's family, belonged to an uncle of hers, I think. Anyway, Dad built the house we've been staying in so I bought this one from him."

"There's a stream in the back," Steve added, running along beside them as they walked up the steps. "But it's off limits 'cause I could drown."

Inside, the house was comfortably modern in warm earth colors with polished wood floors and bright scatter rugs in every room.

Mari and Melissa were taken upstairs to a large bedroom overlooking the garden in the back of the house. It was decorated in shades of green, and a private bath led off of it. Jim set up the portable crib they had brought along and pointed to the electric baseboard heating unit. "Turn it up as high as is comfortable." Then he glanced at his watch. "I'll get some lunch going. And I don't think a bath would do either of you any harm, but, of course, I wouldn't suggest it to a young lady of your independent capabilities."

The pillow would have hit him squarely in the face had his reflexes not been so quick. But a large hand intercepted it, and he looked back at the devilish sparkle in her eyes with wickedness flickering in his. He came toward her threateningly while the children giggled, and she backed away, coming up against the wall. When he was within a foot of her, he tossed the pillow back at her with a roguish grin.

"Try that again," he said for her ears alone, "after the children are in bed." Then he turned to the boy and beckoned him to follow. "Come on, Steve. If we produce a good lunch, Aunt Janie might provide us with dessert."

Mari's blush was the only indication that Steve alone thought he was talking about cookies.

After a delicious lunch of chili, salad, and chunky bread, Mari insisted on clearing away.

"I'll help you," Steve volunteered, standing and stacking dishes.

Jim, who had been carrying his plate to the counter, turned back to put a diagnostic hand to Steve's head.

"Son, you must be feverish!" he said dramatically.

Steve punched him playfully. "Oh, Dad, I always help you."

"Yeah, but I have to beg and plead and promise you a raise in allowance."

"Well, Aunt Janie's prettier than you are."

"Aha! We've had a woman in the house a whole hour and already your loyalties have shifted."

"What does that mean?" Steve grimaced.

"That you already prefer your aunt to me." Jim looked the picture of affronted dignity, and Melissa, misunderstanding, ran up to him and clutched his leg.

"Love, Daddy!" she said warmly, smiling up at him.

His face softening, he reached down to pick her up and settle her on his hip, giving her a hug. "Love you, too."

"It's not a matter of loyalty, Dad," Steve laughed, coming to put his short arms around the man's waist. "It's a matter of cookies."

Looking at Jim, his arms filled with the children and laughter in his eyes, Mari felt a shaft of pain and busied herself with the dishes so that he wouldn't notice. But, though he said nothing, the mood in the room altered subtly, and Jim finally excused himself to make a telephone call. Mari and the children finished clearing away the lunch dishes and were combining ingredients for the cookie batter when Jim reappeared, shrugging into his parka.

"Computer problems again," he explained briefly. "I'll be back by dinner." Then with a grin at Steve, "Save me one or two, please."

"We won't have any until you get back," Steve promised nobly, then glanced at the batter and obviously had second thoughts. He looked back at Jim. "Well, maybe one to make sure they're all right. But that's all."

Missy chorused a good-bye until the door closed behind Jim, then she dipped a finger into the batter and put it in her mouth.

"Yummy!" she declared.

"Now, no more of that!" Mari said firmly, shaking her finger at the little girl who stood beside her on a kitchen chair. "I know you, Melissa Kate. You'd eat the whole bowl of batter, and we wouldn't even get one cookie."

"I usually eat the chocolate chips," Steve confessed winningly. "And we don't even get the batter."

"Well, once we get these cookies finished, you'll both see how worthwhile it is to wait to get the job done correctly. A good cookie is better than the chips or the raw batter. Now, we need cookie sheets."

Steve produced them from the bottom of the oven, then preheated the oven according to Mari's directions.

"Okay," she said, moving the bowl of batter and the sheets to the table where Steve could reach more easily. "Take two teaspoons from the drawer and bring them here."

When he had done as she asked, she explained the process of dropping the batter by teaspoonfuls on the sheets and placing them far enough apart to allow for the batter swelling in the oven.

While Steve followed her instructions, he concentrated industriously, then he put that tray in the oven and set the timer and began another. He glanced up at her shyly.

"Dad said I wasn't supposed to bring this up, but can I ask you a question, Aunt Janie?"

The question itself gave her pause for a moment, but then she realized that whatever it was, Jim wasn't here to hear the answer, so there was no need to be alarmed.

"Sure," she said. "What is it?"

"Well, you and Dad are gonna get married, right?"
That was safe enough. "Yes," she replied.

"Well, what if you have..." He paused again as
though phrasing the question was difficult, and when
he glanced up at her, his blue eyes were troubled.
"What if you have...a baby?"

She would have groaned aloud if she hadn't been so
sure that he was already upset enough about something. Unsure of his point, she asked gently, "What if
we do?"

He dropped a dollop of batter on the last vacant space
on the pan and stopped to look up at her. He swallowed. "Will I...still be able to...to live here?"

"What?" The question escaped her in shocked surprise before she could stop it, and before he could
think that she meant that negatively, she sat down in a
chair to look at him on his own level. "Of course, you
will," she said earnestly and saw the cloud in his eyes
waver. "I think you're a wonderful boy, and I'm as
anxious to have you for a son as I am to marry your
father."

He laughed, relieved. "I tried to ask Dad, but he said
you didn't really want to discuss getting married right
now. And anyway, he didn't really let me finish the
question."

"Steve." Mari took hold of his chubby hands and
pulled him to her. "Your father would never leave you
out of his life for any reason. You know that, don't
you?"

"I know he loves me," he said gravely. "But I know
he loves you, too. And when you're all one family,
that's neat. But when you're still"—he shrugged,
unable to find the right word—"you know...sep-
arate...not a family yet...then his loving me and his
loving you might not work together. I mean, you might
not want him to love me because you'd want your own
kid. And I might be jealous of you."

"That's pretty heavy thinking," Mari noted, wondering if it had all sprung from his own mind.

"Dad and Mrs. Savage...you know, she's our case-worker... well, they talked about it last week when she was here," Steve explained. "It was private stuff. But I forgot something in the house, and when I ran in to get it, I heard them."

"What did your father say?" she pumped gently.

Steve shrugged. "He said he had enough love for all of us. You and me and Melissa and more kids, too."

Mari swallowed and closed her eyes a moment. "And what did Mrs. Savage say?"

"She asked Dad if he thought you had enough." Steve shrugged as though embarrassed. "He said lots of nice things about you; then he said that you were very warm and very loving and that any kid would be lucky to have you for a mother. That he knew you'd be good to me and Missy and that if you guys had other children, you'd be able to handle everything and we'd all be the same."

It was a moment before Mari could swallow the lump in her throat.

"Well," she said finally. "We both know that your father knows everything and that just proves it." Mari hugged Steve and kissed the top of his head. "Now, you take this potholder and remove that tray of cookies from the oven."

While he was occupied, she checked on Missy who was working on a TV tray with her own little bowl of dough and a small pan, then poured herself a cup of coffee, resisting the urge to pour a dash of brandy in it.

The trap was tightening. Not only was she futilely fighting her own love for Jim and losing, she was now being ensnared by Steve, and any attempt on her part to resist marrying Jim would look to the boy as though he had been responsible. And, though nothing could be further from the truth, she could not be responsible for creating a situation where he would think that.

Knowing that Jim thought her warm and loving

made her feel as though she stood a foot taller, but hearing him describe her as able to handle more children only reinforced what she already knew, that he would love to expand their family.

It seemed to purge her guilt to spend the afternoon tidying the house once the cookies were finished and Missy was down for a nap. Steve helped her find cleaning supplies, and she scrubbed the kitchen floor, both bathrooms, vacuumed upstairs and down, and generally picked up.

As the afternoon wore into evening, she found chops in the freezer, put potatoes in to bake, and, hearing that Steve was fond of green beans, found a can in the cupboard and made a casserole with onion rings and gravy she felt sure he'd enjoy. There was ice cream to go with the cookies for dessert, and she had the table set and delicious aromas blending when Jim arrived home.

He pushed his way into the kitchen, lines of weariness marring his brow. Tugging off his jacket, he stopped on the threshold to see Steve pouring milk and Melissa carefully placing spoons to the right of the place settings Mari had already arranged. The lines of weariness softened as both children went to him, Steve with a cookie that he passed temptingly under his nose.

Scooping Missy up, Jim took the cookie from Steve, studied its prefectly browned, neat circular shape and took a contemplative bite. Then he closed his eyes and popped the rest of it into his mouth.

"Did you take notes on how that was done?" he asked Steve, putting an arm around him.

"I didn't have to," Steve said. "Aunt Janie's here to help me do it now. She said so."

Jim's arched eyebrow questioned Mari, but she pretended concentration on the casserole she was lifting out of the oven.

"Hungry?" she asked casually.

"Famished!" he said, putting Missy on the stack of books used to prop her up at lunchtime. He looked around the neat kitchen and the carefully set table, then fixed his gaze on Mari, his eyes so warm she had to turn back to the oven to pull out the potatoes to pretend interest in something else. "You know, a man could get used to this," he said, going to the refrigerator where a bottle of wine lay on its side. "I was going to suggest going out to dinner, but I should have known you'd have it all under control."

There was no barb in the remark, and Mari smiled, forking the chops onto a platter.

"Thank you. Coffee now or later?"

"Later," he replied, taking his place at the table and pouring two glasses of wine. "We can have it with the cookies." He glanced at Steve with feigned threat in his eyes. "You did save me more that that one, didn't you?"

"We sampled a couple," Steve said, and Mari grinned over his head at Jim, remembering how she finally had to put the cookie jar out of reach. It was the first time they had shared a happy thought, and he looked startled for a moment, almost as though he expected her to look away as she always did when his eyes grew intimate. But she smiled at him instead, and he smiled back. Mari couldn't decide if she had just cleared a hurdle or snipped the wire that held her suspended over this tenuous relationship.

Jim dropped Mari off at work the following morning after leaving Missy at Janet's. With Toni on a buying trip to Portland, Mari managed the store alone. Between customers she was taking tedious inventory of a display case. By closing time she was on her knees working on the bottom drawer.

"Excuse me." An attractive middle-aged woman leaned across the counter. "I'm looking for a book, but I don't know the title or the author."

Mari smiled, putting down her pen and a box of refills. She would have loved to have a dime for every request that began just that way.

"What's it about?" she asked, getting to her feet, slipping on the shoes she had discarded during a quiet moment.

"There were two sisters on *Good Morning America* this morning who've written a book about organizing your housekeeping," the woman explained with a puzzled frown. "They said the first letters of the words in the title spell HER, but I've looked on your shelf and don't find anything like that."

Mari nodded, crossing the shop to the shelf even before the woman had finished speaking. She pulled out a thin volume with a comic cover and handed it to the customer with a laugh. "The acronym is SHE not HER," she said. "That's probably why you couldn't find it. It's called *Sidetracked Home Executives*. It's hilarious. You'll love it."

"You're wonderful!" the woman praised. "I'd like two copies, please. One for my daughter. She's a terrible housekeeper, too, but then what can you expect? She learned from me." Laughing at her own joke, the woman paid for the books and left the store with a friendly wave.

Smiling after her, Mari reflected that that was the kind of encounter that made it all worthwhile, even during inventory.

"Could I have some help please?" a deep voice demanded peremptorily, and Mari spun toward the voice, bracing herself for the type of customer to whom the opposite applied, and found herself face to face with Jim. He wore a denim jacket and jeans over a chambray shirt, and he had a slightly mussed and very sexy look about him.

"I'm looking for a book," he said, leaning across the counter toward her, his eyes dancing. "I don't know the whole title, and I don't know the author, but it's something about *The Joy of...*" He closed his eyes as though in concentration.

Stifling a smile, Mari suggested, "*The Joy of Barbecueing*?"

"No."

"*The Joy of Crochet*?" she asked brightly.

"No."

"*The Joy of Taxidermy*."

"That's not it."

"Sir." With a quick look to assure herself that there were no customers in the store, Mari said in her most professional voice, "The book you're referring to is *The Joy of Sex*. Were you hoping to learn something from it?"

He smiled boyishly. "I wanted to look at the pictures."

"Jim!" She swatted his shoulder. "Are you here to take me home or to check out our human sexuality titles?"

"Actually," he said, walking briskly down the aisle of books, looking from left to right at various displays, "there was something I wanted . . ."

"Oh?" Suddenly all business, she caught up with him. "What is it?"

They had reached a tall display of pictorial books, and catching her arm, he pulled her behind it. "A kiss," he said, his eyes now dark in the shadows behind the rack. "I'd like your finest edition, engraved . . . right here." A long finger tapped his lips.

Excitement rose in her, flaring in her cheeks. "Sir," she said with a Victorian inflection. "We keep those under lock and key."

"That makes it difficult for the connoisseur to shop," he said softly, his eyes now riveted on her mouth.

"We could have one specially made for you," she suggested as his arms snaked around her and the clean smell of wood and his musky cologne mingled in her nostrils.

"That would be nice," he said distractedly.

"Delivery in a few weeks?" she teased in a whisper as his head came down to blot out the shop.

He kissed her hungrily, as though starving for her,

and she was not surprised to find herself as voracious as he, straining closer to him, running her fingers inside his jacket. She felt the warmth of his fingers through her silky blouse, then through her woolen skirt as they strayed further.

She wedged a space between them, her breath coming in gasps. "We're in the store!" she protested.

He frowned, pulling her back to nibble her ear lobe. "Why are you always reminding me of where we are? 'Jim, we're in our parents' living room.' 'Jim, we're in a state park.' 'Jim, we're in the store.'"

"Because you, sir, tend to forget yourself." She forced the space between them again and, pushing her hair back, drew a deep breath. "Now, can you behave yourself while I lock up and close out?"

Leaning a hip on her stool, he watched as she rang the till out, counted the following morning's advance, then tallied the day's sales. "Did you call the oil company today?" he asked when she had finished counting the change.

She nodded. "They said maybe Wednesday. I suppose that means they won't get it installed until Thursday."

He groaned. "Three more days."

She feigned hurt feelings. "I thought you liked my cooking. Hold your first two fingers out please."

"I do," he said, obliging her while she threaded the register tape through his fingers and began folding it into a manageable length. "But my halo's tarnishing. I don't know how much more of living with you I can take."

"You have to take three days more," she said heartlessly, dropping the day's files in the safe and slamming it shut, then rolling the dial. "Or my stepfather will hurt you."

His smile was warm and lazy as he opened the shop door for her. "You're right. Then considering the mood I'm in, we'd better not go home yet. Let's get the kids and go for pizza."

She reflected later that it must have been the pepperoni and Pepsi that made her toss restlessly for several hours that night before finally falling asleep and then to find herself in a black void in which she could not see. All around her babies were crying, but they were invisible to her. When she tried to escape the sound, she was unable.

She put a foot out, but there was nothing beneath her to stop it, and a step forward would have resulted in a fall; how far down or to where she could not see.

She began to cry, and the babies cries grew louder and louder until she thought she would go mad. She cried for Jim repeatedly, but he did not appear. She was alone, totally alone, except for the desperate voices of babies somewhere in the darkness.

When she awoke, she was sitting up, her pajama top plastered to her body by perspiration, and she was being shaken. She reached out to grip something solid and connected with the softness of a flannel shirt. Her scream still hung in the air, and when she opened her eyes, tears fell from them and she was sobbing.

Jim's face appeared before her as though through a mist, and she murmured his name with a trace of disbelief in her voice.

"Jim? I...I couldn't find you!" And with that admission she fell against him, and his arms came around her, enveloping her in the warmth and strength that were so much a part of him.

She could not stop crying, and he rocked her gently, pulling the blankets up around her shoulders and holding them in place with his embrace until heat finally began to permeate her chilled body and frightened mind, and she relaxed. She heard him say over her head, "It's all right, Steve. She's just had a bad dream. Go back to bed."

"Melissa?" she asked weakly.

"The sleep of the innocent," he said. "She didn't even stir. How do you feel?" He held her away from him and looked down into her blotchy face, the horror of the nightmare still standing in her eyes. "Do you want to tell me about it?"

She put the back of a trembling hand to her mouth and shook her head, still disoriented. "It...it wasn't much really. Except...that it was black...and I...I couldn't..." Fresh tears came and he pulled her back against him, chafing her arm and back.

"You couldn't find me," he finished for her, his lips at her brow. "Well, I'm right here. I was here by your second call, but I couldn't bring you out of it."

"Stay with me," she heard herself say.

There was a fractional pause, then he said softly, "I'm not going anywhere." He stroked the damp hair back from her face and held her closer. When she finally stopped trembling, he laid her back against the pillow, but she resisted, clutching his shirtfront. He laughed softly.

"I'm only going to get you a brandy and another pair of pj's. I'll be right back."

"Promise?"

"Promise."

He was back in thirty seconds with a small shot glass full of amber liquid. He handed it to her, then pointed to the dresser.

"Pajamas in here?"

She took a sip of the fruit-flavored brandy and grimaced as it bit its way down. "Second drawer. A red flannel nightgown."

Jim held it up in the dim light from the bedside lamp and grinned at her over it. "This does not look like something an independent, capable career woman would wear to bed."

"I bought it here because what I brought wasn't warm enough." She took another sip and coughed. "People drink this stuff for pleasure?"

"It's an acquired taste." He sat on the edge of the bed, holding the nightgown, and urged the glass back to her lips when she would have put it aside. "Come on. Two more sips won't kill you, and you'll sleep better."

She drew a deep breath and frowned at the glass. "Right now I feel as though I never want to close my eyes again." The black feeling came back vividly, and she shuddered.

"Finish it," he said brisky. She did and obediently raised her arms when asked to do so. Her damp pajama shirt was pulled off and her fresh-smelling nightgown lowered over her head. Then he pushed her back against the pillows, and his warm hands reached up under the nightgown to pull off her pajama bottoms. She was sure she was crimson to the roots of her hair, but he was operating with clinical detachment.

"Warmer?" he asked.

"Yes. Thank you." He looked down at her for a moment as though trying to decide for himself whether or not she was telling the truth. And Mari, reacting out of leftover fear, gratitude for the warmth and comfort he had provided, and the desire for him that could be turned aside no longer, whatever the conditions, reached up her arms to him. He resisted her for only a moment, then his heavy chest lay across hers, his mouth came down on hers, warm and satisfying.

"Jim," she whispered. "Jim, stay with me."

"Janie..." He pulled away from her confining arms, but she pulled back, arching her body to meet his when she hadn't the strength to force him back to her. She moved subtly against him, putting her lips to his throat, finding an out-of-control pulse and flogging it with the tip of her tongue.

With a low sound that was half growl, half groan, he fell down beside her, and every argument she had ever held against wanting him and needing him fled. He was so deliciously warm and strong, and she had been so confused and so alone for so long. She kissed him feverishly, raining small caresses all over his face and along his strong neck; his hard shoulder was stroked by her flushed cheek. Her hands strayed across his chest to his waist, and he finally caught it to him and turned his face into the pillow breathing hard.

"Jim?" she asked tentatively.

"Oh, Janie!" He laughed hoarsely and rolled onto his back, his deep chest rising and falling with apparent effort.

"Are you okay?" she asked, getting up on her knees to lean over him in concern.

"I'm fine," he said, hands on her forearms preventing her from getting too close. He drew one more deep breath, closed his eyes for a moment, then sat up to lean against the headboard. Mari still sat on her knees, watching him cautiously. The only reason she could think of for his stopping her, clouded her eyes with uncertainty.

"You don't want me after all?" she asked.

He laughed again. "Hardly, Janie. But suddenly having you willing and pliant, I find myself becoming the moralist."

"I love you," she said urgently.

He smiled gently, reaching a hand up to pinch her chin. "And I love you. But there's your mother and my father...and it'd kill me to hurt either of them." He shook his head as though helpless to understand much less explain what he was trying to tell her. He drew a steadying breath, then said evenly, "Let's get married Saturday."

Mari wasn't even startled by the idea, knowing now that it could be no other way. "All right," she said, bravado warring with panic in her voice. "Saturday."

Her instant agreement surprised him. "You're sure?" he asked suspiciously.

"Are you?" she counter questioned.

"I've been sure since the day I met you."

"Then so am I. We'll get married Saturday."

He folded his arms across his chest and studied her face with a frown. "Why do I get the feeling you're agreeing to this just to challenge me?"

"Marriage is always a challenge, isn't it? For both parties?"

He was right, she admitted to herself, turning her

face away so that he wouldn't read her thoughts. She was throwing down the gauntlet. If he really loved her, then he would be able to accept her sterility—even if she didn't tell him until after the wedding.

"All right," he said, a hand to the side of her face forcing her to look at him. "I accept the challenge. I'll call Father O'Shea in the morning."

"And we'd better see the folks."

"Right." Jim looked at her a long, steady moment, then with a hand around her waist, pulled her down into his arms, propping himself over her on an elbow. His eyes were deep and tender. "Do you have any idea how hard it is for me to leave this bed?" he asked.

She smiled up at him, small fingers tidying a stray lock of dark hair. "As hard as it is for me to let you go."

"Think you'll be able to sleep now?"

She laughed. "I doubt it seriously. I probably won't sleep a wink until Saturday."

"We'll have to save our honeymoon trip until spring," he said. "I can't leave the mill right now."

She shrugged. "After only three weeks on the job, I don't think I can ask for the time off anyway."

"We'll honeymoon at home," he said softly. He kissed the palm of her hand, then swung his legs over the side of the bed and stood. He looked down at her saying nothing, reluctance to leave her in his eyes. Finally he said quietly, "Good night, Janie. I love you."

As the door closed on him, Mari felt two emotions with an intensity that was new to her. She felt love that she knew to be real love, love that could last forever. And she felt fear, deep and abiding fear, that she had dared that love by setting a wedding date without telling Jim the truth.

Chapter Ten

Mari stood in the bathroom of her mother's house, pouring water into a champagne glass. The coronet of white silk flowers Jasmine had made for her rested on the tile counter top next to the two aspirin she had just tipped out of the bottle. As she tossed the aspirin down, she caught sight of her reflection and was reasonably proud of what she saw.

Her red-brown hair hung to her shoulders in a shining sheet, light moving in its careless waves. Delicately made up, her face shone with color from the frantic preparations for her wedding this morning and the champagne this afternoon. Her eyes were bright, and she knew that only Jim saw into their depths and recognized a flicker of pain there. But he had not reacted to it except to keep her close beside him and to watch her guardedly when her mother spirited her away to introduce the small knot of friends invited to the reception.

Mari pulled a comb through her hair then put it down and smiled grimly at her reflection. No one would ever guess, she thought with satisfaction, the private agony of guilt she was going through.

She could not quite believe that she had married Jim without telling him the truth. One moment her conscience would prick her unmercifully, then the next, she would remember what he had said when they had left the party New Year's morning.

"You can take your secret to the grave as long as it

doesn't get between us. I love you totally and that's what I expect from you.''

It didn't matter that she hadn't told him. He didn't care whether she shared her secret with him or not as long as she didn't let it get in the way of their marriage.

The problem now was, would she be able to behave as though she was a complete woman when they came together tonight?

She had sailed through these last few days, busy with preparations, showered by everyone with good wishes and congratulations, and had been able to convince herself that she was doing the right thing. Jim loved her and really wanted to be married to her. Melissa loved Jim and needed a father. Steve loved her, Mari, and was looking forward to having a mother. And she... well, she loved them all and told herself that by being what they all needed in all ways, she could expiate her guilt.

Then a few words spoken during the wedding ceremony this morning jolted her out of her euphoric mood and brought the enormity of what she had done crashing down around her. "Your wife shall be like a fruitful vine in the recesses of your home," the priest had intoned, smiling benignly on both of them. "Your children shall be live olive plants around your table."

Her body had reacted to that, an almost fractional start, unnoticeable to anyone she was sure. But she had felt Jim glance down at her, and he had been watching her closely ever since.

With a sigh she smoothed her long-sleeved, ruffly white dress and angled her chin. All she had to do was stay with her plan to make the best she could out of this marriage and hope that Jim would understand when she finally gathered the courage to tell him.

She emerged from the bathroom straight into her sister's arms. "There you are!" Jazz exclaimed. "We were getting worried about you. Are you feeling all right?"

"Just a little headache," Mari said truthfully.

"Well, listen, Mari," Jasmine drew her toward the bedroom where coats had been thrown across the bed. "Dave and I have to leave. Jim was telling us that you won't be able to get away for a honeymoon yet, but when you do"—she had pulled a tailored gray wool coat from the pile and now emerged with Dave's beige trench coat—"we want you to use our place at Salishan."

"Oh, but—"

"No!" Jasmine held up an imperious hand. "No protests. I'll be hurt if you don't let me know when the time comes. Jim said it sounded like a good plan to him."

"Thanks, Jasmine," Mari replied, wondering if he would still think it a good plan then. "That's very generous of you. Of course, I'll call you."

"Good. Mom's in the kitchen and wanted to talk to you. I'll say good-bye now. Don't worry about seeing us out." The older girl wrapped Mari in a fragrant embrace, then fixed her with a sparkling smile. She was all sparkles lately, Mari noted with a wan look as her sister walked away.

Mari found Katherine placing small sandwiches on a silver tray.

"You wanted me?" she asked, taking a decorative carrot curl from the tray.

"Yes," Katherine smiled at her fondly. "But I imagine your new husband wants you even more. You two sneak off whenever you're ready. It looks as though our friends will be here for a while, and there's no reason for you to sit around being polite."

"And we'll keep the children for you until next weekend," Terry said, coming up behind her and placing warm hands on her shoulders. "I know you can't get away yet, but you still need some time alone."

It was such a thoughtful gesture and one she really welcomed. She turned in Terry's arms and planted a kiss on his cheek. She had grown quite fond of him during the past several weeks and fiercely regretted her reluctance in accepting him.

"Thanks, Dad," she said, and got a crushing bear hug in return.

Jim appeared in the kitchen with the two children in tow, Missy clutching Duck by the neck. Steve had been playing in the basement with several neighbor children and gave Mari a perfunctory hug, obviously anxious to get back to the video game.

"See you next week, Aunt Janie," he said and dashed away.

Missy, too, had made new friends and suffered a quick hug before disappearing into a group of giggling little girls.

"Do you get the impression we won't be missed?" Mari asked Jim.

He grinned down at her. 'Would you think me a rat if I said they wouldn't be missed either?"

Terry laughed. "All right. Get going. Slip out the back door. We promise not to bother you all week, but if you need us for anything, don't hesitate to call."

Katherine hugged Mari, tears in her eyes. "Be happy, darling."

"I will," Mari promised a little weakly.

Terry and Jim shook hands, then Jim reached down for Katherine's embrace. "You be good to her," she said with mock ferocity, "or you'll have me to answer to."

Terry rolled his eyes. "Talk about a deterrent."

Rain fell heavily as they drove home to Jim's house, the trees and bushes along the way looking soaked and battered. The windshield wipers swept away a constantly reappearing sheet of water, and the road ahead was barely visible, yet Mari felt perfectly safe.

Sidled up to Jim in the front seat of the Malibu he used for occasions when his beloved truck just wouldn't serve, she felt as though a wall stood between her and whatever could hurt her. There was pain inside for her weaknesses and her cowardice, but there was pride, too, in this man who was now her husband.

And she had never appreciated his calm or his irrepressible sense of humor more than she did at this moment. It made her able to put her guilt aside and surround herself with loving him. He glanced down and, noting her vaguely anxious expression, put a hand on her knee.

"You're safe, you know," he said. "I wouldn't cross your mother and my father for anything."

"We're friends now," she said, referring to herself and Terry.

"I noticed," Jim smiled at the road ahead, the hand holding her knee giving it a squeeze. "I'm very pleased about that. I think you have a lot to offer each other."

"My mother always glows." Mari smiled fondly at the thought. Taking the hand holding her knee, she lifted it to her lap and held it in her two. It was so reassuringly strong. "I love him for that."

"Jazz is wearing a bit of a glow, too," Jim commented. "Did you notice?"

"Who could have missed it?" Mari asked dryly. "She's gorgeous under most circumstances, but deeply in love again she almost puts one's eyes out." A stab of nostalgia nudged Mari, and she leaned her head against Jim's arm and sighed heavily. "Thea was very beautiful."

"But Thea is apparently very selfish," he said in a tone that held no sympathy. "And beauty doesn't count unless it goes all the way through. Like yours."

The compliment jolted her, and she raised her head to look at him as he glanced down at her, smiling at her surprise. "That nose does prevent you from having perfect features, but it doesn't pale your beauty one bit." In her surprise she had relaxed her hold on his hand, and he raised it to catch her nose between his first two knuckles and tweak it. "And it looks as though I'm going to have to devote my life to making you glow."

After their conversation about her mother and older

sister, she was afraid he would think her lack of sparkle was his fault.

"I do love you," she said quickly.

"I know you do." His reply was gentle, his hand stroking her face, then pushing her head back to his shoulder. "But something inside you is hurting. I imagine it's hard to glow when you're hurting."

There was no point in denying it anymore. "But it won't get between us," she promised, praying that she was speaking the truth.

He said nothing to that, and she raised her head again to look at him. They were pulling into the driveway of his home, and he braked to stop, turning off the motor.

"You don't believe me," she said softly.

He turned to her, tenderness in his eyes. "I believe that you mean you don't want it to."

Tears sprang to her eyes because she so wanted to begin this marriage with hope and love and to convince him that she would be the best wife she was able to be.

"Dont't cry," he directed with gently authority. He cupped her face in his hands and pulled her forward, kissing her forehead. "If it gets in the way, we'll move around it. But nothing...nothing...will ever separate us. Ever."

She nodded desperately, too full for words.

"All right. Let's get inside where it's warm."

Though it was only midafternoon, the house was already dark, and Jim flipped lights on as they went through to the kitchen.

He opened the refrigerator door, pulling at his tie. "How about crackers and cheese and another glass of wine?"

That sounded appealing because she had been unable to eat anything at the reception. She sank into a kitchen chair, still too chilled to remove her coat. "That sounds wonderful," she agreed. "But could we have coffee, too? I'm frozen."

"Why don't you go upstairs and"—he paused in the

act of removing a box of crackers from an upper shelf and turned to waggle wicked eyebrows at her—"slip into something comfortable."

Despite her nervousness, she had to giggle at that. "Would you believe all I have is that red flannel night-gown?"

He gave a shout of laughter, nibbling on a cracker as he filled the coffee pot. "That'll do nicely. Go on up and take a hot bath, and I'll build a fire in the bedroom."

Half and hour later, Mari emerged from the bathroom off the room she had shared with Missy. She had washed her hair, hoping to relieve the last remnants of her headache, and donned the notorious red nightgown. It was large for her but blessedly warm, and she smoothed it in place, then went in search of Jim.

She knew his room was the one that ran the length of the back of the house, but she had studiously avoided it before. Now she peered around the open door and looked into an enormous room decorated in brown and cream with a hardwood floor like the rest of the house but with an enormous dark fur rug in front of the fireplace. Jim knelt on it, pouring coffee from a hot pot into two mugs, a fire blazing merrily behind a screened grate.

Mari walked over to him to frown down at the rug. "What was it?" she asked, disappointed that he would own a pelt.

He looked up at the tone of her voice, then grinned into her judicious expression. "Mostly polyester. It's phoney, Janie."

She smiled in relief. "Good. It didn't fit you somehow."

"Properly undertaken and for the right reasons, hunting is a fine sport." She sank down beside him on the rug, and he handed her a steaming mug. "But not for me."

They sat cross-legged on the hearth rug, the plate of crackers and cheese between them, sipping wine and coffee and getting acquainted in a way that the reunion and the tense weeks that followed had not allowed. Jim had changed into jeans and a green turtleneck that made his hazel eyes take on the same color as an Oregon fir.

"How do you feel about Astoria now?" he asked, leaning back on an elbow and stretching his long legs past Mari's curled-up form.

"I like it," she said unequivocally. "Rain and all." It pattered down above their heads, a steady, romantic melody in the firelight. "I like my job and the people I've met." Her next thought made her falter for an instant, but she shook it off and proceeded. "And it's a good place to raise children. It's a stimulating environment without being filled with crime and pollution."

"Do you want to continue working?" he asked.

She passed him a cracker, considering the question. "Yes, I would. It's just a couple of days a week, and the kids seem to enjoy being with the other kids at Janet's."

Jim grinned. "Steve's already sold on you. Don't be surprised if you end up on display at the next session of Current Events at school." He popped the cracker in his mouth, then sat up to pour more champagne.

"That's all right. If you can handle Melissa living most of her life in your lap, then I can put up with being shown off."

He leaned back with his champagne and laughed softly. "She's just buttering me up until she turns sixteen and wants a Ferrari or something."

Mari laughed, putting the glass to her mouth, then Jim added, "Steve told me this morning that Melissa was okay, but he'd really like a little brother."

The spilled champagne drenched the front of her, as the glass tumbled out of her lax grasp, and also managed to soak Jim's jeans below the knee. He sat up, tossing the two small napkins on the tray into her lap, but when they were immediately soaked without doing much good, he pulled her to her feet and said gently,

"Well, we were just about to dispense with clothes anyway, weren't we?"

She closed her eyes for an instant, the truth on the tip of her tongue while their marriage could still be annulled. But his face was so loving, the hands on her arms so exciting, so promising, that she closed off the words and smiled at him. "Yes, we were."

When Jim's face disappeared as the gown came slowly over her head, she closed her eyes again, saying a silent prayer that her feelings of guilt and inadequacy would remain hidden tonight. But she need not have worried. The moment she was free of the gown, she felt his lips come down on hers, and she forgot everything but how it felt to be kissed after not having been touched in so long, to be stroked and caressed on her bare skin, every nerve ending leaping up to await the feeling again.

She slipped her hands up under his sweater, nibbling at his ear while his mouth played havoc with her neck and shoulder. Then he tore his sweater off, and the tickle of his chest hair against her breasts made her shudder and breathe a little sound of satisfaction. She twined her arms around his neck, straining to be closer. Then he swept her up in his arms, held her high against his heart and placed her gently on the bed.

In a moment he was beside her, all warm delicious flesh against her own, and she seemed to lose all coherent thought. She became a receptacle of feelings, warm, comfortable feelings and new, elusive feelings that came and went as his hands probed her secret places. There was pain briefly as she took his weight and tried eagerly to accommodate him. Then pain was gone and there was another new sensation, an ensnaring rhythm that seemed to promise something out of reach. Caught in its tempo, she clung to Jim, moving with him in this mysterious dance until the world exploded, showering stars all over her. Points of fire touched her everywhere, and she was convulsed with exhilaration, hanging suspended for moments as though balanced on the tip of a flame.

Then her body seemed to slip back into itself, and she fell back against the pillows exhausted. Jim pulled her into his shoulder and gently stroked the damp hair away from her face.

"Are you okay?" he asked.

She replied like someone emerging from a fog. "I... I think so."

He laughed softly. "Aren't you sure?"

Looking into his eyes, now lazily half-closed, passion satisfied in them, her own eyes reflected the awesome excitement she had experienced. "Yes, I'm sure I'm fine," she said finally, a delicious lethargy settling over her. She snuggled against him, burrowing her nose in his neck. "But... I'm sleepy." The tension of the past several weeks finally dissipated, she drifted away, one hand resting on the shoulder that pillowed her head, the other wrapped around his neck.

"Comfortable?" he asked with amusement.

She replied with a little purring sound and fell asleep.

When she awoke, the room was bathed in darkness and only the embers of a fire glowed across the room. Mari stretched languorously, not quite awake, and felt the furnacelike heat of Jim's naked body. She stopped still for an instant, startled, then, drowned in a flood of remembered feeling, of a tenderness so complete and a passion so full she had felt both cherished and desired, she lay gracefuly against him, offering herself.

With a growl he held her to him, and it began again, the wild giving ritual, and Mari gave herself eagerly because now she had begun to learn its secrets and was anxious to know more. Not unsurprised to discover it, she found that Jim had yet new delights to teach her, and she learned the endless reciprocity of getting and giving back and getting more.

When they lay apart, she thought she had never felt so complete, so perfectly in tune, so much a part of the natural process. She almost believed for a moment that a child could come from this delicious afternoon and evening, and then reality dawned. But she refused to let it invade the perfection of this day.

She turned her head sideways on the pillow to find Jim propped on an elbow, looking down at her indulgently.

"I'm hungry," she said, smiling.

"Sandwich hungry or meal hungry?"

She thought a moment, and as she did, her stomach grumbled loudly and they both laughed.

"That sounds like seven courses at least. Do you want to come down to the kitchen and join in the search, or do you want to wait up here and be served?"

"I think," she said, affecting a pompous tone of voice, "that I should like to be served."

"Think again," he suggested, teasing her with a frown.

"No?" she asked.

"No. You make the toast, I'll fry the bacon and eggs."

Mari was to remember the early hours of that morning in the dark weeks that followed their honeymoon at home. They worked together companionably, planning next week's menu, a garden in the spring, a vacation to Canada the following year. They sat across from each other at the small table and laughed, made more plans, and wondered how their parents were coping with the children. Mari made a second batch of toast and more coffee, and it was almost dawn before they finally went back to bed.

They went to church Sunday morning, then out to breakfast, and spent the rest of the day reading the paper on the sofa in the living room, the fireplace blazing warmth and comfort.

Monday morning Jim went to the mill and Mari went to work, feeling a strange deprivation when he wasn't there every time she turned around. When he picked her up in the truck, she threw her arms around him, confessed that she had missed him abominably, and plans for dinner out were abandoned as they drove home.

The rest of the week followed much the same pattern,

and Mari was becoming so sure of his love that telling him the truth no longer held horror for her. She needed only a little distance from him to think it through.

The day before they were to pick up the children, Katherine telephoned.

"Darling, I have a *big* favor to ask." There was dramatic emphasis on the word "big" and Mari braced herself.

"Okay."

"Terry has to go to Seattle this weekend. He'll only be away one night, but you know how I hate to stay alone." Katherine drew a breath and plunged on. "Well, I wouldn't even have brought it up with you being a newlywed and all, but Terry happened to mention that Jim will be spending Saturday and Sunday nights in Portland. Anyway, would you come and spend the weekend with me, and we'll make candy or do something fun with the children?"

Mari looked up in alarm at Jim who was refilling the coffeepot now that dinner dishes were put away and they were settling down for an evening before the fire. He came to her instantly, his eyes concerned. "What is it?" he mouthed.

"Mom, hold on a minute," Mari said, covering the mouthpiece with her hand. "Mom says you're going to Portland."

He chuckled in relief. "Yes, for a couple of days. Why?"

"Terry's going to Seattle, and Mom wants me to spend the weekend with her." She looked so stricken that he kissed her gently.

"Tell her you'll go," he said. "Then I'll pick you up from work Monday night."

"Mari?" her mother's voice asked.

"I'm here," she said. "Yes, I'll come, Mom."

"Tell her I'll drive you up tomorrow morning," Jim whispered.

"Jim says he'll drive me up tomorrow morning," she repeated dutifully. "Are the kids okay?"

"Just fine," Katherine assured her but added with a self-deprecating little laugh. "But I'm getting old. Missy keeps me running from morning until night!"

The conversation ended with Mari saying good-bye to Melissa and Steve and promising to see them the following day. She turned away from the phone with a grim smile for her husband.

"I hate to sound like a wife," she said quietly, "but you might have told me."

He put his arm around her shoulders and led her into the living room to the sofa. "I was going to tonight. I didn't want to think about it until I absolutely had to." He sat in a corner of the sofa and pulled her down beside him. But she sat stiffly away from him, hurt by the last-minute news. She looked into the dancing fire, ignoring him.

"I'm going to miss you," he said softly and with such sincerity that she capitulated and melted against him, allowing herself to be lifted into his lap. She snuggled into his shoulder, wrapping her arms around his neck.

"I'm going to miss you, too. I've just gotten adjusted to being separated from you during the day. Two days and two *nights* will be awful!"

He laughed softly, the hand resting on her hip, caressing her. "I'm sorry. Someday I'll take you with me. Portland isn't LA, I'm sure, but there are lots of big stores, quaint little shops, and the old river front is being restored. I think you'd enjoy it."

"That settles it," she teased. "I'm coming with you."

"You mean you'd saddle your mother with our little monsters for two more days?" he teased back.

"She said she didn't want to be alone," she laughed softly. "Why is Terry going to Seattle?"

"Same reason I'm going to Portland," he said. "We have lumber brokers in both places. They do our selling for us. Incidentally"—he paused, his expression sobering as he changed subject—"Mrs. Savage will probably call you while I'm gone. She called at the mill today to set up a visit, but I didn't want to make a date without talking it over with you first. She'll be handling Missy's placement, too.''

"When is Steve officially yours?" she asked.

"June. And he'll be officially ours." Jim smiled, firelight trapped in his eyes when he looked down at her. "Jasmine and David are untangling the red tape.''

Mari sat up in his lap, surprised. "Have you spoken to them?''

"At the wedding," he said, grinning. "You did seem a little out of things, but I was tending to business.''

"You're so efficient," she complimented, running her finger along his bottom lip. "You just have a poor memory, that's all. Forgetting to tell me you were leaving town.''

"How long are you going to use that against me?" he asked, trapping the tickling finger between his strong, white teeth.

"I suppose," she said thoughtfully, leaning back down to nibble on his earlobe, "you could make me forget it.''

"That's an interesting prospect. Ah!" He gasped as she bit a sensitive spot and, taking a handful of her hair, sat her up again. "Shall we explore it?" he asked.

"No, I don't think so," she said lightly, feigning a change of mind, "because, actually, the whole thing shouldn't have happened in the first place. I mean, you... Ah!''

She was flat on her back on the sofa cushions, and Jim was leaning over her threateningly, propped up on his hands.

"Do you or do you not want me to bring you something back from Portland?" he asked.

"I can't be bribed," she said nobly.

"Isn't that what you just tried to do to me?" he asked, fighting back a smile.

"Yes, but only because you were at fault in the first place." Her tone was righteous but her eyes were full of laughter. She pushed feebly against him as he lowered his weight, giggles making her helpless. "Oh, all right," she conceded. "What do you want to bring me?"

He kissed her soundly, then pulled away to look at her with an arched eyebrow. "How about something to replace the red flannel thing?"

She smiled tauntingly. "I never wear it."

He kissed her again, lingeringly. "But the kids will be home now."

"True," she acknowledged. "Okay, you can bring me a nightie."

"Now," he said, getting to his feet and pulling her up with him, "about the other bargain..."

She shook her head. "I think it's morally improper to bargain with sex."

"You're right," he agreed, lifting her into his arms and heading for the stairs. "We won't bribe or bargain or discuss. We'll just do it."

Sighing contentedly, she wrapped her arms around his neck and leaned her head on his shoulder. "As I said before, you're so efficient."

Though Mari missed Jim abominably, the weekend with her mother and the children gave her the distance she needed to think through the problem of explaining her sterility to Jim.

During the hours spent stirring candy, looking through old photo albums, or simply sitting on the sofa reminiscing, Mari established a new relationship with her mother. Seeing things from a new viewpoint, Mari now understood Katherine's love for Terry and the need to be with him though her father had been gone such a short time. Now that love for a man was a shared experience, they met on a new level, and Mari felt closer to her mother than ever before.

Her thinking time came at night when the house was dark and quiet and she didn't have Jim's arms to protect and distract her. She was forced to face the issue squarely and reach a decision. He loved her, she knew he did, and he would understand. She would tell him Monday night when the children were in bed.

When Mari locked the door of the shop at five thirty on Monday, Jim was waiting for her in the truck. He had already collected the children and smiled warmly over their heads at her, reaching along the back of the seat to put a hand to her face.

"How are you?" he asked gently.

"Wonderful now that you're home," she replied, turning her lips into the palm of his hand. "How are you? Did you accomplish what you had to?"

"It was quite a trip," he said expressively. But that was all he was able to say before Steve began interrogating him, then told him about their weekend of candy-making.

"We rolled these gold things in chocolate and then in nuts. They're yum!"

At Jim's look of confusion, Mari explained simply, "Almond rocca."

"Ah!" he smiled. "Is there any left?"

"Right here." Mari held up a stationery box in which she had carefully placed the candies between layers of foil. "But we'll have to stop at the market or that's all you'll have for dinner."

"How about going out?" he suggested.

"Sounds wonderful. No dishes."

He raised his eyebrows wickedly. "Just what I was thinking."

During their honeymoon week, doing dishes together had been a prelude to retiring upstairs to sit on the rug in front of the fire, sipping wine, before making love. His remark implied skipping a nuisance step and getting straight to making love to her. She blushed, yet managed to look eager at the same time, and he pinched her chin and laughed. But as he checked the rearview mirror, concentrating on pulling out of their parking space, she remembered her promise to herself to tell him the truth tonight, and a little niggle of fear sat in the pit of her stomach.

It stayed with her through dinner at the Thunderbird Coffee Shop and on the drive home. Faced with the moment of truth, she was suddenly frightened. It had been one thing while he had been away to convince herself that it would be easy, but now, looking into his loving eyes, eager for the touch of his hands, the reality was looking much more difficult than the plan. But it had to be done. She could put it off no longer.

After bathing Missy and putting her to bed, Mari fussed around the kitchen, waiting for nine o'clock to urge Steve up to bed. Now her stomach was tied in knots, and her behavior so unlike the woman she had been since their wedding that Jim was watching her with concern.

"Something wrong?" he asked, stopping her scurried movements around the kitchen with a warm hand on her neck. She jumped as though a spider had landed on her, and he dropped his hand, looking both surprised and a little impatient. "What is it?"

"N—nothing..." she denied unconvincingly.

"Janie..." He took hold of her shoulders and she did not react this time. His eyes were intense and he looked weary. "We're not back to that again, are we?"

"What?" she stalled.

"You know what. The fear in your eyes, the furtive looks at me."

She forced a smile that was almost her own. "I'm just tired. Would you tuck Steve in, and I'll just take a minute to freshen up. I'd...I'd like to talk to you."

He looked back at her steadily, trying to read her eyes, but she lowered them, not wanting him to see anything until she had organized it into words that made sense. "All right," he finally agreed. "I'll pour the wine and meet you in the bedroom."

With hands that shook, Mari tied her hair back and bathed her face with cold water. She splashed repeatedly, trying to organize her feelings of inadequacy and guilt into coherent thought. Reaching blindly for the linen closet, she found the old-fashioned latch, turned it, and groping inside for a towel, found bare shelf. Then remembering that she had done a large load of towels just that morning before leaving for work, which were still in the dryer, she reached back into the rear of the cabinet where odd towels were kept.

Her hand connected with a soft, filmy fabric and she grasped it and pulled it out, wondering what it was doing there. Opening her eyes, she found herself looking down at a handful of turquoise silk chiffon trimmed in ecru lace. Holding a wispy strap in one hand and gathering up the hem with the other, she held the negligee up to the light, its transparency acting like a window so that through it she could see herself reflected in the bathroom mirror.

For an instant her heart leaped in excitement, thinking it was the gift Jim had promised and hidden to surprise her. But on closer inspection, a catch or two on the long skirt indicated that it had been worn. Her heart beating faster, Mari reached back into the cabinet, found an old towel on an upper shelf, and dried her face. Then she tossed the towel down and studied the garment again, fury and shame rising in her. A fragrance Mari had noticed only one other time drifted from the garment to her nostrils, a fragrance from New Year's Eve at the Thunderbird, and she knew suddenly to whom the negligee belonged. It was Julia's.

As though struck by lightning, Mari suddenly saw the truth of the last six weeks of her life. Beguiled by this beautiful, historic spot on the wide, wild Columbia, she had become ensnared by a handsome face and a gentle manner. With the lack of romance in her life and the recent jolt of Kent's defection, she had been easy prey for the Northwest man who needed a mother for his child and a bedmate for the cold winter nights. Plagued by guilt because she had not told him her secret before they were married, she had failed to notice that he was able to allow the secret to exist between them because he simply didn't care. A secret of his own was able to remain so, because Mari was wrapped up in her own problems. Remembering all the times he had left for the mill after a telephone call or spent twelve-hour days there, she wondered how much of that time had been spent working and how much time enjoying the fringe benefits of the job.

She remembered suddenly his emphatically spoken, "It was quite a trip!" and realized that the passion in his eyes had been leftover feeling from a weekend spent with Julia, not impatience to be alone with her, Mari.

Fastening the top buttons of her blouse that she had undone to wash her face, she gave one more disgusted look to the garment in her hand, then clutching it like a rag, stormed down the hall to the bedroom.

Jim was kneeling on the rug, adding kindling to a reluctant fire, and looked up at her when she slammed the door behind her. A smile had formed on his lips but when he saw her expression, it died and a frown replaced it. He got to his feet but remained near the fireplace, his hands loosely on his hips. His eyes went to the gown in her hand, then to her eyes, and she saw a flicker of change in his expression. Anger had replaced the momentary confusion, and she knew that he knew what was on her mind. It was there in his hazel brown eyes. He made a fractional gesture, as though he would speak—explain perhaps—what such a seductive negligee was doing in their linen closet, when he appeared to change his mind. That, too, was in his eyes, a hardening.

But it did not intimidate her. No one made a fool of Marijane Westridge. Only she wasn't Marijane Westridge anymore. She was Marijane Sullivan. A violent sense of loss touched her, but only for an instant. She could cope with that later.

Mari shook the offending garment, the velvet of her eyes now darkest steel. "What is this?" she demanded, her voice a choked whisper.

He looked from it to her face again with a weary disdain that infuriated her further. "It appears to be a negligee," he replied.

"What is it doing here?" Her voice rose in pitch and intensity.

"What do you think it's doing here?" he asked, shifting his weight and folding his arms across his chest. His eyes were obsidian, and when they clashed with Mari's, the contact was almost audible.

"I think that while you were supposed to be in Portland, you were right here, with Julia." She spoke that accusation calmly, but her voice flirted with hysteria when she continued. "And I think that this afternoon, in your last passionate lovemaking when you tore it off her and tossed it to the floor, that it lay there forgotten. Then either she, or maybe even you, noticed it and tossed it in the back of the closet, thinking that I wouldn't notice it. But I have."

"Mmm," he said, as though giving the matter thought. "And when I planned this little tryst," he said, taking several steps toward her, "I mentioned it to my father so that he could tell your mother who could casually mention it to you."

That gave Mari pause for a moment, but only a moment. "You probably did go to Portland and took Julia with you. Then, loathe to end a stimulating evening, brought her back here to stage the denouement you're so damned good at!"

"Thank you," he said quietly, his eyes even blacker than before. "But if you recall, your mother was the one who suggested you leave the house and visit her. That wasn't my idea."

"Yes," Mari snapped. "But it didn't have to take place here, did it? You could have been together in Portland or in half a dozen motels along the way. I just conveniently chose to leave the house vacant for you."

For a moment Jim simply looked back at her, a hard cold anger emanating from him. Mari angled her chin and looked back, her free hand balled into a fist, the gown torn by the fingernails of her other hand.

"And it hadn't occurred to you that it might not be that way at all?" he asked.

"Why should I believe otherwise?" she shrieked, throwing the fistful of chiffon at his feet.

She had not thought he was close enough to reach her, but in an instant he had both her arms in a biting grip and had brought her up so that she was on tiptoe, her face a mere breath away from his. A storm raged in his eyes, and a muscle ticked out of control in his jaw. "Because for six weeks I have loved you despite some secret you're keeping that sits between us like a wall! I have trusted you and given you everything I have anyway. And what do I get back?" He reached down to scoop up the nightie and shoved it at her, leaving the question unanswered because her accusations still stood between them. "Thanks for *your* trust, Marijane."

Tears stung her eyes as she spun away, headed for the door. "I'm leaving, James." She tore the door open but his voice halted her exit.

"And how do I explain that to Melissa?"

She turned, leaning back against the cold door, fear in her stomach. "What do you mean? I'm taking her with me."

"Both our names are on the adoption papers," Jim said calmly. "I told you Jazz and David were working on it."

"*I* am adopting Missy."

"Not since we got married," he corrected. "The legal paperwork says we're adopting her together as husband and wife. Mrs. Savage will expect to see us both here when she comes."

Mari swallowed. "And if she doesn't?"

Jim shook his head, jamming his hands in his pockets. "Well, I'd say if she discovered that you've left your husband of nine days, she might consider your stability suspect."

Mari stood frozen, her eyes wide with fear at the pos-

sibility that her leaving could interfere with her adopting Missy.

"If you want Missy," Jim said, "you'd better stay."

"When is she coming?"

"I'm not sure. Did she call while I was gone?"

"No."

"Then she might not. Sometimes she likes to drop
in."

Mari closed her eyes at the thought of having to stay
indefinitely while waiting for the caseworker to "drop
in." Now she wanted nothing more than to pack her
things and return to Los Angeles and forget she had
heard of Astoria and James Sullivan.

She looked up at Jim with a frosty glare. "All right.
I'll stay. But I'll sleep with Melissa."

Jim reached to the head of the bed for her pillow and
tossed it to her. "Good night," he said.

Choked with indignation, Mari spun on her heel,
tore the door open, and slammed it behind her.

That life could go on, even find a relatively peaceful
plateau from which to pass day into day, amazed Mari,
then finally provided a measure of comfort.

February wore on, and no one suspected that ani-
mosity was a tangible thing between her and Jim. Even
Katherine and Terry, whom they saw every weekend,
noticed nothing amiss, though Katherine did tell Jim to
be sure Mari didn't keep so busy with the children and
her job that she forgot to eat.

There was a slightness about her now, a fragility in
her face that gave her a look of drama. She saw it in the
oval mirror when she brushed her hair in the room she
shared with Missy. But the look never left the room
with her. When the bedroom door closed behind her,
she smiled from six in the morning when she made
Jim's breakfast before he left for the mill, until ten at
night when the children were in bed and Jim was at
work in his office. In between, there was breakfast for

the children and rushing Steve off to the school bus; there was cleaning and baking and the increasing responsibility of her job.

"You don't have to do all this," Jim had said one Sunday afternoon, wandering out of his office for a cup of coffee to find her engaged in housecleaning. "A girl from town used to clean for me before you came."

"I'll bet I know which one," she had said caustically.

His eyes flashed angrily at her, and he turned away.

Despite the tension, the children seemed to be thriving; Steve enjoyed making cookies and bread with Mari, and Jim was often joined in his office by Missy and Duck.

Melissa now apparently found it easier to drop the Jane and call Mari simply "Mommy."

Mari's only real problem with the children was finding enough dry days in the Oregon winter to allow them play time in the fresh air. Jim had fenced a large yard behind the house to protect Missy from the always-swollen, swift-running stream a hundred yards beyond. It was a beautiful spot, but when Jim took Mari to the edge of it one afternoon, she understood his adamancy that even Steve not go near it. The bank was steep, the water not very deep, but moving almost like rapids over rocks and gnarled roots. A small head could be cracked so easily, young feet knocked off balance in an instant. Steve knew that the stream was out of bounds, and on the few occasions when the sun had shone, and Missy had played in the yard, Mari tried to impress upon her that she must remain behind the fence.

She had watched nervously from the kitchen window and had shaken her head in frustration when Missy went directly to the latch as she suspected she would. She had brought her into the house and scolded her and Missy had cried, but the next try had ended with the same result.

Jim, home early, came out to the kitchen to investigate the cause of Missy's indignant tears and frowned at Mari's explanation. He dropped to one knee, holding

Missy's sweater-clad arms firmly and giving her a gentle shake.

"Play outside!" she wept plaintively.

"You can play outside if you stay in the yard," Jim said, his face grave. "If you leave the yard one more time, Daddy will spank you. Do you understand?"

Missy looked deeply back at him and apparently deciding that he meant it, said with a quivering lip, "Want Mommy!"

"No, Mommy's not going to come to your rescue, Missy," he said sternly. "If you leave the yard, I'll spank you."

"No."

"Yes. Now you'd better go upstairs and talk it over with Duck and decide what you're going to do."

As Missy toddled away, baggy corduroy rompers waddling, Mari turned back to her task of relining the kitchen cupboards.

"Well, m'lord, now that you have all the subjects quaking," she said, measuring a piece of green paper rolled out on the counter. "Would you like something to eat before you return to the throne room?"

"Better quaking, than fearless and drowned," he returned, unperturbed by her caustic remark.

"She's merely interested in what's beyond her confinement," she said testily, aggravated by his calm when his presence always put her back up. "She can't help it."

"I never said her intent was criminal." He reached out to stop the paper when it would have rolled back on her. "But she had to know what's beyond the fence is dangerous and she can't go out to investigate. What reason won't accomplish, a good swat might."

He was right, she knew he was; she often applied the same principle herself. But she hated to admit it.

"You know, if you keep this cleaning up," Jim changed the subject, "it's going to be so antiseptic around here, we'll all have to wear white."

"Cute." She cut the paper and climbed up on the

kitchen stool to install it. "We don't want Mrs. Savage to think I'm a slob."

He leaned back against the counter to watch her. "She'll be interested in your qualities as a mother not a maid."

"It's all part and parcel of the same thing. You have to be able to make a comfortable environment for kids to be comfortable in."

"Comfortable, not vacuum-packed."

The sheet installed, Mari slammed the cupboard door, glaring down at Jim from her now superior height. "Our point in this charade is the children," she said, brushing aside a strand of hair that had escaped her barrette. "If anything messed that up, I'd never forgive myself. Our relationship I can fake when she comes, but housework shows; neatness counts." Then, because his steady hazel gaze was affecting her pulse, she glanced at her watch and asked imperiously, "Don't you have something to do?"

The movement that swept her off the stool was so swift, the hands so biting, that Mari screamed, and when Jim held her forearms and pulled her up so that her face was bare inches from his, she felt herself tremble. His eyes were almost black and his mouth was set in a grim line.

"Now you listen to me, Marijane Sullivan," he said with a quiet intensity that resounded in her ears. "I've put up with a month of your smart mouth and condescending behavior, and I've had just about enough. Don't you ever...ever!...dismiss me in my own home." He dropped his hands but his eyes held her to the spot. "I think your problem is that you're frustrated. Insulated and virginal just isn't fun anymore, is it?"

Jim looked down at Mari for a long moment, the edge of anger suddenly dissipated, his dark eyes lingering on her wide ones, her pale, hollowed cheeks, the pink bottom lip caught between her teeth. When she felt strained to the breaking point, sure those cool, mobile lips were going to come down on hers, he drew a deep breath and the spell was broken. "But you created the situation. You're the one who has to fix it."

She watched him stride away and felt the shell she had built so carefully these past weeks cracking under a surge of longing so strong she was tempted to run after him, to beg his forgiveness and promise him anything if he would be the man he had been before.

But she resisted the impulse because that was the real root of the problem: the man he had been before didn't exist. The James Sullivan of that week after their wedding was a figment of her imagination. The gentle man, the tender lover, had never been; she had wanted to see love in his eyes and in his manner because it restored the self-esteem Kent had destroyed.

As the matter of Missy and the backyard turned out one cloudy weekday afternoon when Jim had come home early to make some phone calls in the quiet of his office, Duck had not been a responsible confidant.

It had been the first day without rain in a week, and Missy had been impatient to venture out. But Mari had promised cookies for an event at the school Steve attended, and she was too busy with them to keep checking on the child.

"When Steve comes home you can go outside with him for a little while, okay?"

It had not been okay; Missy was in a fractious mood, but Mari stood firm. When Steve ran up the drive in his slicker, hitting every puddle on the way, he was greeted at the door by Missy and Duck, the former pulling on a jacket, the wrong arm in the sleeve, Duck trapped between her knees while she struggled.

"Yard, Seevie!" she demanded.

Having sniffed the air as he came in, he ignored her and went to Mari who was rolling dough into little balls in the palm of her hands.

"Peanut butter cookies and chocolate chip!" he cried, delighted, scooping up one of each then asking belatedly, "Can I?"

"Sure. Want some milk?"

Missy had a hold of his coat and was pulling him toward the back door, only one arm in her coat.

"Wait, Missy." Mari went to her and pulled the jacket off and replaced it properly. Then buttoning it, she leaned down and said firmly, "Now don't forget what Daddy said. Stay in the yard."

"Yard," she repeated, nodding. "'Mon, Seevie!"

Steve rolled his eyes in a very adult gesture of tolerance and followed Missy out the door.

For more than half an hour, their high voices—Missy's a little petulant—assured her that all was well. She finished the cookies, stacked the cool ones in the cookie jar, and set the last batch out to cool. Putting the cookie sheets and utensils in the sink, she ran hot water over a squirt of suds, then turned off the tap. It was then that she noticed the silence.

Brushing the curtain aside, she looked out the window and caught her breath in an audible gasp. The gate stood wide open and Steve and Missy were nowhere to be seen.

She was out the door in an instant, checking the garage, the front of the house, the wood pile where they sometimes played, but to no avail. She thought of running back for Jim but knew he had just taken a long distance call he'd been waiting for all afternoon. She hated to disturb him if it was something she could handle herself.

But at this point there seemed only one more place to look. Mari ran through the trees toward the stream, heart pumping anxiously. Branches caught at her face and her ankles, but she ignored them and flew down the gradual slope to the bank of the stream. She felt relief like a warm blanket on her chilled nerves when she saw Missy, her red parka hanging open, looking down into the stream. It was a moment before it registered that she stood alone.

"Missy!" she cried, skidding to a halt as she reached

the bank. "You're a bad girl!" she declared firmly. "Where's Stevie?"

Missy pointed into the stream. "Seevie! Duck!" she said happily, the admonishment unnoticed. "Swimming!"

In horror, Mari looked where Missy pointed and saw Steve, his slicker discarded, making his way carefully to the middle of the murky, swirling stream where Duck lay apparently caught between two rocks. Even while she watched, a large tree branch moving swiftly caught the back of his leg as he bent for the sodden duck. Her "Stevie! Watch out!" was too late, and she was skidding down the bank as he fell sideways into the water.

Though it took her only seconds to reach the water, the swift, swirling motion had carried him several yards. She ran laboriously, up to her hips in icy water, tripped and fell and rose and ran again.

"Catch the branch, Stevie!" she shouted, noting frantically that he was being carried toward a large boulder from which a grotesque branch grew. For a moment she thought the panic he must be feeling would make controlled reaction impossible, but as he reached the rock, she saw him flail against the current and throw out a grasping hand. The stream's movement was strong, and he was able to hold his grip on the branch for just a moment. But it was long enough for Mari to reach him. She caught his chest, felt her fingernails scrape his skin as she tore through his shirt in her effort to hold him.

"Put your arms around me!" she shouted, trying desperately to hold him with one hand and the branch with the other. She was panting heavily, her breath coming in painful gulps, her legs feeling rubbery and frozen and lacking the strength to make it back. She clung to the branch and to Steve as water roared around them, trying to regain her strength, but feeling deep inside a terrible fear.

Then she felt Steve's gasp of surprise and heard him

whisper, "Dad!" Before she knew what had happened, Steve was taken from her. Jim slung him onto his hip as though he were Missy's size, and Steve wrapped his legs around him saying joyously, fear evaporated, "Hi, Dad!"

His strong legs braced against the current, Jim looked in no mood for conversation. As he pulled Mari to his side, she wondered if she mightn't be safer at the mercy of the stream.

But he was striding comparatively easily toward the bank, and she had no choice but to move with him. She stumbled once and his hand bit into her side, holding her upright.

When they finally gained the bank, Missy was waiting for them, her dark eyes wide and uncertain. Jim paused long enough to set Steve on his feet and ask him sharply, "Are you all right?"

"Yeah, Dad."

"And you?" The flashing eyes swung to Mari. She nodded, still speechless.

"All right," he said quietly but with a determination that gave the word an ominous quality. He scooped Missy up without his customary gentleness, and the child frowned, saying anxiously, "Want Mommy."

"Be quiet, Melissa!" Jim ordered, giving her a dark look. She subsided instantly, her eyes widening. "We'll discuss this in the house. Come on!" And he headed off, leaving Mari and Steve to follow in his dust.

Jim stopped them right inside the kitchen, set Missy down, and loomed over the three of them, thunder on his brow. "What happened?" he demanded.

Steve, completely drenched but impressed by his father's rescue, was glowing. "Missy wanted to go out in the yard when I came home from school," he explained, his mood dampening a little at the look on Jim's face. "We were playing with my Matchbox cars, and I started building a road and a tunnel and she was helping me, then"—he shrugged helplessly—"then she was gone. When I found her, she had thrown Duck

into the stream, thinkin' he was gonna swim, I guess.
but he got stuck in some rocks, and she started to cry
and was gonna go in after him." He paused and went
on a little nervously. "I know the stream's off limits,
but...I...I thought it was the right thing to do. But it
was rough goin', and I fell and Mom came in after
me."

Mari, cold and trembling, started at the title Steve
had given her and saw Jim note it, too. But he was
distracted for only an instant before turning to her.

"And what in the hell were you doing?"

After what she had just been through, Mari bristled
at his attitude. "What do you think I was doing?" she
screamed up at him. "Our son was drowning!"

"Why didn't you call me?"

"You were on a long distance call."

"If our son is drowning, I don't mind being interrupted."

"Next time I'll remember." Mari turned to Steve
and said conversationally, "Remind me, darling, next
time you're drowning to call your father before I try to
help you."

But Steve wasn't looking at her, he was looking at
the open kitchen door where a plump, middle-aged
woman stood, clipboard clutched to an ample bosom, a
look of vague apprehension on her face.

"Is this a bad time?" she asked.

Jim glanced dryly at Mari and replied easily, "Not if
you don't mind fixing your own coffee while we dry
off. Come on in, Mrs. Savage."

Chapter Eleven

Sitting in the bathtub, Mari wept freely, considering all hope of keeping Missy gone. In the room next door, Missy had just been soundly spanked while Mrs. Savage, the long-awaited caseworker, sat in the dining room alone, hearing her mighty screams. On top of having witnessed the loving adoptive mother and father screaming at one another, the caseworker had seen the kichen still strewn with dozens of cookies, flour, dirty dishes, and the puddle of stream water they had left while they shouted. Mari was certain that had clinched Mrs. Savage's report. It would probably recommend immediate removal of both children, followed by the arrest of Jim and herself for child abuse.

The bathroom door opened, and Jim, in the act of rolling up the sleeves of a fresh flannel shirt, frowned at her. "What are you crying about?"

Too miserable to even be embarrassed by his presence, Mari shook her head hopelessly. "We blew it," she sobbed. "She'll take Missy away for sure."

"That's nonsense." He took a thick blue towel from the rack and crossed to the tub, holding it ready. "Come out of there; you're getting water-logged."

"We were yelling, you had to go and spank Missy, and the kitchen's a mess!" She stood and was enveloped in the towel, then lifted out onto the rug. "Poor Stevie was soaked and shaking, and she's sitting down there all by herself..."

Jim rubbed the towel roughly down her back and

over her hips, then wrapped her in it. "Steve's changed and is entertaining Mrs. Savage right now, telling her in dramatic detail how Mom came to his rescue. I had to come and bail you out, of course, but he's making you look pretty good. She liked your cookies, too. You're worrying for nothing. Now, hurry up and get dressed. You'll like her."

She did. Instead of the critical, exacting bureaucrat she had expected, Mari was introduced to a warm, motherly woman who laughed about the scene she had witnessed.

"I'm sorry you were greeted that way," Mari apologized, dressed in the jeans and red turtleneck Jim had put out for her. She would have opted for something more impressive, but Jim had insisted that she hurry.

"Actually it was good to see all that feeling," Helen Savage laughed, brown eyes behind large glasses smiling at Mari. "Steve explained to me what happened. That does get the adrenaline flowing."

"Missy..." Mari began to explain.

"Steve explained that, too. Your husband was right to carry through, Mrs. Sullivan. Failing to, simply because I was here, might have resulted in tragedy the next time. Don't worry"—she patted Mari's hand— "I'm not here to criticize and find fault. I just want to get acquainted and ask a few questions. Maybe even help, if I can."

Jim came in with coffee mugs and a plate of cookies, Steve bringing up the rear with his mouth full. He murmured something unintelligible, then swallowing, repeated, "These are great, Mom. She made them for Cub Scouts, Mrs. Savage. I finished my knot board. Want to see?"

While Steve disappeared for his collection of knots mounted on a board Jim had cut and painted for him, Mrs. Savage took a cookie and dunked it in her coffee.

"Steve seems very pleased with his new mother," the caseworker observed. "How does he get along with the little girl? Was there any jealousy or resentment?"

"None at all," Mari was quick to reply. "He's very thoughtful of her and pretty tolerant. He does get impatient sometimes because she follows him everywhere but on the whole I think he likes her."

"He said he did," Mrs. Savage nodded. "I just wondered if you had noticed any grievances he might be reluctant to tell me."

Mari looked at Jim for help, knowing the boy was more frank with him than anyone. He shrugged. "No more than the usual sibling rivalry. They get into it now and then but Janie's an expert at diplomatic negotiations, and most problems are resolved peacefully."

"And if you left them to solve it themselves, would it end peacefully, do you think?"

"I tried that once," Mari replied candidly. "Missy wanted something Steve had and when he wouldn't give it to her, she took it when he wasn't there and broke it accidentally. He was angry but he wouldn't do anything because she's so much smaller than he is. That seemed as harmful to him as the reverse would be so I do step in to try to make sure Missy doesn't bully Steve."

They were laughing at her explanation when Steve returned with his board. Mrs. Savage admired the carefully worked designs in jute, then looked up at Jim inquiringly. "If you don't think it would upset your discipline, could I meet Melissa?"

He nodded. "Of course. Do you want to get her, Jane?"

Mari found Missy sitting up in her crib, looking forlorn, her dark eyes bright with tears, her ponytails awry.

"Come on, darling," Mari said briskly, fighting a catch in her voice at the sight of Missy without Duck. "We're going to meet Mrs. Savage, so you be a good girl, okay?"

Sitting on the sofa beside the caseworker, Mari held the child on her knees. "This is our friend, Mrs. Savage, Missy."

Missy's large brown eyes studied the stranger solemnly, then suddenly, unexpectedly, her bottom lip began to quiver. "Want Daddy!" she said plaintively.

Looking up to Jim in surprise, Mari met his arched eyebrow as Missy ran across the room to where he sat in an easy chair. She clambered into his lap and settled into the crook of his arm, apparently without a doubt that she would be welcome.

"It appears you're forgiven," Mrs. Savage observed.

"I don't know." He looked down into the child's sober face as she snuggled her head into his shoulder. "She still looks pretty grim."

"We lost a favorite toy in the stream," Mari explained.

"No Duck," Missy said, a tear spilling over.

"Poor Missy." Jim hugged her and kissed her disheveled hair. "But Duck got lost because you left the yard."

"Missy bad," she agreed and sniffed.

"Leaving the yard was bad," Jim corrected. "And you won't do that anymore, will you?"

She shook her head penitently.

"Good girl. How about a cookie?" She nodded instantly.

Jim set her on the soft carpeting and pointed to the caseworker seated near the tray. "Go and see Mrs. Savage, and she'll give you one."

Missy hung back a moment, then looked longingly at the plate of cookies. Mrs. Savage chose one, broke it in half and held one half out to Missy, who finally succumbed.

Jim took Steve with him into the kitchen, leaving Mari and Missy alone with Mrs. Savage. They talked for the better part of an hour, and just as Mari was beginning to feel that perhaps the afternoon wasn't a total failure, the caseworker asked the question that Mari feared.

"Tell me, Mrs. Sullivan," she began carefully, as though wary of how her question would be received, "you seem a very qualified mother to me despite your youth. But what if you become pregnant? Could you manage?"

The room swam in front of Mari for a moment, and she tried to reply several times before an answer came. But when it did, it was direct and firm because it was true. "I love my husband, Mrs. Savage. I want to have his children." No lie in neglecting to add that he didn't return that love and that even if he did she was unable to have his children.

"Good enough," Mrs. Savage pronounced and stood to leave. It was only as Mari walked her to the door that she saw Jim leaning against the molding, his eyes dark with a look she couldn't interpret. There was no doubt that he had witnessed her declaration.

After the children were in bed, Missy cuddled up to a decrepit teddy bear Steve had dug out of the bottom of his toy box, Mari sought to avoid a confrontation with Jim by cleaning up the kitchen. But he was there before her, half-sitting on the kitchen table, a glass of wine in his hand.

Wanting to discuss anything but the remark she knew he had overheard, she began clearing dishes to one side of the counter and said stiffly, "I suppose I should thank you for saving our lives."

"That would be gracious of you," he said dryly.

She drained the cold water she had run to do the dishes what seemed an eternity ago, then ran hot water and added a splash of detergent. She turned to the table to collect some utensils Missy had been playing with and glanced up at Jim, who hadn't taken his eyes off her.

"Thank you," she mumbled.

"Anytime," he said lightly, then his tone changed and he added, "Thank *you* for going in after him. I'm sure you sold Mrs. Savage without having to say a word."

"Then..." She carried the utensils to the counter

and dropped them into the sudsy water. Glancing over her shoulder at him, she began again. "Then . . . there's no longer any point in my staying."

"Unless you consider the fact that she'll be back again every month for a year." Jim pulled a dish towel out of the drawer and stood ready to dry. "And that your leaving would destroy Steve."

Tears sprang to Mari's eyes as she added the other dirty dishes to the water. She couldn't hurt Steve, but she couldn't take much more of loving Jim and never being near him because he loved someone else.

"How can we live like this for a year?" she asked, her voice quaking. She ran the rinse water and passed a clean cup to Jim. He took it, wandering to the cupboard as he dried it.

"We've done it for a month," he pointed out calmly. "We can do it for a year."

"There has to be another way," she said feebly.

"As I see it . . ." He reached for another cup she held out and grabbed quickly as it slipped out of her hand. He glanced at her pale face and trembling fingers and dropped the towel, pushing her toward a kitchen chair. He put the wine he'd been drinking in her hand and sat across from her. "As I see it," he repeated, "there's no way you can leave without risking Missy and hurting my son."

Remembering how she had felt seeing Steve swept away from her, she corrected softly, putting the wine to her lips, "Our son."

"Which only goes to prove my point," he said.

The hopelessness of it swept over Mari, and she collapsed in sobs, resting her head on her arms on the tabletop. "I . . . can't stay! And I c–can't . . . go!" she wept. "What do I do?"

Jim made no move to touch her, and she felt isolated in her own little hell.

"Sometimes," he said, his voice drifted around her, "it's best just to coast along until a solution presents itself." He was silent for a moment, then added in that brisk tone she was now so used to, "If it helps any, I'll be leaving for Portland Sunday."

She looked up at him at that, in her eyes a tear-filled mixture of relief and regret. "For how long?" she asked cautiously.

"Until Thursday or Friday at the latest." He said that almost as though he was reluctant to leave and anxious to be home again, she thought, sniffling, a little pulse beginning to tap at the base of her throat. He was looking at her deeply, the green in the plaid of his shirt darkening his eyes.

"You look as though you might miss me," he said.

"You sound as though you don't want to go," she countered.

"I don't," he admitted readily. "We've become quite a family, the four of us. Even Mrs. Savage thought so."

Because that remark brought to mind the subject she had come here to escape, Mari sought desperately for a diversion and found it, as was becoming a habit lately, in needling him.

"Are you taking Julia with you?" she asked lightly, tossing down the last sip of wine.

His eyes flared, going almost black as temper altered his expression. He was the only man she knew, she thought idly—fascinated for the moment by his face— who became more handsome when he was angry. There was no sneer, no out of control tic. All his features hardened into line, forming an awesome symmetry. But when he spoke, the blade edge to his voice sliced into her absorption.

"Is that a question you'd ask a man you've just professed to love?"

A warning signal clanged in her brain, and she quickly lowered her lashes, afraid that he would see it was true. She stood and walked casually away from him toward the coffeepot. "It is unfortunate that you overheard that. I was trying to impress Mrs. Savage with what a loving wife I am. Only you and I have to know that you don't really want one."

She poured coffee into a brown pottery mug and turned to Jim with an artificial smile. "Want a cup?"

He looked back at her evenly. "No, thank you. I want you to come back here and sit down."

"Jim, I came here to clean up."

"You came here to get away from talking about us. Come and sit down. It won't take long."

Not surprised that he read her so well, Mari was nevertheless annoyed with herself for being so transparent. "No, it won't take long," she returned hotly, wildly stirring her coffee, forgetting in her agitation that she hadn't put anything in it, "because I refuse to discuss it!"

"Why? Afraid you'll discover something you don't want to recognize?"

"Like what?"

"Like the fact that you still love me."

She looked at him in shock for a moment, then turned away, her spoon still noisily banging in her cup. "Hah! Whatever gave you that preposterous idea?"

"Your eyes," he replied softly. "They melt when you look at me."

"Hah!" she said again, thinking abstractedly what a foolish sound that was, and continued to stir her coffee. Her exaggerated motions caused the hot brew to slosh out of the cup onto her arm. She yelped, jumping back as the hot liquid stung her, and splashed herself again, finally dropping and shattering the cup, watching its contents puddle on the brown tile floor.

Jim was beside her in an instant, drying her arm with the dish towel, rubbing a thumb gently over the red spot. "You're becoming a basket case, Janie," he observed dryly.

"I'm tired," she evaded.

"So am I. Of a lot of things."

"All you have to do," she said huffily, "is say the word and Missy and I will go!"

"Will you stop it!" he growled at her, shoving her none too gently into the chair. He turned to sit on the edge of the table facing her, and she saw again the symmetry of anger on his face. "We've just been all through that. You can't leave."

"It's a farce!" Mari shouted. "I can't go on like this."

"You're making it a farce." he accused. "You haven't let the kids see it, I'll say that for you, but pretty soon the wall between us is going to be visible. What do we do then, Janie?"

"I'm making it a farce!" she screamed hotly. "I loved you!"

"Then what in the hell happened?" He leaned down to her, the vehemence of the question snapping in his eyes. "When you love someone, you don't make wild accusations without knowing the facts. You don't jump to conclusions."

"The conclusions jumped at me," she retorted. "How else would you explain the negligee?"

"I wasn't asked."

"All right!" she cocked her head sarcastically. "Why was there a blue negligee in our linen closet?"

For a moment he looked as angry as he had the night she had found it and made her accusations, then he seemed to collect himself and straightened up to look down at her, a challenge in his eyes.

"All right, I'll strike a bargain with you. You tell me what you were going to tell me the night I came home from Portland, and I'll explain the negligee."

Her heart thudding, panic rising in her at the prospect of having to explain now, she looked down at the table and shook her head. "No," she said.

There was a moment's tense silence, then he walked across the kitchen to lean against the counter as though he needed distance from her. "Actually I might have it figured out myself before long."

Just as Mari's pulse was dribbling back to normal, it picked up a wild beat at his statement. She looked up, her eyes wide and wary, waiting for him to explain.

"It's not another man," he said, his brow furrowed. "I think I can be pretty sure of that because of the way you react to me."

"Pretty sure of yourself, aren't you?" she asked weakly.

"No, sure of you," he amended. "I know you're not a woman to give yourself casually, and your commitment to me was total. You couldn't have done that while loving someone else."

She stared at her lap, afraid of what was coming next.

"Then I thought you might have a child somewhere. Everytime someone mentions babies, your eyes explode, and I drew the obvious conclusion." His voice gentled. "But you were very much a virgin on our wedding night, so that eliminated that solution."

The pain of this discussion was becoming unbearable, and she pushed away from the table. "I'm too tired for this," she said wearily, her eyes closing heavily, her face pale. "Could we go into it another time?"

"And what excuse will you find then?"

"Could we talk when you come back from Portland?" she asked on sudden inspiration, the idea instantly gaining appeal. She glanced up at him hopefully. "It'll give us both time to think."

He studied her for a long moment, his eyes so reluctant she was sure he was going to refuse and shake an answer from her right then. But he finally nodded.

"All right. But we're going to settle up then, whether or not you're still willing to talk. I won't let you back out on me."

"I won't."

"Good. We'll settle a few other things then, too. Like the fact that I don't plan to spend the next year celibate."

Color flooded Mari's face, but she struggled to maintain her dignity. "A celibate Sullivan is probably unheard of."

To her surprise, he grinned. "It's been a long four

weeks. My patience is worn down to a nub. You'd better give that a little thought while I'm away.''

"You said yourself that I'm not the type to give myself casually,'' she reminded him. "I'm also not the type to give myself where I'll receive nothing in return.''

"Have I been ungenerous in returning what you gave?'' he asked, an eyebrow raised.

"Quite the contrary,'' she replied. "But I'd prefer to be the only recipient of your generosity.''

To her surprise, he grinned again. "We'll lay that ghost to rest, too, when I come home.''

The three days before Jim left were an eternity; the three that had passed since she and the children waved him off had flown frighteningly, and Mari was no closer to a resolution to her dilemma.

Steve and Missy were constructing a Tinker Toy castle in the middle of the living room floor, since it was raining again, and she was leafing through a magazine, unable to settle down to anything constructive.

"Would you two like some hot chocolate?'' she asked, tossing the magazine down and stretching to her feet.

Steve looked up and smiled. "Yes, please. It's lonesome without Dad, isn't it?''

"Daddy today?'' Missy asked for the tenth time that afternoon.

"No, darling,'' Mari answered. "Not until Friday.''

"Lonesome,'' she said, mimicking Steve.

"I know, love. But two more days and Daddy will be home. Want some cookies, too?''

The answer was unanimously affirmative, and Mari went to the kitchen, turning on the kettle and taking the cookie jar down from the shelf. She heard the doorbell ring and, thinking it was one of Steve's friends, continued her task while the boy went to the door.

A vaguely familiar voice asked, "Does Mari Sullivan live here?''

"Mari?" Steve asked.

"Marijane," the voice corrected.

"Oh. That's my mom," he said, then in a blood-curdling shout, "Mooooooooom!"

"Coming!" Mari called, turning the burner on low under the kettle. She hurried into the living room to find both Steve and Missy staring up uninhibitedly at a fair-haired young man shivering in a pale blue suit of a light fabric.

"Kent!" she gasped, as shocked as though the President himself had appeared on her doorstep.

He smiled bleakly, shoulders hunched up against the cold. "Can I...come in?"

"Oh, yes! Of course." She stepped back, pulling the children with her, then closed the door behind the man she had thought she would never see again.

Kent shivered exaggeratedly and rubbed his arms, moving toward the fire, asking, "May I?"

"Yes. Please," Mari said, feeling suddenly very uncomfortable. She shooed the children back to their project on the floor and went to the kitchen. "I was just making coffee," she called over her shoulder. "Sit down and..." She was going to say that she would bring him a cup but discovered him right behind her when she reached the stove. His eyes roamed her face hungrily.

"Oh!" she said nervously, "I thought you were warming up by the fire." She fiddled with knobs and spoons and cups and saucers, all the time keeping her back to him.

"Mari," he said heavily, his voice close to her ear.

"How did you find me?" she asked brightly, moving away from him to pull a tray down from the cupboard.

"Your boss told me where you'd gone for Christmas, so I stopped there and your mother told me, with great hostility I might add, that I'd find you here." He turned her firmly around, his pale eyes roving her face as he frowned. "That you had married and had two children after only three months." He grinned. "You always were exceptional."

"The boy is my husband's," she said, relaxing. "And you remember Melissa."

He nodded. "Thea's away again?"

"Yes. But she's given Missy up for good this time. We're adopting her."

Kent studied her moodily another moment, then, hands in his pockets, he wandered slowly the length of the kitchen. "How long have you known this guy?" he asked suddenly.

Mari smiled at him as he spun around because an issue had just resolved itself in her mind. There was no reason to feel nervous or guilty about Kent's presence because it meant absolutely nothing to her. They had been more than friends once; she had liked Kent because he was quiet and easygoing and never wanted more from her than she wanted to give. But now the only man on her mind was aggressive and demanding, always pushing her, always prodding, but touching her with life, with a stirring awareness she'd never known before. Even when she had pitted herself against him and was fighting tooth and nail for whatever liberty she felt he had usurped at the time, there was more feeling in one minute spent with him than in the whole of her life before Jim walked into it.

"We knew each other a month before we were married," she said, smiling again as she thought about it.

"A month!" he said, aghast. "I can't believe that of you."

"It's true. Would you like something with your coffee?"

"You don't look particularly happy." He came back across the kitchen to stand before her, looking down into her upturned face. "In fact, you even look unhappy."

"I'm not," she lied, turning away to put cookies on a plate. "You're just imagining it."

She turned her back to him, fingers pinching painfully into her upper arms. "No, I'm not! What's happened, Mari? What would make you move to this god-forsaken place and marry a man with a child after only knowing him a month? What's he holding over you?"

My heart? she thought with a little wince. "Nothing," she said, disengaging herself from his hands. "I needed a father for Missy and he needed a mother for his son. It's working out very well."

"You're lying!"

"I'm not!" Beginning to get impatient with him, she excused herself and took cookies and cocoa out to the children. When she returned to the kitchen, he was frowning into a cup of coffee. Accustomed now to Jim's height and vibrance, Kent seemed suddenly ineffective, dull for all his apparent anger and concern.

"Where is he?" Kent asked quietly.

"Away for a few days," she replied, taking a sip from her cup. "Forgive me if this sounds rude, Kent, but what right have you to be concerned about why I married or how I'm treated?"

"The right of somebody who loved you once," he said, putting his cup aside, his face contorting in emotion. "Somebody who loves you still. I was an idiot to let you go."

"Let me go?" she repeated, her voice shaded with mockery. "*You* told *me* it was over. It doesn't matter now, anyway."

"Come back with me," he said urgently, reaching for her with a suddenness that surprised her into immobility. "You can't be happy here. Come back to LA with me."

"Kent!" Finally coming to life, Mari struggled, pushing him away. "Stop that! I'm a married woman with two children."

"You can bring Melissa."

"Nothing else has changed, Kent," she said, angry now. "I still can't have children."

He ran a hand through his fair hair, a little desperately, she thought. "Today, there are test tube babies, artificial..."

"No!" she shouted, hot color flooding her face, disgust filling her being. "You'd better leave, Kent."

"Doesn't he care that you're sterile?" he asked coldly, angered by her rejection. The word made her flinch, but she didn't answer and he nodded, sneering. "I suppose it doesn't matter to him because he already has a son."

In answering that, Mari straightened up and played out a little fantasy she had dreamed a hundred times. "The boy is adopted, and Jim doesn't care because he loves me, as I am and for what I am. Good-bye, Kent."

He chuckled brutally and, turning to leave, stopped at the door to the living room and turned back to her. "No man is that big, Mari. Good-bye."

She sat at the kitchen table with her coffee for twenty minutes, unable to stop trembling. What she would have done to have Jim sitting across from her, absorbed in the morning paper, his very presence making her feel secure. She closed her eyes and imagined him there and slowly a sense of peace closed around her. She would tell him the night he came home. She would be totally honest and unafraid because there was a vast world of difference between the man Jim was and the man who had just left, Julia or no Julia.

Strange, she thought, how the quality of her bitterness over her sterility had changed. She no longer felt incomplete or half a woman as she had so often thought of herself. When Jim was near, he seemed to cancel out all that, making her feel feminine and all woman. But how much she regretted the fact that there would be no Jim in miniature, no little boy with that devilish grin, no little girl with soft hazel eyes.

"Mom, could you help us?" Steve appeared before her, cocoa on his upper lip. "We're trying to put a tower on the castle, and it keeps falling down."

Putting aside the children who would never be for the children who unmistakably were, Mari left her coffee and followed Steve.

That afternoon Katherine stopped by, stylishly dressed in a silky, light-green raincoat.

"Hi, darlings!" She greeted the children in a slightly preoccupied fashion, then shooed them off to play while pulling Mari into the kitchen.

"Did he come here?" she asked in a whisper, shrugging out of her coat while Mari made fresh coffee.

"Yes, he did," Mari replied, no question in her mind of who "he" was.

"The nerve!" Katherine exclaimed, sitting down at the table and crossing long, brown-knit-clad legs. "I didn't like him!"

Mari smiled at her mother and sat across from her. "I didn't either. Were you afraid I'd run off with him?"

Katherine's eyes widened. "Is that what he wanted?"

Mari nodded. "Even told me I could take Melissa with me."

"No!" Katherine gasped, leaning on her elbows to stare at her daughter, her gray eyes even wider than they were before. "What did you say?"

"I said good-bye."

"Thank goodness!" Katherine's mood suddenly altered, and Mari was shocked to see her mother's eyes moist with tears.

"Did you really think I'd go with him?" Mari demanded.

Katherine shook her head, making a helpless gesture with her hands. "No. I don't know," she replied, her voice hoarse. She looked at Mari sheepishly. "Terry told me that he suspected you and Jim were having problems. He said Jim hadn't been himself lately. When Ken—whatever his name is—appeared at my door, I thought you had called him, or..."

"Mother!" Mari interrupted, torn between laughter and indignation.

"Well, I didn't know!" Katherine defended herself quickly. "I know how you are about...you know. I thought maybe Jim got upset about it, or you..."

Mari got to her feet and went to pour the coffee, letting the unfinished sentence hang there. The silence stretched while Mari put the cups and cream and sugar on a tray and carried it to the table. Avoiding her mother's eyes, she put a cup before her, then placed the other items on the table.

"Want to try my cookies?" she asked.

"You haven't told him yet, have you?" Katherine asked quietly.

"No." Mari's reply was swift, and she tried to convey an unwillingness to discuss it in her tone of voice. But Katherine ignored it.

"Why not?"

Mari sighed impatiently. "First, because I was afraid to lose him; then because I was angry with him."

Katherine frowned, raising the pottery mug to her lips. "So you are having problems."

"It's very complicated."

"Problems usually are or they wouldn't be problems."

Mari gave her mother a dry smile. "That was very sage, Mother."

"I'm sorry," Katherine sighed. "We've got Jazz and David on the right track, and now there are you and Jim to worry about."

"There's nothing to worry about," Mari insisted, then changed the subject. "Heard anything from Thea?"

"Jasmine said she got the release form back from her this week. That means she has formally given Missy up."

Mari frowned. "Why didn't she tell *me*?"

"I spoke to her on the phone this morning because they're coming up for the weekend. I'm sure they'll call you today. I think we should all get together for dinner. How about Chinese?"

"That sounds good," Mari said absently, her mind amuddle with the events of the trying day.

They finished their coffee, and Mari walked Katherine to the door, assuring her again that she needn't worry. She was sure that she, personally, was doing all the worrying necessary.

Katherine started down the walk, and Mari was about to close the door when her mother turned back abruptly. "I keep forgetting to ask you, darling. Have you found a nightie that doesn't belong to you?"

Mari's breath stopped for an instant, and Katherine prompted, "It's turqoise with a pretty vanilla lace. I wore it the night Terry and I were stuck in town because of snow. It was a few days before you came."

Feeling as though she'd just been grabbed by the scruff of the neck and shaken, Mari cleared her throat and said, "I'll institute a search. It must be here someplace."

"Thanks, Mari, I wouldn't care if it were any other gown, but that was a rather romantic evening. Terry bought the gown for me and a bottle of perfume. The fragrance wasn't really me, but the gown has some great memories attached to it! See you on the weekend."

Mari closed the door behind her mother, then leaned against it, closing her eyes against the pictures forming on the screen of her mind. She could see herself abristle with righteous indignation, flinging the turquoise nightie at Jim and accusing him of infidelity and treachery. She could see the hurt in his eyes clearly now, in retrospect, when then she had only seen anger and what she thought had been disdain for her own anger. In truth it must have been an unwillingness to defend himself against unfounded accusations.

With an audible groan, she went upstairs and hand laundered the notorious nightie and hung it over the bathtub to dry.

When the sound of the Malibu's motor filtered into the kitchen Friday night, it was all Mari could do to stop the children from running into the garage. When the door opened, Missy hurled herself at Jim, and Mari hurried to relieve him of his suitcase and raincoat before he was forced to drop them.

"Hi, Daddy!" Missy squealed again and again when he scooped her up in one arm, circling the other around Steve and holding him close. There was incoherent jabbering and excited questions, then Mari peeled the children from him.

"All right, now. Dad's had a long, hard trip. Let's let him have some breathing space. Finish setting the table for me, please?"

They went off obediently, giggling together, and Mari reached up to help Jim with the jacket he was shrugging off. She slid a hand under his lapel, up to his neck, to pull the jacket out from under his shirt collar, and stopped, feeling the warmth of his body through the cotton, looking into eyes that were consuming her, feature by feature. It was the most natural thing in the world to reach her other hand up, join them behind his neck and stretch up on tiptoe to meet his lips. Reacting to a surge of joy at the sight of his familiar grin, she approached the kiss with enthusiasm and sensed his surprise. Then she lost awareness of everything as he responded in kind, ardently, lengthily.

When she came down to earth again, it was to feel him laughing softly against her. She pulled away and looked at him inquiringly.

"Well, that's a hell of a thing to do to a guy when his hands are trapped," he said, indicating his arms still caught in his partially removed coat.

She blushed. "I'm sorry."

"I'm not." Pulling the coat the rest of the way off, he flung it at a chair and pulled her back to him. "Let's give it another go."

Mari wrapped her arms around his broad middle and felt his close around her, strong, almost hurting. Feeling his hands on her back, moving down her spine to her hips to linger there, gently tracing the curve, she was transported. It took Steve's cry of "Mom, do something! It's boiling over!" to bring her back to earth.

She tried to wriggle out of Jim's arms, but he held

her fast, kissing her eyes, her nose, her ears. "He means me," he said absently.

She giggled. "He means the green beans. And if you don't let me go, your roast and vegetables are going to be ruined."

"It smells like a feast!" Jim said, releasing her reluctantly and following her to the stove where she lowered the burner under the beans. She peeked into the oven and lowered that, too.

"Do I have time for a shower?" he asked, both children clutching his hands again, their table setting completed.

"Yes. I can hold it off until you're ready."

"Fifteen minutes?"

"Fine."

"Okay, you two." Jim pulled the children along with him. "Help me unpack, and you might find a few surprises."

Her heart racing in exhiliration, Mari heard the sounds of their conversation in the bedroom, the children's squeals of delight, the sound of the shower.

When the shower stopped, Mari took the juicy roast and golden vegetables from the oven, poured wine and milk and was just pouring coffee when the three appeared together, Jim smelling of soap and after-shave in clean jeans and a white turtleneck.

Missy held a large brown stuffed cow with white spots, feminine eyelashes, and a sunny smile. "Mommy! Moo!" Missy cried, holding it up for her inspection.

"It's beautiful, darling. What have you got there, Steve?"

The boy put a large metal box on the floor and opened it reverently. "Tools!" he said, his eyes shining. "A saw, a wrench, a hammer . . ." He enumerated everything for her, then closed the top of the professional-looking case lovingly. "It's the best present I ever had." He looked up at Jim and grinned. "Except for Mom, of course."

"Of course," Jim laughed. "Now why don't you put your things aside until after dinner."

Steve placed his toolbox under his chair, but Missy clutched her cow maternally when Mari tried to extricate it.

"Cow hungry!" she insisted.

"Darling, there isn't room for both of you in the high chair," Mari reasoned.

Unmoved, Missy clutched Cow while Jim picked her up and put her in the chair. The tray, obstructed by the smiling animal, would not slide into position.

"How about if Cow sits on a chair beside you?" Jim suggested.

"Cow hungry!" Missy repeated.

"I'll donate my vegetables," Steve quipped. Jim brought his fist down playfully on the boy's head, then went to the cupboard for another plate.

"She can have a plate, too, just like yours," he bribed, placing the plate on the table in front of the chair pulled up for Cow.

"Share plate!" Missy said, indicating that another plate was unnecessary.

"You'll have to give Cow half of your ice cream, too," Mari said on sudden inspiration.

Missy considered that, then handed Mari the cow to be placed in its own chair, to eat its own dessert without tampering with hers.

"Clever girl," Jim praised, pulling Mari's chair out for her.

It was the liveliest dinner and yet their most relaxed evening together, Mari thought, bringing more coffee to the sofa where Jim and Steve sat discussing a building project. Missy, Cow hugged lovingly, had been put to bed without complaint.

"Dad's gonna help me make a chair to go with my new desk," Steve announced. "Then we're gonna make you a desk so you don't have to write letters and stuff on the table. Want a rolltop?"

"Hey, Steve!" Jim laughed. "We're not that good."

"You are!"

"Well, that's very loyal of you, but let's try to talk

Mom into something simple." Jim leaned against the back of the sofa, stretching long arms over his head. "It's been a long week."

He turned his head to look at Mari, and she knew he was reading her thoughts, that she too had had a long week without him and that she was remembering the agreement made before he left.

Mari angled her chin. She was going to apologize to him, then she was going to tell him everything.

"How'd you fare while I was gone?" he asked, propping his feet up on the coffee table.

"Pretty well," she said, tension mounting in her. She longed for privacy and time to talk.

"No problems?"

"We all missed you," she said with sincerity. "And Missy asked twenty times a day when you were coming home. But apart from that, we were fine."

"It's good to know the old man was missed," Jim grinned. Then he reached down to poke Steve gently with his toe. "Got that all packed up yet? It's about time for you to hit the sack."

"I guess so," the boy said reluctantly, snapping the lid closed on the toolbox. "But can we get up early since tomorrow's Saturday and work on Mom's desk?"

"Not too early. I might want to sleep in a little." Though he didn't even glance at her when he spoke, Mari presumed the inference and felt a ripple of excitement up her spine. Her pulse quickened, and she fought the betraying color rising from her neck.

"Go on to bed, Steve," Jim went on. "Call us when you're ready and we'll come and say good night."

When Steve had disappeared, Jim set his coffee cup on the table and took Mari's from her, replacing it also. Then he pulled her into his arms and kissed her with agonizing slowness, his fingers tangled in her hair, his body forcing hers down onto the cushions.

Feeling the lick of flame from her lips to the tips of her limbs, she fell victim to a languor that left her sweetly paralyzed. Her fingers clung to each other behind his neck, her heartbeat merging with his while a delicious insanity stole over her. He wanted her as much as she wanted him. He loved her as much as she loved him.

But the nagging thought emerged gradually, demanding recognition, and a little cloud of black entered her crystalline euphoria. They must talk first.

"Jim..." She pushed weakly at him, not really wanting his weight moved from her. "Jim?"

"Hm?" His lips were tracing a line from her ear to the spot where her blouse closed at the hollow of her breasts.

"We...we have to...talk." She was pushing a little harder now, feeling herself drowning in the warmth of his body. "Jim..."

"Talk?" he murmured vaguely, nibbling at her collarbone.

"Talk," she repeated. "You said...before you... left..."

"I missed you," he groaned, his arms crushing her, his lips bruising her soft skin. "Janie, I missed you so much!"

"Jim!" With a little cry, she forgot the need to talk and responded to the need to find other means of communication. She stopped pushing him away and pulled him closer, kissing his freshly shaven chin, nipping his ear.

She was spiraling away, then suddenly Jim's weight was lifted from her, and she looked up, confused, to see him standing over her, the passion in his eyes momentarily banked, his grin wide.

"Steve's calling us," he said, reaching down to pull her to her feet. "We'll tuck him in, then we'll...talk."

Led along to Steve's room in the crook of his arm, Mari resolved that she was going to have to keep her distance if they were ever going to have this talk. She was thrilled that he was so hungry for her, but a little sanity was called for here.

Steve's toolbox was in bed beside him, but Jim removed it to the floor within reach. "You thrash around a lot in your sleep, Steve," he explained gently. "If you bumped your face on one of those corners, you could get a nasty cut or worse."

"I was gonna build some dreams," Steve joked, heavy-lidded, a sleepy contentment on his pink-cheeked face.

"You don't need a hammer and nails for that," Jim laughed.

"I used to do that at first," Steve said, suddenly serious. Jim sat on the edge of the bed beside him.

"What's that, Steve?"

"Build dreams about having Mom and Dad back. Not that I didn't like you," he was quick to explain, and Jim reassured him with a nod. "But I was lonesome. Like at Christmas. But it got better, even when it was just you and me. Then I'd dream about if we had a mother," Steve smiled at Mari, then at Jim. "And now we do, and it's better than any dream."

"Thank you, Stevie," Mari leaned down to hug him, leaving a tear on his pillow. "You're a very special boy. Good night, darling."

"I'm glad you didn't marry him!" Steve said emphatically as Mari straightened up. Jim had risen and stood behind her, and she felt her back stiffen as he inquired in puzzlement, "Who, Steve?"

"The guy who was here while you were gone."

Mari heard cymbals crash in her brain and struggled to retain a hold on her composure as she turned to Jim to explain, and Steve, thinking the delay meant she didn't remember, added: "You know, Mom. That Ken somebody. The one that hugged you when you went into the kitchen."

There was a moment of charged silence, then Jim said calmly, putting the light out by the boy's bed, "Well, she didn't marry him, so don't worry about it. Good night."

"'Night, Dad."

Jim took Mari's arm in a grip that almost made her

cry out and pulled her into the hall, closing the door quietly behind him.

"Jim, I . . ." she began feverishly, pulling at the fingers that felt like they would break her bones.

"Save it!" he snapped and, applying more pressure, pulled her with him down the hall to his room, locking the door behind them.

"So you had a good time while I was gone?" he asked quietly, anger emanating from him in pulsing waves. He stood before the door, arms folded across his chest, biceps intimidatingly round, his eyes burning in a face gone almost white.

"Don't be stupid!" she said hotly, trying not to betray fear, though it battled with her own anger for supremacy.

"Apparently I have been. And I believed you when you said you missed me." There was self-mockery in his voice and a flash of pain crossed his eyes, cutting at Mari like a dull knife. Forgetting her own anger, she took a conciliatory step toward him. "Jim . . ."

He watched her, completely unmoved.

"Jim, please . . ." she whispered, fear beginning to take the upper hand, fear that after coming so close, she was going to lose him to a misunderstanding. "I didn't know he was coming! He . . . he just . . . showed up."

"So you made the most of it."

Mari looked back at him helplessly. "Steve misunderstood . . ."

"How do you misunderstand an embrace?" he asked, the coolness of his anger becoming more dangerous by the minute. "If one of the parties isn't willing, it would be obvious, even to a child."

"He wanted me to . . ." she began, making an effort to explain.

"He wanted you," Jim cut her off, advancing toward her. "Just leave it at that. I suppose you forgot to mention that you're married now?"

"He..."

"Or had you forgotten?" He stopped in front of her, so close she would have touched him had she moved a fraction of an inch. An angry pulse worked at the base of his jaw set in an uncompromising line.

Mari was afraid of his anger but suddenly angry enough herself to put her fear aside. "How you under-estimate yourself, husband," she said, standing toe-to-toe with him, her slight frame straining to avoid being dwarfed by his. "No woman could be married to you and forget it."

Surprise registered in his eyes, replaced by a curious combination of wariness and anger. He inclined his head in question.

"A compliment?"

"A fact," she returned. "But don't let me stop you. Your macho tirade was going so well. But if you were planning to remind me that I was married to you by forcing me to bed, don't forget that it's now illegal to rape your wife. I could have you arrested."

"Perhaps you could convince me that reminding you of anything is unnecessary," Jim said quietly. "Why was he here, Jane?"

"Why do you think he was here, James?" she countered, shades of a conversation that took place a month ago.

"I think he was here because you're convinced that I'm seeing Julia on the side and decided to pay me back in kind by reviving an old flame." His words were clipped and angry.

"And while I was planning this little tryst," she said, her own voice reflecting fury, "I had two children play-ing in the living room and my mother over for coffee in the kitchen."

His jaw hardened. "Stop playing with me, Janie."

"Well, isn't that what you did with me?" she de-manded. "You let me believe that you were messing around with Julia, when just a few words would have

cleared up the issue! But, no. You had to play the outraged, misunderstood husband. Well, how does it feel
to be on the other side?''

"What brought this on? You weren't ripe for ven-
geance when I came home."

"You hadn't accused me of fooling around on you
then," she said bleakly.

"Ah," he nodded. "And how does that feel from
the other side?"

She walked away from him to stand on the hearth
rug and stare into the empty fireplace. "Kent came to
see if he could talk me into going back with him to Los
Angeles. Obviously, I refused. What Steve saw was
Kent grabbing me and holding me, and my being too
shocked to react, until a moment later when I pushed
him away and asked him to leave. Fifteen minutes after
that, my mother arrived. She asked me if I had found a
nightie that wasn't mine and explained to me about
Terry and her spending the night here because the road
home was impassable." She glanced at him over her
shoulder to find him right behind her. "I'm sorry about
that."

He was silent for a long moment, and she began to
fear that he was refusing her apology. Then he turned
her gently around, his eyes dark and warm.

"Julia Kramer and I spend a lot of time together at
the mill out of necessity. As I explained before, the
computer is a new thing for us. I learned to operate it,
then hired Julia and taught her. It's tricky and perverse,
and sometimes two minds can see what escapes one.
Apart from that, I like her a lot. She's intelligent and
capable, and I admire that in anybody. But I don't love
her romantically. I love you." He leaned down to kiss
her lightly. "And I got a little wild at the thought of
anyone else touching you. Forgive me?"

Mari was tempted to adopt an indignant attitude, but
another idea tempted her even more. She appeared to
consider his apology. "I think I should be allowed the
same tactics you tried," she said.

He arched an eyebrow. "And that is?"

"I should be allowed to force you to bed," she said boldly. "And there's no law against that."

"How expedient." Something glinted in his eyes, and he slowly held his hands away from his body in a gesture of defencelessness. "I'll try not to fight too hard."

Giving him a seductive look under her lashes, Mari reached up under his sweater to gather the fabric to slip it over his head. Deliberately, with the tips of her fingernails, she left a trail of feeling from his waist to his shoulder blades. She saw him close his eyes against it as he raised his arms to allow her to pull the sweater off. Tossing it aside, she stood on tiptoe and combed his hair with her fingers to smooth it, then molded his shoulder muscles with gentle hands, following a path down his upper arms to follow the contour of his torso to his waist.

Reaching up again with her mouth, she teased his lips with hers and slipped her fingers inside the waistband of his pants to his belt buckle. But she got no further. Suddenly they were both on the bed with no clothes to impede the exploration of their fingers, and Mari had lost the initiative. Jim's hands were everywhere and hers followed their lead. All the longing of the past month was in her efforts to please him, and he made love to her as though they had forever.

She didn't remember until she lay beside him in the small hours of the morning, curled into his chest, his even breathing sweet music in her ear, that she'd had something else to tell him.

Chapter Twelve

By the time Jim awoke Saturday morning, Mari was showered and had been sitting in the chair by the window for several hours. She alternated between watching the stormy sky lighten from deep blue to muddy gray, the naked maple on the front lawn a grotesque silhouette against it, and studying Jim's peaceful face against the ivory pillowcase. He slept deeply, without moving, his arm flung across Mari's side of the bed, his hand cupped as though he still held her.

Jim stirred, and Mari's heart began to race, her blood moving through her limbs with the sudden flow of adrenaline. She was going to tell him now about her sterility, and she was determined that nothing would stop her. She could hear the children downstairs watching cartoons and knew they would be hypnotized for the next hour, at least.

As though hypnotized herself, she watched Jim move toward her side of the bed, saw his hand groping for her. Her eyes filled as the enormity of the risk she was taking registered in her frightened mind. The casual affection she had grown so dependent upon and the burning love that sustained and renewed her every day could be lost in a moment. And that little gesture of his seemed to spell it out for her. Because of what she was about to tell him, Jim might never reach for her again.

He raised his head, a frown forming as he saw the empty expanse of sheet. Then he spotted her in the chair and sank back against his pillow with a laugh. "Thank God!" he said feelingly. "I was beginning to think last night was a dream I had in a Portland hotel room." Then he leaned up on his elbows and frowned teasingly at her. "What are you doing way over there?"

She studied him a moment, his face flushed from sleep, his brown eyes bright and laughing, so endearingly glad to see her that for a moment her resolve was shaken. Then she forced herself to her feet and walked to the bed. "Gathering my thoughts," she said with a grim smile. "Remember our agreement before you left? I . . . we have to talk."

As he studied her face, his expression sobered, and he sat up to lean against the headboard. He patted the spot beside him. "All right. Come and sit down."

"No." She smiled a refusal and perched instead at the foot of the bed facing him. "It'll be . . . easier . . . if you don't touch me."

"All right." Though he frowned, he folded his arms across his bare chest, ready to listen.

Mari put a hand to her forehead as a moment of pure pain overtook her and her head spun. The silence was loud, broken only by the distant sound of cartoon hilarity. She drew a deep breath, trying to fortify herself with the thought that whatever came of this morning, she would at least be free of the deception.

Mari looked up into Jim's eyes, found them waiting but kind, and tried to force the words from her brain to her lips before anything could hold them back.

"I'm . . . I'm . . ." She had always hated the word sterile and now, as she groped for another word, the silence rang loudly. She finally blurted, "I'm barren!" She closed her eyes, afraid to watch his reaction. How ugly a word that was, too. It called to mind dusty fields and dead orchards. It made her think back to their wedding ceremony and the words that had jolted her. "Your wife shall be like a fruitful vine . . ." Tears squeezed out from between her lashes.

"Barren?" Jim's voice sounded puzzled, and when

she opened her eyes to look at him, he was frowning in confusion. "Barren," he said again, then looked up at her as understanding dawned. "You mean... unable to have children?"

Mari nodded, then felt her heart plummet when he looked at her blankly another moment. Then, as she watched his eyes, anger began to build in their depths. But before either of them could say another word, a crash and a blood-chilling scream came from downstairs. In the split second that it took Mari to react, she saw the frustration at the interruption register in Jim's face, mirroring her own.

As Steve called urgently, "Mom! Daaaaad!" Mari was flying down the stairs in her bare feet, her heart thumping. What she found in the kitchen flipped her stomach, and she had to consciously take hold of herself.

Missy lay on the tile floor in her pink sleepers, blood streaming from somewhere in her hair. She was screaming hysterically. Cereal and the contents of a full carton of milk lay on and around her. Mari pushed aside an up-ended stool to kneel beside her.

"I tried to tell her to wait!" Steve, also in pajamas, his face pale, knelt on the other side of her as Mari wet a kitchen towel and put it to Melissa's head. "I was watching *Superfriends*..."

"It's all right," Mari said calmly, though her voice trembled. "You can explain later. Right now..."

Steve was lifted bodily as Jim, clad only in jeans, took his place. "How bad is it?" he asked tightly, reaching down to hold the tiny hands that were trying to halt Mari's probing. Missy's screams were deafening, and Mari winced against them, shouting to make herself heard. "It's a good inch long and deep," she said, rising to rinse the cloth again, then reapply it to the gash. "It'll need stitches, I'm sure."

"I'll get my keys." Jim sprang to his feet, pulling Steve with him as he headed for the stairs. The damage assessed, Mari sat on the floor, cradling Melissa in her

arms, applying pressure to the wound. She rocked her
back and forth, shushing her, wanting to scream herself. Superimposed on her fear for Melissa was the
sight of Jim's angry face.

Closing her mind against that image, she concentrated on trying to quiet the child.

At the hospital Jim stayed with Steve in the waiting
room while Mari watched the nurse and doctor literally
mummify Melissa in a sheet to immobilize her flailing
arms and legs. She knew the terror and trauma of being
overpowered in that manner were secondary to the doctor's swift and efficient attention to her wound. But
Melissa's pathetic cries of "Mommy!" tore at her, and
she stood in a corner of the emergency room, weeping
quietly.

"She should be just fine," the young doctor assured
her as he put Melissa in her arms. "This sheet of paper
has a list of symptoms to watch for on the chance that a
problem does develop."

"Thank you."

With Melissa clutching her neck, her small legs
wrapped around her waist, Mari walked the long corridor to the waiting room. Subdued, the little girl was a
deadweight in her arms.

Jim was on his feet instantly, Steve at his heels.

"The doctor says she'll be okay," Mari replied to his
unspoken question. "We're supposed to watch for
these symptoms." She waved the sheet of paper caught
between the first and second fingers of her right hand.
"But he doesn't foresee a problem. The X rays were
fine."

"Do you want me to take her?"

"No," Mari replied simply, holding her a little
tighter.

Though she knew his concern was genuine, his manner was stiff, and she started toward the door to termi-
nate the conversation. The explanation she had begun
so bravely just an hour ago now lived like a nightmare
in a corner of her brain. Remembering Jim's expres-

sion, she couldn't raise the subject again because she somehow knew it would mean the end of their life together. Wearing Melissa like a shield, she walked out to the car.

Melissa seemed good as new once home again in her corner of the sofa. She became absorbed in cartoons, and Mari, watching her from the kitchen, felt as though she had stepped into the Twilight Zone and the past hour and a half had happened only in her imagination.

Pouring a glass of juice, Jim asked tentatively, "Janie...?"

Terrified that he meant to bring up their uncompleted conversation, Mari went to the refrigerator without looking at him. "How about some breakfast? You must be starved. We could have bacon and eggs and potatoes or pancakes. Or we could just have French toast. Oh, but there's no milk."

"Janie..."

"Maybe I should just run down to the bakery for doughnuts."

"Janie..."

"I think I'll just have coffee, but you and Steve..."

"Janie!" he shouted, and Mari jumped, letting the refrigerator door close.

He looked hurt and angry. Unable to face him, Mari turned to fill the coffeepot. She heard him draw a breath to speak when the telephone rang. With a murmured oath he snatched the receiver off the wall and growled a greeting. Then he seemed to make a distinct effort to adjust his voice. "Hi, Katherine. I'm sorry. We just made a trip to the hospital with Missy. No, she's fine now. Just a few stitches. She was trying to fix her own breakfast and fell off the kitchen counter." He paused to listen. "No, I guess Janie forgot to mention it. I just got back last night, and it's been rather an...eventful morning." He paused again. "House of Chan? What time?"

Mari closed her eyes, realizing that her conversation with her mother about Jasmine and David visiting had been completely forgotten. She shook her head at Jim, urging him to refuse the invitation.

"Yes," he said forcefully, an eyebrow arched at Mari. "We'll be there. Six thirty. I think Missy will be okay. If anything changes, we'll call you. All right. Bye."

"We can't go," Mari said flatly, the moment he hung up the phone. "Melissa won't be up to it."

He looked at the child happily laughing at the television. "She'll be fine. If she doesn't seem to be later, we can change plans then."

"I don't want to go," Mari said stubbornly.

"We don't really have a choice," he replied. "If we refuse to go, they'll either think something's seriously wrong with Melissa or that something's wrong with us."

She turned away from him to put the coffeepot on the stove. "Is there?" she asked quietly.

"There sure as hell is!" was his angry reply. "I'll be at the mill." She felt him storm past her, then the front door slammed with a resounding bang.

The day was agony for Mari. Steve went out to play and Melissa fell asleep in front of the television. Mari covered her with an afghan and noted that her color was good and, except for an occasional groan when she turned the wrong way in her sleep and disturbed what was now a good-sized lump, she seemed fine.

But it was Mari who had the fatal injury. Had she held the smallest doubt about how Jim felt about her revelation, his parting remark laid it to rest. It was over. Had he not promised their presence at the party tonight, she would have left with Melissa this afternoon, but she couldn't do that to their family. Instead she would have to sit through an interminable dinner, pretending that the bottom had not just fallen out of her world.

She had the children bathed and dressed and was fighting with the back of a small pearl earring when she heard the front door slam. Her heart began to pound, and tears welled in her eyes. She heard Jim speak to the children then race up the stairs. When he came into the bedroom, he saw Mari standing before the mirror in a red wool dress, brushing her gleaming hair with studied nonchalance. He stopped to stand behind her, studying her reflection with a grave expression. He looked tired and tense.

She considered turning into his arms, explaining how it had all happened, how she had lost control of what had begun as an innocent deceit, how she would give her soul if it could never have happened; but she knew she would not be able to deal with the rejection a second time. Instead she said coolly, "You've left it rather late, haven't you? We're due there in fifteen minutes."

His expression hardened to anger, and after a long, dark look at her, he went into the bathroom and closed the door.

Had circumstances been different, Mari would have found the House of Chan an adventure in Chinese cuisine. The restaurant was full to overflowing with families chatting and eating under gaily colored pagoda-shaped lanterns. The walls were decorated with paintings on silk, and dining areas were sectioned off by large terrariums peopled with ivory figurines among the thriving foliage.

Instead of cheering her, the warm atmosphere seemed only to intensify her little hell. But Jasmine's mood would allow no frowns at the table, and Mari tried to follow Jim's lead and behave as though all was well. Her mother and stepfather still looked blissful, but Mari found Terry's eyes on her, apparently puzzling over her quiet demeanor.

"Let's have some of everything!" Jasmine was saying, her gray eyes jewel-bright as they scanned the long menu. She looked particularly beautiful in a lavender sweater and slacks. David, wearing a pale blue sweater over an open-necked shirt, kept glancing at her, his love there for everyone to see.

Jim looked away from them to his menu as though their distraction with one another upset him. "One of everything sounds good to me."

Steve watched a tray piled high with dishes that made the adults groan in anticipation as it passed and looked doubtfully at his father. Jim smiled back at him. "Hamburger and fries for you, right?"

Steve looked relieved. "If that's okay."

"Sure. What do you want for Missy, Janie?"

Absorbed in checking the menu for something suitable for the little girl, Mari was able to avoid Terry's now very watchful eye.

"How was Portland, James?" Katherine asked, putting her menu aside and leaning eagerly toward her son-in-law.

He shrugged indifferently. "Big. Noisy."

"I thought you enjoyed the trips to the big city," Terry said, frowning.

Jim glanced at Mari and in a teasing manner that didn't quite come off said, "That was in my wild youth. Life's gotten a little heavier since then."

Dinner was long and delicious, but Mari tasted nothing. The children were well-behaved and Missy, finally transferred to Jim's lap, was absorbed with sleepily rocking Cow. Jim was more subdued than he usually was with the family, but he seemed to be making a genuine effort to appear relaxed and untroubled.

But in the light of David and Jasmine's love, Mari was feeling her own misery more deeply. And watching a secretive look pass between the two several times, Mari was beginning to see a reason for their visit that was totally unrelated to her adoption of Missy.

A cold pain knotted her stomach muscles.

After dinner there was throat clearing and that look passing between Jazz and David. "We're going to have a baby in September," Jasmine said softly. "Terrence James or Katherine Jane. And . . . and we're both thrilled to death!"

There was a general commotion, chairs scraped back, hugs and backslapping uninhibited by the presence of other diners. Mari, at the far end of the table next to Missy's high chair, was the last to congratulate the beaming couple.

She saw the sympathy in Jasmine's eyes as she hugged her but held fast against it, steeling herself to force a smile and offer cheerful congratulations that rang with sincerity. But when she pulled out of Jasmine's arms, it was to find the rest of the family staring at her, and that was her undoing. There were tears in her mother's eyes for her and a poignant compassion in Terry's. David looked caring but pitying in his exhuberance, and Jim looked angry enough to kill her.

And that was when she had to escape. The touch of Jim's eyes was like a plunge in ice water, and she felt as though her heart would snap with the pain.

She ran for the door, weaving her way between the tables, her path a blind tunnel of garish impressions, streaks of red and yellow and lanterns swinging drunkenly. She heard activity behind her, the sound of china crashing to the floor, but panic lent her sufficient adrenaline to race past the stunned cashier and reach the door before Jim could cut her off. She ran out onto the darkened sidewalk and across the street toward the car. Escape was uppermost in her mind but without a particular direction; she wanted only to reach the car and not have to face her husband.

The screech of brakes halted her frozen in the middle of the street. With a sensation of watching it happen to someone else, she saw a blinding light coming at her, hot white at the center with a corona of misty glare surrounding it, and heard screams, shouts, and Jim's voice, husky with fear, shouting "Janie!" As she slipped quietly into a cold void of black, she thought sadly that no one would ever call her that again.

Mari came to, enveloped in something scratchy and hard, aware of a strong pulse beating against her chest. As though from a distance, she heard her mother sobbing and Terry's firm voice.

"Katherine, stop it! It didn't hit her. Jim pulled her back in time. She's just fainted."

Mari stirred and discovered that she was wrapped in Jim's arms, and the pulse rocketing against her was his heartbeat. He held her away from him and looked at her, his face so tortured she was rendered speechless and could only stare back at him, wondering what could have caused him such pain. Shock, she supposed, that an accident could have been that close. Then he closed his eyes and crushed her to him again, holding her with such force she half expected to hear the snap of her bones.

"Come on, you two." Terry tugged Mari free, pulling her to her feet, then reached down to help Jim. "That ground's going to get awfully cold in a minute."

Katherine and Jasmine, clinging together, parted to draw Mari in between them. Wordlessly Katherine hugged her, her face wet, her arms trembling.

"Let's all calm down," Terry said firmly, his voice betraying a lingering trace of emotion. "Everyone is all right. Katherine, stop crying. We've got to do something positive here."

"Right, darling." Katherine straightened immediately and took Mari's face in her hands. "You and Jim need time to talk. Why don't you let Terry and me keep Steve and Melissa tonight?"

"Where are they?" Mari asked, suddenly aware of their absence. "They didn't see...?"

"No, they're still inside," Jim replied. He was pale under the glaring streetlight.

"Take her home, Jim," Terry said firmly. "We'll take care of everything here."

As Mari followed Jim away, she paused to force a smile for her sister. "I don't want you to misunderstand," she said, her voice tearful. "I'm really very happy for you."

"I know that." Jazz hugged her, tears falling freely.
"And I'm sorry for the casual way I've always told
you that being unable to have babies didn't matter. I
know how I feel now that having one is happening to
us." Her eyes clouded and she clutched Mari's hand.
"When I saw that look on your face, I finally understood what it means to you. I'm sorry I've been so
unfeeling."

"You haven't," Mari insisted, sniffing. Realizing
how she had destroyed what should have been a warm
family evening, she said guiltily, "I'll call you in the
morning, and we can get together before you go back
home. All right?"

"You bet," Dave replied, drawing Jasmine back as
Jim opened the car door.

Mari watched her husband warily from the far corner
of the front seat as he turned the key in the ignition,
listened to the quiet motor for a moment, then pulled
out into the street. He raised a hand to Terry and Katherine who were leading the children out of the restaurant as they passed. He braked for a red light at the
corner and turned to Mari as the Malibu idled quietly.
There were too many emotions in his eyes for her to
interpret that look, and she looked away, her eyes
burning.

The house seemed strangely unfamiliar when they
arrived home, as tidy as she had left it, toys picked up,
coffee table clear of projects. It seemed empty and un-
real without the children.

Jim gestured toward the stairs and like an automaton
Mari climbed them, following the hallway to their
room. She guessed that she was about to become part
of Jim's past, and she could think of no argument in
her defense.

Jim followed her, detouring into his office to emerge
with a bottle of brandy and a glass. Pouring the brandy,
he inclined his head toward the bed. "Sit down," he
said.

While Mari sipped the burning liquid, watching him

under lowered lashes, he removed his jacket, pulled at his tie, and rolled back his sleeves, then knelt to build a fire. In a moment it blazed cheerfully, and he got to his feet.

As he turned to face her, Mari downed the rest of the brandy, anxious now to have the confrontation over with. She was tired beyond describing, and she was almost glad there was nothing left to fight for because there was no fight left in her. All she had to do was take the punches for a few minutes and it would be over. She could do that.

"All right," she said, looking out at him from eyes that looked bruised. "Go ahead."

He went to the chair by the bed and fell into it, looking as tired as she felt. "You go ahead," he said, his voice cold. "You're the one with something to explain."

"There's nothing to explain, really," she replied quietly. "I'm sterile, and I married you without telling you. I believe that gives you legal cause for divorce."

He was out of the chair so fast she jumped as he approached the bed. There was fire in his eyes, and she braced herself for the crash of his fist against her jaw. But he turned away from her at the last moment, pacing toward the door, jamming his hands in his pockets. Then he spun around and paced slowly back to her, his body stiff with anger. "Do you realize," he demanded, his voice hardly recognizable as his, "the time we've wasted..."

He had a right to be furious, to say every cruel thing that came to mind, to consider their time together wasted because she could never give him the children he wanted so much, but the time they had together was all she had left. The future stretched before her, black and empty, but it would have been easier to face had she known he held warm memories of the last few months.

Mari tucked her legs up under her on the edge of the bed and closed her arms around her in an unconscious effort to make herself a smaller target as he approached the bed again. Tears slid silently down her face.

He stood over her, his voice dangerously quiet. "Why in the hell did you wait till this morning to tell me?" He took her face in one angry hand and turned it up to him. "Why?"

"I'm sorry!" Blinded by tears, she tried to shake her head, but his hand had violence in it and she was afraid to move. "I...didn't mean to...keep it from you. At first...it was because I was waiting for the right time...then I was afraid of..." She broke down and had to finish between sobs. "Afraid...of losing you!"

With an angry exclamation he dropped his hand and turned away from her to wander toward the window. Her velvet eyes, spilling tears, followed him.

He spun around again, one hand leaving his pocket in a despairing gesture. "What in the hell do you think of me, or of yourself for that matter, to have even considered that your inability to have children would make a difference to my love for you?"

For a moment Mari was sure she had misunderstood, and she just stared at him, her eyes uncertain. "Doesn't it?" she whispered, time suspended while she awaited an answer.

When it came, it was like a clap of thunder. "No, it doesn't!"

"Then why," she whispered, "have you been so angry?"

"Because you thought it would!" he roared. "We've wasted two months dancing around each other, you afraid of me and I uncertain of you, just because... God, I don't believe it!"

"I tried to tell you several times," she said raspily, her heart picking up a swift, unsteady beat, "but I was always stopped by something. First it was Steve running in with a bloody nose the day he had the accident on the sled, then it was that accursed nightgown." She shook her head, sighing wearily. "I was so sure I'd lose you if you knew. I hated myself for not telling you, but

I couldn't make myself do it. That's why I seemed so hot and cold. One day I was sure I could make you love me enough that it wouldn't matter to you, then you'd mention children and I was terrified again.''

He came toward her, his eyes still angry, and looked down at her disheveled figure near the edge of the bed. Then his eyes softened fractionally and he sat beside her. "Tell me about it," he said.

Mari put a trembling hand to her eyes, a look of exhaustion about her. "I am...sterile," she forced herself to say. "That's really all there is to it."

"How did it happen?"

She lowered her hand and stared at it, afraid to look at him. "The summer when I was seventeen, Mom and Dad took me to the hospital with what we thought was appendicitis." Her voice constricted, but she swallowed and went on. "It turned out to be an ovarian cyst, and when surgery was performed to remove the ovary, cysts were found in the other as well and it...it was removed also." She did look up then on the barest chance that she hadn't misunderstood him a moment ago. "I can never, ever, conceive a child."

He looked back at her steadily as though trying to see something she hadn't told him. "That's it?" he asked warily.

She frowned. "Isn't that enough?"

A sigh that mingled relief and frustration broke from Jim as he reached out gently to touch her face. "Look, Janie. I don't mean to minimize it; I can see that it hurts you. But for my part"—he paused to emphasize with a shrug—"I don't care."

While she stared at him, trying to absorb that, he asked unexpectedly, "Is that why you and Walters broke up?"

She nodded.

With a grim smile he shook his head. "You're better off without him, Janie. Any man who could walk away from you for that reason doesn't have both oars in the water."

Trying to ignore the compliment, she felt forced to point out, "You can't blame him. He wanted a woman who was...complete."

Jim growled impatiently and sprang off the bed. "Is that self-pity, or are you really that blind to everything else you have to offer?"

"What else?" she demanded, her voice breaking. "A not-too-ugly face and a so-so body? Will that satisfy you ten years from now when all your friends are carrying around pictures of sons who look like them? You want your own children, Jim. You said so. And you can't have them with me."

"I already have two of 'my own' children!" he shouted back. "Missy is mine, Steve is yours, and they are ours together because we love them. My God! Do I have to explain to *you* that there is no difference in the love you feel for an adopted child?"

"That's not what I mean," she said softly, eyes downcast.

"Then please explain what you did mean. That certainly sounded like you were rating them second-class citizens to me."

"I was not!" Tears of frustration stood in her eyes, and brushing them away impatiently, she wondered if she would ever be able to stop crying. She took hold of herself and forced a steady tone of voice. "I couldn't love a child more than I love Missy or Steve, but I'm not the issue here. You are." She looked up at him, trying to be calm. "I have no choice in the matter, Jim, but you do."

"Okay, before I answer that..." He sat on the bed again and pulled her over to sit facing him. She could see the flecks of green in his brown eyes and the tiny laugh lines raying out from their corners. "...tell me this. Do you think of the kids as mere substitutes for what you can never have?"

"Of course not!" she replied hotly. "They're special little people, and I thank God that He brought us to-

gether. They're not substitutes, they're mine! Ours,"
she corrected more quietly. "But you..."

He shook her lightly, and his eyes, black with feeling, bored into hers. "I have no choice either, Jane. I
am totally, two hundred percent, committed to them
and to you."

"This is no time for nobility!" she said forcefully.

"Nobility has nothing to do with it," he said evenly.
"I love you, Janie, though at this moment I'm beginning to doubt my sanity. Had we been able to have
children together, it would have been wonderful, but
we can't. Frankly I don't see the trauma in the situation. We have a gentle, intelligent son and a beautiful,
spunky little daughter. What more can two people
ask?"

Confused, overwhelmed, Mari put her hands to his
chest and swallowed a sob. "Jim, I love you, too. And I
want you to have everything you want, even if I'm not
the one who can give it to you."

Jim took her face in his hands and held it firmly, his
eyes intense. "Listen to me, Janie. Because if I don't
come through this time, I have to conclude that you
don't want to understand and that it's over."

"No," she whispered.

"Then listen! Everything I want in this world is
wrapped up in you, Marijane Sullivan, as you are!" He
punctuated that with a shake for emphasis. "So, bio-
logically you're..." He frowned. "Where in the hell
did you get a word like barren?"

"I've always hated 'sterile,'" she said.

He nodded. "Equally foolish. With the children,
with me, you are as warm and loving as any man could
hope for. You know what I missed most in Portland?"

Mesmerized, feeling light enough for flight, Mari
shook her head.

Jim smiled. "I missed the kitchen. Portland is fairly
big and exciting, and I've always enjoyed trying new
restaurants...until this trip." He shook his head, his

smile waning. "Do you know how awful it is to eat alone in elegance when you've become accustomed to a small round table, children's conversation, peas flying and spilled milk, and you across the table from me, pink and glowing, comfortably quiet yet refreshingly alive. Janie..." He stopped, his voice heavy, and she saw desperation in his eyes. "Do you understand?"

She threw her arms around his neck and fell against him with such force that they landed stretched out on the mattress, she crying and he kissing away her tears.

"This morning I thought you hated me," Mari said, her voice choked.

"I have never hated you," he said, a smile in his voice. "When we came back from the hospital and I wanted to talk it out with you and all you'd do was discuss breakfast, I could have cheerfully killed you. But I have never hated you."

She pulled away from him to look into his eyes, her own clouded and grave. "When Jasmine told us about the baby tonight, I thought you looked as though you wanted to kill me because I could never give you one."

"No!" he barked again, and she looked at him doubtfully, marvelling at the temper of this man who had been so kind and so gentle for so long. "I was angry because they were so happy, and we should have been, too. Not because of the children, though Steve and Missy are as much ours as if I had planted them in you and you'd carried them for nine months. But because we're in love. That's the one element you forgot in all your secret-keeping. I love you. Love can deal with anything."

"I didn't forget it," she explained in a strained voice. "I didn't want to lose it."

"You can't lose it," he said firmly, pulling her back against him. "Ever. I am yours and you are mine. Come hell or high water or sterility. We are Jim and Janie Sullivan, together for all time."

Basking in his declaration, Mari nestled her head into his shoulder, happiness warming her chest like a drink of Jim's brandy. "I feel like I did the night I had the bad dream that I had lost you and then woke up and found you holding me." She looked into his face and his eyes stroked her. "Imagine waking up, all alone in the universe, and finding a soul-mate." She smiled. "And a saint, at that."

Chapter Thirteen

It had been a brisk November day, the sky a bright blue, the air a fragrant collection of every perfume carried on the wind from Singapore to the Oregon Coast. Amber and flame-colored leaves tumbled and drifted across the lawn as the day waned, and heavy clouds marched in to lend drama to the sunset.

Terrence James Bennett had been baptized that morning, and Mari and Jim, his godparents, had hosted the reception that followed the ceremony. It had been a beautiful day. There had been no pain in watching the baby for Mari, no longing for what she could never have. There was just pleasure in being part of Terry's life and a new excitement in simply being alive herself. She had accepted the fact that pregnancy and childbirth were things she would never experience, but the last eight months as mother to Melissa and Steve had taught her that, while those were exciting and rewarding events in a woman's life, they were just a small part of the total experience of motherhood.

Mari had just waved off their guests with the agreement that they would all meet at Jazz and David's for Thanksgiving. Despite the chill air, she sat on the front step, wrapping her arms around herself. She knew this sort of treatment was not the best thing for her emerald wool dress, but she would just sit for a moment.

It was that time of the day when the pace of the world slowed, birdsong stilled, and the sun began to slip away. The stillness always turned Mari to reflection, and today her thoughts brought happy tears to her eyes.

The front door burst open and Mari turned toward it, startled.

"There you are!" Jim said, one hand still on the knob as he held the door open.

"Was that the mill on the phone?" Mari sniffed and forced a smile for him. "Do you have to leave?"

He closed the door and came, frowning, to sit beside her. "It can wait until morning. What's the matter?"

She smiled again. "Nothing. Really."

"Janie." He put an arm around her shoulders and pulled her close. "We've talked about this a couple of times. Don't close me out. Tell me how you feel, even if you think I won't like it. It's easier on both of us."

"Darling, nothing in wrong," she said forcefully, but the sincerity of his concern seemed to contribute to her pensive mood, to a tear spilling over.

As his concern deepened, she shrugged her shoulders helplessly. "It's...just...woman stuff."

"Woman and baby stuff?" he guessed.

She smiled up at him and clasped both arms around his middle, settling into his shoulder as a long sigh escaped her. "Not at all. I was thinking about how happy I am and how much I love you. My mother and your father still seem so happy, and Jazz and David are doing so well with little Terry." She pulled away to look into the quiet depths of his eyes, hers molten with emotion. "Haven't you ever been so happy that it's actually painful?"

Jim kissed her temple and pulled her back to his chest. "I am right now. I was afraid holding Terry would be hard for you."

"It wasn't. It was wonderful. I'm just so happy to be you and me...here...now."

"I wish," Jim said feelingly, "that we were, you and me, in bed."

Mari laughed, pointing to Steve and Melissa bounding toward them from the neighboring field where they'd been playing. "We'd have to chloroform the kids."

Jim straightened away from Mari, preparing to receive Missy, who had acquired the habit of leaping into his lap from whatever direction she came. "I'm beginning to understand," he said dryly, bracing himself as Missy raced up the walkway toward them, "why some people chain their children to bedposts in the attic. Oof!"

Missy loved the dramatic way he reacted to her landings and giggled helplessly. "More cake, Mommy?" she asked as Mari scooted over on the step to make room for Steve between them.

"You have to have more than cake for dinner, Missy," Mari insisted, the battle for nutritious food a major and constant altercation between her and her daughter at this stage of the child's development. The beautifully decorated cake had had Melissa's attention all afternoon.

"Cake," Melissa said, her little brow pleated, wondering why the obvious solution wasn't clear to her mother, "And ice cream."

Jim turned his face away to hide the grin, and Mari sighed defeatedly.

"Your daughter is hopeless!" Mari exclaimed to Jim's averted profile.

"Your son," Steve said, leaning against her shoulder, "is hungry. How about a leftover ham sandwich?"

"That sounds great!" Jim said. "Anyone who eats a sandwich can have cake and ice cream. What do you say, Missy?"

"Small sammich," she compromised.

"Small cake," Jim warned.

Then she yawned mightily, and her wide eyes drooped slightly. "Okay," she agreed.

Mari set up TV trays and made up sandwiches while Jim kept the children busy in the living room. She came out with glasses of milk to find Missy already asleep in Jim's lap and Steve in a beanbag in front of the television.

Mari shook her head. "She managed to get out of eating again."

"She did so much running around today, it's amazing she's lasted this long."

"She'll wake up early and hungry."

"Now that the cereal's on a shelf she can reach," Jim grinned, shifting Missy to his shoulder and standing, "all we have to worry about is spilled milk. I'll put her to bed. Don't eat my sandwich."

Mari put a tray on the floor beside Steve who was watching the TV screen as a gigantic, scaley monster consumed a radio tower. "Godzilla is eating his dinner," Mari said firmly. "I expect you to do the same."

Steve laughed and sat up. "He counts volts instead of calories." Then he looked around furtively and whispered, his eyes alight with mischief, "Wanna hide Dad's sandwich and say we ate it?" Steve's wit and sense of fun kept both her and Jim on their toes.

Mari wrapped Jim's sandwich in a napkin and hid it under the Sunday paper on the rack under the television.

When Jim returned to the living room, he found that the beanbag chair had two occupants, both munching on sandwiches and both apparently engrossed in the complete destruction of downtown Tokyo.

Mari was aware of the long, strong legs standing near her as Jim studied his empty sandwich plate. "Where's my sandwich?" he asked mildly.

Ignoring him, Steve pointed to the screen as a bridge collapsed. "Look, Mom! Gosh! What if Godzilla came to Astoria?"

"Where's my sandwich?" Jim growled.

"I think he just arrived," Mari said to Steve in a stage whisper. She and the boy looked up at Jim innocently.

"What's the matter, Dad?" Steve asked, as Mari questioned, "Something wrong, dear?"

He looked down at the angelic faces presented to

him and squatted down, pointing to the empty plate.
"My sandwich. Where is it?"

Mari swallowed and looked at him over half of a ham
on whole wheat. "Sandwich?"

"Sandwich," he repeated, snatching hers from her
and tossing it on the plate. "Like that one. Only big-
ger."

"Oh, that one," she said dramatically, turning to
Steve. "Remember that one?"

"You mean the one we ate?" Steve asked blandly.

"What?" Jim demanded.

"Well, darling," Mari said, shrinking away from him
as Steve decided the better part of valor was to flee the
scene altogether and scrambled out of the beanbag.
The stuffing shifted and she sank into the chair. "You
were so long coming back we thought you'd lost interest and...well, I mean...it was so juicy and delicious..." She rolled her eyes descriptively. "We
couldn't let it go to waste."

"You ate it?" Jim's frown darkened ferociously as
he bit back laughter. "Then you'll just have to make
me another one."

Mari widened her eyes dramatically, putting a row of
fingernails to her teeth. 'But it's all gone! All that juicy,
succulent, pine-apple-glazed ham is gone!"

Jim snatched one of the slippers Mari had donned
for comfort when their guests left and wielded it threateningly. "Steve, leave the room," he ordered, his eyes
dancing behind the scowl. "I'm going to beat your
mother."

"All right," Steve said readily.

"All right? All right!" Mari shrieked after the boy,
straining against Jim's restricting hand. "You're going
to leave me at your father's mercy? Who's idea was it
to hide the sandwich?"

"You're always telling me," Steve said over his
father's shoulder, "that bad companions can't make
you do what you don't really want to do."

"I think," Mari said to Jim with narrowed eyes, "that you should beat him first."

"Suits me," he said, reaching around to catch Steve behind the knees and tip him into the beanbag.

Laughing, Steve capitulated immediately. "It's under the Sunday paper! It was my idea but Mom did it!"

"You traitor!" The boy had fallen into Mari's arms, and she tickled his ribs until he pleaded for mercy.

"I'm sorry! I'm sorry! I'll do the dishes! I'll mow the lawn!" He smiled at Mari winningly. "I'll clean my room."

"Goodness. He really is contrite." Mari laughed at Jim as he dropped the slipper and shuffled through the Sunday paper for his sandwich.

"Then he'd better go do the homework he's been putting off all weekend before I change my mind."

Steve groaned. "Why don't you beat me instead?"

Getting to his feet, the sandwich retrieved, Jim reached down to help Steve up. "Why don't I beat you, *then* make you do your homework?"

Steve acknowledged defeat. "It's not nice to hold a grudge against a little kid."

Jim laughed and gave him a gentle shove toward the stairs. "Get going. There might be dessert in it for you when you're finished."

Too tired to fight her way out of the beanbag, Mari kicked her other slipper off and settled back comfortably, listening to the small sounds of Jim making coffee in the kitchen. She felt warm and deliciously relaxed. She closed her eyes thinking that she really should turn off the television, clear away the tray, change out of her dress...

When she opened her eyes again, she saw the soft pool of firelight across the room and realized that she and Jim were locked together in the well their bodies made in the beanbag. Mari rubbed her forehead against his warm, scratchy chin, an overwhelming feeling of contentment filling her. She ran her stockinged foot up his jean-clad leg and uttered a little moan of bliss.

"Hi," she said sleepily.

"Hi," he replied, his strong hand running along her spine, pulling her even closer. "I thought you'd never wake up."

"Why?" She forced her eyes open and attempted to sit up, but in the beanbag, with him beside her, the effort only resulted in her falling back on top of him. "Is Steve ready for dessert?" she asked, pushing against him to try again.

He pulled her back, and she fell on her arms across his chest. "We've got to get rid of this thing!" she complained of the chair.

"I like it," Jim said. "And I brought Steve his dessert two hours ago. It's almost nine o'clock, Lady Jane."

She kissed his chin. "And I'll bet his lordship is ready for another sandwich."

"No," he said gently, his large hand shaping her head. "You're the only thing I'm hungry for right now. But before we get to that...I've been thinking about a honeymoon."

"Oh!"

"How does Acapulco for a couple of weeks sound? Then we can still go to Salishan this summer with Jazz and David."

"Acapulco?" She got up on her knees in excitement and fell sideways as the stuffing shifted and Jim slid under her. "Acapulco? Really?"

"Really. Janie, your elbow is in my ear."

"Oh, sorry." She moved her arm and Jim, bracing with one long arm on the floor, pushed himself to a sitting position, pulling her down into his lap.

"Now, we might finish this conversation," he prophesied, "if you don't move. Where were we?"

Her hands clasped around his neck, she hugged him noisily. "On our honeymoon in Acapulco! When?"

"Whenever you like. Your mother and my father said they'd watch the kids."

"You spoke to them about it already?"

"Today, as a matter of fact. Katherine said just a day or two's notice will do. Want to go next week?"

Mari felt instant excitement at the prospect of two full weeks alone with her husband, but then her brow furrowed. Her boss had also raised an exciting prospect Friday evening that, due to circumstances at home, she'd been unable to discuss with Jim. She winced now, half afraid of turning aside his offer.

"Well..." she began uncertainly, "maybe... I mean, I don't think so... that is..." She ended in a groan. "Oh, Jim."

He frowned, his eyes sharpening. "What's the matter?"

"Well, I've been trying to tell you since Friday, only you got home from the mill so late and you were so tired. I didn't want to bring up anything that would end up in a long discussion." She paused for breath, her eyes wide with dismay. "And last night, after we put the kids to bed, you didn't give me time to talk about anything!"

He smiled reminiscently; then aware of her distress, he sobered and gave her his full attention. "Okay, well there's time now. Have we got a problem that requires a long discussion?"

"Maybe," she said, heaving a deep sigh as his calm calmed her. "But knowing you Saint James, maybe not."

"You think you know me, do you?" he asked idly, rubbing the spot between her shoulder blades.

She smiled gently. "Yes, I do. You're gentle, kind, and understanding, and the only thing that seems to make you angry is being powerless to take action, like when the kids are ill or I'm blue."

"I think I recognize a setup." He leaned against the plumped up back of the beanbag to be better able to face her. "All right. I'm ready."

"Well. Guess who was asked to become the new manager of Columbia Books?" She smiled tentatively, waiting.

"Ah." Jim's smile was broad. "It must be the young woman who can put her special order success average up against the major chains."

"Right!" She couldn't suppress her exuberance. "Oh, Jim! What do you think? I'll get to do *all* the book orders and some gift buying!"

"That's wonderful, Janie. I'm proud of you," he said.

"Are you sure?" She looped her arms around his neck, her eyes intense. "The honeymoon sounds heavenly, but between now and Christmas I'll be swamped. And after that there's inventory."

He nodded calmly. "There's every likelihood that Acapulco will be there in February."

"Oh, Jim." She kissed him, her adoration for him in her eyes. "But do you realize what that means for the month of December?"

His eyes wandered distractingly to her mouth. "What?" he asked absently.

She loosened one hand to poke him. "Are you listening to me?"

He seemed to call himself around. "Yes, I'm listening. You're about to give me some horror story about the month of December."

"I'll be going in early and working late. You'll have to feed the kids and get the groceries—"

"Have you forgotten," he interrupted, "that you're dealing with the original bachelor father here? I was parenting before you were, remember? I do not foresee a problem."

"No, you never do," she said softly, tracing the line of his bottom lip with her fingernail. "I want this job, Jim. But your career is very demanding of you, and I don't want to make your life miserable."

"The nice thing about being boss is setting your own hours and calling the tune." He captured her finger and kissed it. "For the month of December I'll work my schedule around the kids. We'll cope." He grinned lasciviously. "But you'll have to make it up to me in Acapulco."

"Gladly," she said, settling down against him, nipping his earlobe. "Want a deposit now?"

"Mmm." He made a throaty sound of approval while nuzzling her neck. "Here in the beanbag?"

She giggled. "Seriously?"

"Why not?"

"Because it'll take a chiropractor to get us out."

"If worse comes to worst, we'll just unzip the vinyl and let the pellets out."

Jim shifted, turning so that she fell into the depression and he lay beside her, pulling at the small covered buttons of her dress.

Drowning in his eyes, Mari heard a rush of wind, then the now familiar sound of an Astoria storm. "Listen to the rain," she said, holding his hand still against her breast.

He cocked his head. The rain began as a steady tapping, then became a drumbeat of sound against the windows. "That's a hard rain," he said. "Winter's here."

In the firelight, with that look in Jim's eyes, the rain was beautiful music to Mari's ears. She pulled him down, her arms going around his neck. "It's music to love by," she murmured. And they basked in a warmth that would rival Acapulco's tropical sun.